Imminent Domain

Left Behind

Neal JB Verne

Copyright: *APP #: 1-3422313701*

ISBN10: 0-9972280-4-0

ISBN13: 978-0-9972280-4-5

Disclaimer Legal:

Acknowledgements:

- *AVC Proofreading- Proofing: Alicia Carmical*
- *AVC Proofreading- Editing: Alicia Carmical- Thanks for the sleepless nights and dedication to excellence and being so much support!*
- *Chrystinia Joy Carmical- Thanks for the feedback, help with proofing and encouragement!*
- *Holly Mae Carmical- Thanks for proofreading!*
- *JS Scott- Thanks for the inspiration.*
- *Sri Bonthu- Thanks for the advice and answering so many dumb newbie questions!*

Glossary of terms:

- **Buckingham Dolly:** Powered dual-wheel device with a hydraulic lift for moving large, heavy objects.

- **Goldilocks:** A habitable environment. The new world that many inhabitants have relocated to.

- **GPS with Memory:** A mock global positioning system that uses memory, basing its location on physical movement rather than actual satellites.

- **Holograph:** Three-dimensional image producing device.

- **Ionosphere:** Area of the highest layer of the atmosphere between a planet and space.

- **Op Track:** Four-tracked vehicle made to travel within a layer of snow, also can travel on top of snow.

- **Replicator:** Three-dimensional printing device used to reproduce an item. This device can print many different substances, including food.

- **Replicator Fuel:** A base substance that is used to create a substance. It can be solids, liquids, and gases.

- **Tunnel Buster:** A device used in conjunction with a vehicle to make a tunnel within deep snow.

- **WRC:** World Relocation Coalition.

Contents

Chapter 1
Charmed Life

A blonde haired, brown eyed, well-tanned, beautiful young lady walks along a row of tomatoes in her garden. She is carrying a hoe and snipping out stalks of grass that are trying to consume the water and fertile soil she has provided for her plants. She wears blue jeans, a flannel shirt, tied in the front, over a white undershirt, and white tennis shoes.

It is a peaceful morning, but there is no sunrise. There is no change in the weather as she looks out across the large garden to see trees. An enormous domed metal roof is above her, extending up high above the trees, continuing past the garden for miles. She lays her gloved hand across the end of the hoe handle and looks back up to her home. It is a modest cabin with a porch. Her man, Danny, sits with a mason jar of a clear liquid that appears to be moonshine. He wears overalls, with no shirt, and is still wearing his house slippers. He is about forty-one years of age. He is not a huge man at about six feet tall, but he is muscular, with brown hair and a pronounced five o'clock shadow.

She calls out to him, "You best not be getting drunk this early in the morning, you ole motherfucker, you!"

Danny, without saying a word, reaches behind him and grabs a deer rifle, pointing it down toward the garden.
She yells at him again, "You best not be shooting at me, you old bas…"

KaaaBOOOOM.

The rifle is fired, echoing all throughout the closed-in shelter. She _SHRIEKS_ and drops to the ground, lying flat and lifeless.

Danny stands and holds a hand flat out above his eyes, as if to block the light from above, with the rifle in his other hand and says, "I got 'em!"

1

Riddled with fear, she looks toward him on the porch, stands, and turns to look at what he is looking at. She sees a whitetail buck deer lying dead at the end of her garden.

She yells out again, "You about gave me a fucking heart attack, you old son of a bitch!"

He chuckles and says, "Go get my damn deer and skin 'em before I grab the round in there that says *BITCH* on it!" She finishes the row that she is on, then goes and starts dragging the deer back up to the cabin. She isn't a big strong lady and she struggles, leaving a blood trail behind her. She manages to get the bloody carcass back up and into the barn, tying the hooves of the animal to cotton ropes that are threaded through pulleys anchored to a rafter. She then grabs the other end of the ropes that have a hook at the end and connects them to a rack on the back of a large four-wheel drive ATV. She pulls forward, tightening the ropes and dragging the lifeless animal vertical as blood streams from its shoulder and onto the concrete floor of the barn, turning it red.

Danny comes walking in with an ice chest and a knife. He says, "I sharpened your knife." Without speaking a word, she takes the knife and makes an incision in the animal from the groin to the neck and looks at Danny while she cuts. Without hesitation, he says, "I will be in the cabin if you need me." He quickly leaves the barn.

She butchers the animal with speed and precision, leaving the bones and entrails in a large pail beneath the hooves that hang from the ropes she tied earlier. The large ice chest, that he brought, was quickly filled full of fresh meat. She backs the ATV up and struggles with lifting the heavy container with the entrails, and disconnects the ropes. She pulls the four-wheeler up to the cabin and parks it. She steps off and up to the front porch, leaving small bloody tracks on the steps. She sits down on the lawn chair and relaxes, looking out over her garden.

A few moments pass and Danny comes walking out in his overalls, a pistol strapped to his side. Not a word is said as he makes his way across a brilliant green lawn and down to the

ATV. The motor cranks up and he is off to the replicator refueling area.

He travels for about five minutes when he reaches his destination. It is at an outer wall of the shelter. There is a six-inch-wide concrete barrier that protrudes deep within the ground, several feet going along the outer wall, keeping the ground-dwelling creatures from overwhelming the shelter. The area on the other side of the wall is under thirty feet of deep snow now and an ice age has fallen on Earth. The location that he has arrived at is a very large pit with an opening to the ground outside. It is at least twenty feet deep and is lined with a glass-like surface.

It is half-filled with snakes, moles, and other animals that have traveled through the ground, seeking shelter from the cold, and food. He pulls the large bucket from the four-wheeler and dumps it on the top layer of doomed animals, splattering them with blood and the other parts of the deer that are left. He then flips a lever marked "FILL" and a wall begins to traverse across the bottom of the pit like a trash compactor. The sign near the pit reads "REPLICATOR FUEL." He waits while the pit is seemingly cleaned and a green light illuminates on the control panel. He then presses a button on a screen that reads "PUMP A", and a deluge of water overwhelms the area, cleaning it of blood and bodily secretions.

This pit is part of a large system that processes bio-matter and turns it into fuel. The fuel is used for the food replicators that are used to sustain their food supply. He turns a switch to "Automatic" and hops on his ATV. As he pulls away, he wonders how terrible life must be for these poor animals that were freezing to death, finding shelter only to be destroyed in order to sustain human life.

He takes a trail that brings him in the opposite direction of the cabin. He feels as though his female companion would be better off alone for a while. He travels down a trail, looking up at the grow lights as he rides. All throughout this area, the vegetation is plush and green, as it would be during the summer

3

months at his southern Arkansas home. It has been ever since the shelter construction was completed about seven months prior. He makes a trek around the outer wall of the shelter once a week to inspect for collapses, failed lighting, and to ensure nothing or no one has breached it.

He rides and remembers a short time ago when he was on his own hunting grounds and how it would get dark at this time of day. The light remains consistent as he reaches the wall furthest from his home. The interior of the shelter is white sheet metal, with red beams and steel members. He is about a two hour ATV ride from his cabin, stopping at another pit that is marked "REPLICATOR FUEL." It is the same as the other but doesn't have quite as many animals in it. He presses the button and walks over and sits on his ATV.

He sits for a while questioning his decision to wait and not leave on a transport, why he had spent his life as an atheist. He has been in the shelter for about six months now. He wonders about the ones destined for Goldilocks. Were they there? Did God empty the transports? He thinks of all of his wealth that was in the banks across the world. He had amassed great riches in the world as the founder of an investment banking group, Chimera, and it was all gone. All he has now is this enormous shelter and Kelly, his little southern swimsuit model that he was with when the end came. He becomes angry as he recalls the multiple three-hundred-million-dollar installment checks that he wrote to the WRC in support of the relocation efforts.

He hears something at the side of the pit. A small rodent sticks its head out of one of the many holes that are on the backside. Danny pulls out his pistol and shoots it. The animal disappears. He decides that he must have missed and it ran back into the hole, but then he sees blood trickle out and down the side into the pit below. He yells, "Take that! You get some fucking pity, it was over for your sorry little life, just like that. No misery of lying in that pit, feeling like a sitting duck until next week when I come again."

Just then, a very large snake comes straight through the same hole, mouth gaped open with the small animal toward the back of its throat. It widens the hole with its large body and flies across the top of the pit, stretching almost the entire length of the pit, rapidly approaching Danny. He takes a firm grip on his pistol, but as its tail clears the hole, it begins a descent into the blood stained, concrete bottom below. A pronounced slap is heard as the large animal lands on the smooth surface.

Danny walks over to look at this enormous animal. He spits over the side. "Not today, you foul son of a bitch, not today. You get the pleasure of lying in there until I come again next week, for that poor assed shit!" He decides that he will be as humane to the other animals as possible because this snake will eat anything that falls in the pit. He takes a step to the control panel and flips the "FILL" lever, then says, "I hope that hurts, you bastard!" The energetic whine of a hydraulic ram and squishing sound is heard. He flips the switch back to "Automatic" and walks over and jumps on the wheeler and takes off back to the cabin.

He takes a different path home. On his way, he passes large creeks and ponds that are filled with boiling water. The shelter was placed in an area that has natural hot springs. This helps to keep the temperature warm by using the Earth's core heat that is transferred up through the water. He comes to a "Y" in the trail and turns left. As he goes along the trail, he reaches a black and yellow striped paved road. He turns right on the road and after a while, he comes upon a white building with a red cross on the front of it. He slows as he passes, then takes off for another few miles until the road disappears under two large gray metal doors that are similar to barn doors but three times the size and fashioned out of thick, ten gauge metal.

He turns down into a drainage ditch and back on dirt. He follows brown dirt tire tracks, with green weeds in the middle and on each side, through a small patch of woods and into the west side of his field. A large muscular, black pit bull with snipped ears and a bobbed tail comes running up to him as he has slowed to a crawl, trying to ensure that Kelly isn't in a sniper position somewhere. He stops and the dog runs up and puts his front paws up on the gas tank of the ATV. He reaches down to pet him and says, "Chopper, she let you out to play?" The large dog rubs his head against Danny's leg as he strokes the back of his neck. He pushes him away and says, "Come on, boy, let's go see if momma is still mad at me."

He rides up to the cabin. There is no sign of Kelly as he walks up on the front porch. Chopper runs over to a love seat and climbs up and lies down, making a high-pitched moan accompanied by a yawn coming out of his mouth. He looks over at the dog and says, "She got you, too, huh?" Chopper looks like he is getting comfy there and has no interest in going in there with Kelly.

He walks in through a decent sized mudroom, then to the front door of this beautifully constructed log cabin and immediately smells the aroma of freshly cooked deer tenderloin. Kelly walks out with a short pair of Daisy Dukes and long tanned legs. She smells of ladies' soap and shampoo. She bounces up to him and hugs and kisses him.

Danny says, "I guess you are over the whole deer thing?"

"I wouldn't say *over* it, and if you do that again, I have that .40 S&W on my side. I will shoot your ass graveyard dead."

Danny replies, "I understand. I smell something good!"

She looks at him. "Yeah, I know how much you like fresh tenderloin and I figured you would like to have that rather than something replicated. I haven't cooked for you in a few days, so I thought I would be nice."

"Daisy Dukes, too? You must be feeling good. You ain't cooking my last meal are you? Got a little rat poison reserved for my plate?"

"No, honestly. I got a shower and thought about the fresh deer meat. You couldn't exactly yell, 'Hey, there is a deer behind you' without scaring it off. So I decided to let you off the hook. You do not demand that I get and clean it, though. I don't

6

mind doing that, but you could have helped get it. I won't tolerate being disrespected like that again, prick!"

She finishes the meal and they sit, eating supper. After both getting their fill, they decide to go to bed, and enjoy their time in the bedroom.

Chapter 2
Life Out There

Morning comes to find Danny up in the basket of a large bucket truck. The diesel engine roars as he extends a large, white telescoping arm to the top of the shelter. It is on a hill, past a creek, up behind the barn near the northeast corner of the shelter. There, braced out from the wall, is a large pole that extends down into the ground.

He is soon at an electrical panel nearly thirty feet high at the top of the shelter. The panel has a large metal electrical conduit that goes into both ends, and buttons and switches on the door. One switch is labeled "AUTO" and "MAN",he flips this switch to MAN. There are also buttons marked UP, DOWN. He pushes the up button and hears a motor attached to the pole at the roofline groan. The box clicks a few times as he presses the button. He pushes the down button to hear another click, and the pole moves downward slightly. This pole has a satellite dish at the top of it, enclosed within a glass-like dome.

The snow has covered it up, rendering it inoperable. The system has an automatic control, but since it is stuck, it is malfunctioning and not receiving a signal. Danny hopes that it is just stuck and hasn't extended as far as it can reach. They have been without any Internet, news, or television for about two months. It went out in February of 2119 and it is currently the middle of April. They are both getting tired of watching the same old movies they had saved on their computer.

He presses the manual up button and the pole begins to move. He doesn't dare let off of the switch, as it may get stuck again. Soon the unit is moving fairly fast and making a high-pitched humming noise. He decides that it is high enough to be out of the snow. He looks over at a hatch to the side of the pole that has a yellow-caged ladder extending down from it. He is thinking it would be a difficult journey up the ladder. Kelly comes running out of the cabin.

"We are connecting!"

She looks like a midget from his vantage point. Danny hollers back, "That is great news! I didn't want to have to try to melt my way up that ladder."

"You won't have to do that now, babe. It works!"

He lowers the basket down to the ground and they both go into the cabin to see what is out there. The last time it worked, they had several foreign channels, an emergency network that ran the same "END OF THE WORLD" message, and about ten channels from the more populated shelters that are in Dallas, Atlanta, Miami, Washington DC, Boston, Cincinnati, Los Angeles, Seattle, New York, and Toronto. They also had some social media sites on the computer from these areas.

He turns the television on to find the morning news being broadcast from Dallas. He recognizes the channel as one that belongs to a broadcasting group that Chimera owns. He wonders if somehow they are earning money or if it is simply a charity broadcast. *Either way, it is on me. I guess I should enjoy it.*

He sits down to watch as they give an update on news from Alpha Kantabury I. Kelly sits down at the computer and after about thirty minutes, she jumps up and runs over to Danny, throwing her arms around him and explains how happy she is that he fixed their satellite dish.

He says, "I wanted it to work also, you know. A little gratitude this afternoon would be nice." She smiles at him as if to let him know that he has earned it. He gets up with her in his arms. He carries her into the bedroom. The front door only has the screen door closed and all of the windows are open in the bedroom. He throws her onto the bed. They begin to make love when suddenly they hear a low growl at the south window. Danny stops and looks her in the eyes and says, "Talk about a mood killer."

"No doubt," she replies.

He grabs his pistol from the belt hanging from the headboard of their bed and goes to the window. He sees ole

9

Chopper standing out near the garden. He turns and says, "Hell, it's just ole Chopper. He probably seen…" A loud yelp is heard as he turns back to see a raccoon foaming at the mouth, fighting with the large pit bull. A definitive bone crushing, crackling sound is heard. It is obvious the coon was no match for the dog, and the fight was over before it really got started.

Kelly asks, "Danny, what is it?"

"It looked like a rabid raccoon was after Chopper."

"Has he had his shots?"

"Of course, woman. We have that whole medical facility to ourselves also, just down the road. They said it would have veterinarian supplies in it as well. We will keep him up on those shots. Can't imagine that big dog going nuts."

She says, "What medical facility?"

"The one, you know, with the big red cross on the front of it."

"Oh, that is what it is? I thought maybe it was another cabin or something."

Danny says, "You have to be kidding me. You didn't know what the red cross meant?"

"No, am I supposed to know everything?"

"Not everything, but uh…er…*some* stuff other than fucking and cooking."

Obviously and rightly upset, she jumps up from the bed naked and grabs her pink little robe and storms out of the bedroom. Danny looks out at the dog that he had been distracted by and yells, "Chopper, don't eat that, boy, it will make you sick!" He grabs his overalls and makes his way outside to save the dog. He grabs the raccoon and is really unsure of what to do with it. He knows the food replicator breaks down particles to the atomic level prior to processing, but doesn't feel like it is safe. Even if it is, it is really kind of gross to consider eating something rabid, so he carries it out into the woods and throws it out.

He arrives back at the cabin a short time later. This time, Chopper is barking at him as he realizes that he got rid of his coon. He pulls up to the front porch and yells at Chopper as the big dog makes his way to the side of the house and out of sight. He steps up on the front porch to see Kelly on the computer.

He says, "Listen. I didn't mean anything by that. You put me on the spot there. I am sorry."

She stops what she is typing and says, "I know a lot more than you think. Just because I don't know what a red cross represents doesn't make me stupid, you know."

"I know and I said I'm sorry. I am not a nice, kind person inside. I can't help that. I am not mean enough that I want to kill people, but you must realize I have gone from king of the world to pauper."

She looks up from the computer. "You can be a kind person. I have seen it."

They both walk into the bedroom to resume their fun.

They finish a couple of hours later. Kelly walks to a closet in the cabin, where a sophisticated control panel is located and starts navigating on a screen there. Danny gets up to go see what she is doing and she goes into a screen that says "Environmental Controls: Lighting." She presses a button labeled "MIMIC SUN AND MOON PHASE", it lights up green. The lights outside go dark. It is about ten at night.

Danny says, "I didn't know we had that option."

"I know, all you are good for is hunting and fucking."

"Okay, okay, I deserved that. We even?"

Kelly smirks and says, "We will never be even. I have the pussy."

"The only one in captivity! Oh, you bitch, you! Will this be a twenty-four hour day now?"

She says, "You tell me, Mr. Smartass."

They both laugh and go climb into bed.

The next day finds Danny sitting in the living room before simulated daylight, having coffee and stroking the back of the dog. He decides that today he will try his luck at creating a tunnel. He has a GPS locator with memory. The group that

11

designed the shelter built a domed attachment for a truck that can create tunnels under the snow. He walks out to the barn while it is still dark out. There are security lights atop power poles at the barn and on the far side of the cabin that light his way. He steps through the door, flips on a light switch, and looks at the vehicles they left for him. It is a rather large room and there are a few tractors, several different ATVs, two snow machines, a couple of vehicles that are under tarps, a large four-wheel drive Superduty with big mud tires, and a new Jeep with a hard top and various different attachments. He also has a track hoe, bulldozer, and various odds and ends of ditch witches, cable burying machines, and small drilling machines. He stands there and says, "Look at all of these toys. It's like Christmas morning."

He walks over to the aluminum colored dome attachment for the truck. It has steel framework painted black, wires neatly affixed to it, and a generator with an electrical control box in the middle of the inside of the dome. It has two male receiver hitch attachments spaced equally on each side that match the receiving female members on the truck's front end.

When extended, the dome looks large enough to almost cover the hood of the big truck. He looks down at the receiver part and it has something in a plastic bag, with a zip tie holding it to one of the pins. He pulls it off and it is a thumb drive with a note. He opens the note and it reads: Review the files within this thumb drive prior to operation. Caution: Tunnel busting equipment can be dangerous and possibly life-threatening to operate.

He says out loud, "Hmm, I guess they left me instructions. Tunnel buster, huh? Snappy name." He walks over to the excavator and looks at the key with a small plastic bag attached. He says, "I guess a fella could have some fun with this stuff, and it even comes with a manual. Isn't that something."

He goes back into the cabin to find Kelly on the computer. He has her get off so he can insert the thumb drive. It demonstrates how to put the dome on the Jeep or the pickup. It says the generator is used to heat up heating elements that are mounted within the dome and can be used to melt ice or snow in order to make a tunnel. It has two sections; a bottom fixed dome and a telescoping shell-type top dome. When it is down, you can see over it in order to drive and when it is up, it is used for melting extremely deep snow and ice for forming a tunnel. It suggests that you burrow through thirty yards at a time and then back up and widen the tunnel by the width of the device.

The tutorial explains that it must be used in conjunction with a GPS that has memory so you can find your way through the snow. It is necessary to navigate using the GPS locator to guide you, as there is no visibility out of the windshield due to the dome's top half covering the front of the truck, making it impossible to drive by sight. It also explains the snow could be unstable and could collapse, causing you to only move forward. This could dictate that you must burrow a circle in order to turn around. It recommends that you mark a parking lot or some known large area to turn around in if the snow is unstable once the tunnel is created.

The manufacturer had no way of knowing how firm or soft the thirty-foot deep snow would be and warned about the potential of collapse. They also spoke of the need to take precautions, like using a carbon monoxide detector, and making small sections and test it to ensure the carbon monoxide is properly vented from the truck and generator exhaust, as carbon monoxide poisoning could occur.

He finishes watching the tutorial and asks Kelly if she wants to go visiting. She isn't too thrilled about going out tunneling in the snow. She says, "You first." He kind of chuckles as he heads back out to go to the barn, saying, "Ye of little faith," as he reaches the front door. She thinks to herself that if she had faith, she wouldn't be in this predicament to start with.

It isn't long and he has the tunnel buster saddled up to the front of the Superduty. He has the heavy metal tubing protruding under the shiny chrome bumper. It attaches in two

13

places. He starts up the smooth quiet motor of the generator and flips a switch on the side to see the telescoping shell slide upward, away from the bottom half. He pushes the button back down and it moves back in place. He walks over and climbs into the truck, carrying a black box with a flexible antenna resembling a remote control car controller, and a small cellphone looking device that is a GPS unit with memory. He moves the shell up using the remote control and the inside of the aluminum metal dome goes up and the two sections snap into place with a loud metallic pop just as it did with the controls that are on the side of the unit.

The diesel engine of the truck sits there rumbling. There is a display that reads "Temperature"; he sets it at two hundred degrees. The metal of the dome begins to creak and pop a little. He puts his hand near it and feels the heat coming off of it. He wonders if it will actually bust a tunnel in the deep snow outside of the shelter.

Chapter 3
A Prayer From a Sinner

Danny is all set to go out into the snow and see if he can reach other shelters or communities. He has the dome down and backs the big white pickup out of the barn. He pulls across the yard and is ready to go meet up with the road near the medical facility. He pulls up and through the front yard of the cabin and Kelly comes out on the porch and starts down the stairs, with Chopper tagging along behind. He stops, feeling a bit of frustration as she said she didn't want to go. The big truck's diesel engine is rattling and a little black smoke is puffing out of the back. She opens the door and climbs up on the passenger side running board.

Danny says, "I thought you wanted to stay here. You were scared."

"How long will you be gone?" she asks.

"I really don't know. I thought I would go test this thing out. I will put together some supplies before I go on a major journey."

"I wanna go."

"No. I should go it alone at first to make sure this thing doesn't get crushed. That snow has to be pretty packed before it is going to be stable enough to hold up after I melt it at the bottom. If it doesn't work, there is no reason for both of us to die," he replies.

She tells him to wait and runs back in the house, coming back with a walkie-talkie.

"You tell me if you get into some trouble," she affectionately tells him as she throws the walkie-talkie on the brown leather passenger seat.

He revs the engine and she jumps off of the running board and slams the door. He is off to go make a trail in the snow. He drives a little ways and reaches the road. The big Ford growls a little as he climbs up out of the ditch and onto the roadway, turning right.

He gets to the big doors and stops. He climbs out of the truck and walks over to the center of the doors to find a metal tube with a hasp that locks them in place. He grabs the handle protruding from the bar and it is as solid as a rock. He pulls up with all of his might and it doesn't budge. He walks back to the truck to find an orange box in the bed. He opens it to find an assortment of tools. He digs around and finds a three-pound shop hammer. He says, "This should do the trick," as he quickly makes his way back to the frozen latch. He draws back and begins to swing upward on the big metal latch and just stops as if the wind was knocked out of his sails. Questions start popping up in his head. *Will these doors drop ten thousand pounds of snow on my head when I get them busted loose? Will I be able to close them back again?*

He decides to pull the truck up against one of the doors to try to avoid injury. Once in place, he is back and begins to take another crack at it. He continues beating on the latch and it begins to move. He gets the latch up, freeing the doors. The door on the right side moves inward slightly. Since he has the truck against the left side, it obviously stays closed. He pulls it open to reveal about five feet of snow up against the door and a mountain of snow up to the outer eve of the shelter that goes upward for a long distance. It is not as cold as he had imagined. The snow actually served as somewhat of a blanket. The temperature was colder than in the shelter, but it was not cold enough to feel like he could be prone to frostbite.

He climbs in the truck and backs it up, not seeing a need at this point to open the left door. He reaches over and picks up the black box and the familiar sound of a generator starter cranks the big quiet generator. He sets the temperature on the box at eight hundred degrees Fahrenheit, per the video. He pushes a button on the display and the telescoping shell extends up over the top of the large truck. A metallic "THUD" is heard when it locks into place.

He grabs the walkie-talkie and calls out, "Kelly? Kelly, are you out there?" He feels a little strange using this device. He has not used one since he worked the floor at his first factory.

Soon he hears, "This is Kelly. Go ahead. Is everything okay?"

He clicks the button. "Yep, all's well. I am going to take this contraption out into the snow. Hopefully, the shit won't collapse and kill my non-godly ass, cause we both know what I got to look forward to."

The radio comes alive again, "No doubt. Be careful."

"Over."

Then on the other end, "Over."

Not being able to see anything out of the front window and only through the sides, he slowly pulls up to the door. *CRASH!* The loud sound of metal colliding with each other is heard as he ran into the left door. "Shit!" he exclaims. "Hope I didn't fuck it up!"

He backs up for another run and the radio comes alive with Kelly's voice, "Was that you?" He doesn't want to talk about it, or have any more conversations, so he says, "Yes! Who the hell else do you think it was?" The radio is silent. He picks up the GPS and looks down, seeing the path that the road takes. He locks the big diesel truck into four-wheel drive low and proceeds to follow the path on the display.

The black box shows the tunnel buster temperature is at eight hundred degrees. He pulls forward and hears the sizzle of the hot metal coming into contact with the snow. Water is running down over the cab of the truck and he has to turn the heater off in the truck. The metal dome has it hot inside and he is a little anxious. He starts his trek and the snow is just disappearing, from what he can tell in the rearview mirror. He manages to pick up a little speed. It is still just a snail's pace, but it seems to be cutting a path fairly efficiently.

He travels the distance of a football field and remembers what the tutorial said about making a wide path so that it can be turned around. He puts the big truck in reverse and the dome hangs. He revs the big diesel and all four wheels spin. He sees snow clumps fall behind him. He is stuck, all he can do is go forward. He frantically searches the GPS to try and find a parking lot, or a circle driveway, even a three-lane road where he can turn around without having to back up. He has no luck and it appears that he will have to tunnel for a ways before he will be able to turn around. He stops and concentrates on his options, he triggers the dome to go down so that it doesn't hang as he backs up. The dome is exactly the same size as the tunnel and as he backs up it is very difficult to keep it and the truck aligned with the newly cut tunnel. The carbon monoxide detector lying in the back seat begins beeping. The snow above the truck holds, he heats the dome up to a maximum temperature of fourteen hundred degrees and puts the big truck in reverse once more.

He can smell the carbon monoxide from the diesel in the cab and the detector is beeping very quickly. It is almost a solid tone, and he realizes that this could be the end. The truck begins to go backward, with the dome melting away at the snow on the sides. The tunnel is large enough for the back of the truck to fit and have a little control. He works at getting back to the doors for about a half an hour, driving forward a little to get it straight and to widen the tunnel sides and backing up again and making progress moving backward so that he can return to the shelter.

Finally, he finds himself at the large doors. The big truck backs into the shelter. The big diesel bucks and jumps as he is putting on the brakes but not engaging the manual clutch, finally, the engine goes silent. Danny comes bailing out of the truck, running away from it and into fresh air, gasping as he runs. His chest is leaning way out in front of his legs as he staggers, collapsing in the middle of the black abandoned road, near the yellow centerline. As he lies on the ground, he speaks a heartfelt prayer that God helps him to survive this.

He speaks, "Lord, we both know I have done wrong and I hope that you find a way to forgive a sinner like me. Please help me recover from this horrible poison in my lungs." He then succumbs to the carbon monoxide.

A short time passes and the area is becoming quite cold with the large doors standing open. He begins to wake and slowly opens his eyes to see Kelly standing there. A four-wheeler sitting behind her, idling. She says, "What the hell did you do? Have a heart attack?"

19

Dazed and struggling to remember what had happened to him, he looks over at the big doors and struggles to mutter, "Carbon monoxide."

He closes his eyes and Kelly says, "Nope, you aren't dying on me like this!"

She tugs and pulls, struggling to get him onto the back rack of the wheeler. She takes him back to the cabin and up to the barn. He awakes again and she has a cutting torch head in his mouth. He spits it out, struggling, and thinking, "This bitch is trying to finish me off!" She holds him down and continues to pump pure oxygen, from the cutting torch, into his lungs. He is sitting on the ground, with his back against the back wheel of the four-wheeler and she is continually feeding him the oxygen from the torch head. He wakes and takes it from her. He realizes she knew what she was doing and that she has just saved his life.

With a headache, unlike a hangover that he's ever had before, he gets to his feet. He thanks the beautiful young model, in a drunken state, and begins to stagger to the cabin, with her close behind to try to keep him from falling.

Chapter 4
The Tunnel

The next morning he wakes with the same headache from the day before, but realizes he must have missed something on the tunnel busting tutorial. He heads to the computer. It is still dark outside. He says, "Freaking simulated nighttime," as he walks by the window. He has become accustomed to twenty-four hours of daylight.

He brings up the safety portion of the tutorial that he wasn't so interested in the day before and it explains that creating a double width area while building the tunnel is necessary to help disperse the carbon monoxide from the generator and vehicle. He decides he will watch the tutorial once more in its entirety, paying more attention to the details.

It isn't long and he is back in the big truck. He has the large left door standing open this time. He begins and widens the tunnel three times as wide as the original, only progressing the distance of the length of the truck each time he goes forward. He realizes that this is going to be a very long and tedious process.

He makes this his job. Each morning, he goes out, filling up the fuel tank on the truck and generator, and burrows tunnels in the snow. The GPS doesn't show locations of the other shelters, but he gets the data from the Internet feed from Dallas. He is currently outside of the town of Hot Springs, Arkansas, and the nearest shelter to his is in Hot Springs Village. Hot Springs Village was a very exclusive area where quite a few upper-class families lived. This shelter is about fifteen miles away. His tunnel busting speed is about an eighth of a mile in an hour. He tries to get a mile out in a day. This will put him at the Hot Springs Village shelter in about fifteen days if he doesn't have issues.

After the third day, he arrives back home at around two in the afternoon and Kelly is out in the garden picking some green tomatoes, squash, and fresh cucumbers. He drives through the front yard and around by the barn and parks the big truck. He gets out and she comes walking up. She has been thinking of the shelter at Hot Springs Village. She wants to know how he will react if he isn't welcomed there.

She catches him as he is coming around the front of the truck. "How do you know that these people will welcome you there?"

"I contributed over *nine hundred million* dollars to the WRC's relocation, and shelters in Arkansas. It belongs to me, as far as I am concerned. I will put their asses out in the fucking cold if they aren't civil to me."

"I don't think they will care to remember that part. I am just saying you should be ready for them not to roll out the welcome mat. They are not on the Internet and I haven't reached anyone at the bigger shelters that has heard anything from the shelter in Hot Springs Village."

"Maybe it is vacant. I can't imagine all those rich people going to Heaven, though." He chuckles, then continues, "Leave me be, woman. I got shit to do! If you're that worried about it, ride shotgun when I bust in there."

22

"Just sayin', asshole. I am trying to be nice and let you know that there may be issues, and that's the way you have to respond? Prick!"

She takes back off to her gardening duties.

He goes into the cabin and replicates a hamburger and fries. He heads out to the barn to get on his four-wheeler, without saying a word to Kelly, while eating the sandwich. It has been close to a week since he has been at the pits, so he climbs on the big white Yamaha and heads out to check them. He rides along and it begins to rain. The shelter has a large heating element in the roof that melts the snow and provides water for the trees and foliage that is within it. It is usually triggered at night while they sleep, but it does have an override.

He yells, "What a bitch!" He gets to the first pit and finds it about 10% full. Soaking wet, he looks at the far side of the pit where the dirt opening is at, it has holes like a piece of Swiss cheese. There is one hole toward the top that had grown large enough to fit a person through. He looks diligently down at the reptiles below and sees a gray bushy tail.

"What the fuck," he says. It looks like a little squirrel. "Well, I guess I will put the poor little bastard out of his miser…" Then he sees it has a large rattlesnake in its mouth. "Well, I guess the mongoose is going to be put out of its misery." Assuming it must be a mongoose since it has taken down a rattlesnake. He presses the "Fill" button and all of a sudden the little gray squirrel traverses the dirt wall. It runs across the round metal guardrail, with blood all over its mouth, and latches onto Danny's shirt. He grabs the big bushy tail and slings the little rodent back into the pit as the large steel wall is making a trek from the side. He pulls his pistol and POW! The little squirrel lies dead on top of the snakes and moles as a large snake begins to wrap around it. The wall traverses fully closed and they all disappear into the side.

Danny unbuttons his soaking wet shirt to see if it got him. In all of the excitement, he can't be sure. He finds a small laceration on his chest. He thinks little of it as he makes the

23

rounds. He is still driving in the rain, wiping his eyes and going very slow so he can see without the cold drops blinding him. He makes his way to the large building with a red cross on the front. He walks up under the porch and makes his way inside. He finds a small waiting area with no one present. He walks through the door and back past the patient rooms to find a sign that reads "Medicine". He walks in there and finds a large room full of antibiotics, pain medicine, and other various items. It has many shelves with various sized bottles on each. It is essentially a very well-stocked pharmacy.

He had been vaccinated for rabies when he found out that he would not be able to leave. He finds a box labeled PCECV 4.0 mL, along with a small syringe. He grabs them, along with some hydrocodone pills because it had begun hurting. He gets back outside and the rain has stopped. He chuckles. "She punished my ass enough I guess."

He gets on the four-wheeler, still soaking wet and pissed off at Kelly, and makes his way down the wet paved road to the ditch. He drives down and through the ditch, splashing mud up on his ankles, and arrives back at the cabin. He steps through the front door, past the mudroom, and onto the small white ceramic tile entrance, continuing onto the hardwood floor, dripping and stomping mud everywhere. She is sitting at the computer in a small room off of the living room.

"What the fuck? Don't track mud all through the house!" she exclaims.

He stomps through the living room and down the hall to their bedroom.

She goes behind him, leaving the computer. "Why such a mess?"

"You freaking drowned my ass while I am out tending the pits. I get fucking attacked by a squirrel that is probably rabid! I ain't worried about your clean fucking house, bitch."

"Whooooa, mister. I didn't turn on the rain routine. It must have come on by itself. And you know how I feel about being called a bitch!"

He considers that maybe she didn't. "You didn't turn it on because you were upset at me?"

"No, as a matter of fact, after thinking about it, I wasn't really upset with you. I know this riches-to-rags thing has to suck for you."

"Why the fuck didn't I live a better life? My god, forgive my misguided ass. I think a rabid squirrel bit me."

"A squirrel?" She kind of grins.

"Yes, a mutha fucking squirrel and it ain't funny. Little bastard was eating rattlesnakes, climbed up the wall, jumped on my chest and bit my ass." He pulls out the syringe.

She can't contain the laugh, she busts out, covering her face as she does.

He says, "Okay, yeah, I guess the mental image has to be amusing. Now help me treat this shit."

She takes the package and reads. She puts 1.0 mL in the syringe and he pulls off his shirt. She gives him a shot. He thanks her and grins. He walks and gets a glass of water, pulling the bottle of pain pills out of his pocket and taking two. She is standing behind him as he turns around.

"What? It fucking hurts."

"Yeah, Tylenol hurt maybe, not two hydrocodones hurt."

He heads into the living room and turns on the TV.

"Grab me a beer," he yells.

"Are you working on the tunnel today?"

"No, I am going to have a drink and recover from this attack and try to reach someone at the Hot Springs Village shelter. Let's try and see if they welcome visitors."

She hands him a glass of beer and says, "You are becoming wise. You are actually listening to me, maybe we should begin praying."

"I already have, guess it's too late for that. We get this tribulation thing all to ourselves. I guess I could have an ugly ass, old bitch to spend the rest of my life with."

25

"If you keep on with your fucked up attitude, you will at least get the bitch part."

Without any replies from Hot Springs Village, Danny finds his way to the bed and they call it a day.

Chapter 5
Is There Anybody Out There?

Danny spends the next couple of weeks dedicating every day that he can to cutting the tunnel to Hot Springs Village. His tunnel heads north up Park Avenue and turns left on Highway 7. The GPS, with memory, keeps him fairly precise on course. He uses the rumble strips on the side of the road to be able to stay away from the ditches and most of the road signs. He occasionally runs into abandoned cars under the snow. He always pulls them out and pushes them up off of the road.

Finally, the day comes. He is within a quarter of a mile of the shelter at Hot Springs Village. This community had a golf course and several mansions, including one of his homes. He had planned to visit the shelter before the sun failed but had been working on a project in Dallas and didn't find his way back until the snow began. His large home sits in the middle of the shelter. He honestly feels as though he should be there instead of in the cabin where he ended up stuck at.

He has currently made a right onto Desoto Boulevard. This is the road that leads into the shelter, and his day of trail cutting is through. He thinks it best to get back to home base and break into the new shelter tomorrow with Chopper and Kelly.

He drives along the new path, with lights from the top of the truck lighting his way. The road is still slippery from the ice that froze back over from the melted snow. He gets back home to find Kelly inside the cabin, on the computer.

"Damn, girl, is this all you do anymore?"

"What else is there to do other than tending to the garden, cleaning, and cooking? At least this way I can get a sense of there being someone else left on this isolated frozen freaking world. You got all of this money and power. What are we doing stuck here? Did they forget about you?"

Danny obviously was not amused. "The money and power don't mean anything without a society. We have to get on

27

past that. They didn't forget about me. I was invited by Charles Phillips himself to go on the first Armada because of my contributions to the WRC, but I didn't think this was going to happen, honestly. I thought that I would have all of this to myself, to tell you the truth, and they would all come back slowly. That was a bad gamble. Anyway, doesn't fucking matter, it is what it is at this point."

"I did watch some television earlier. It looks like the shelter in Chicago has gone crazy and they are all killing each other."

Danny responds, "I figure all these big shelters will go nuts after a while unless they learn to adjust and start repenting. I am one day away from being at the Hot Springs Village shelter. I need you to come along tomorrow. The tunnel is safe. I have been out in it by myself for the past thirteen days."

"I will come along. Will I need a weapon?"

"Yes, we will be fully armed. I have no idea what we are walking into. It could be full of people or there could be no one. It would be nice if we could reach someone on the Internet."

"No one from Hot Springs Village has answered. We have Texarkana, Little Rock, Cabot, Bentonville, Conway, and the one in Southern Hot Springs all corresponding. They all seem to be making it okay, but nothing from Hot Springs Village, and no one has been able to get there to check on it."

Danny says, "It could be collapsed, for all we know."

They finish out the day in their usual way. Kelly fixes some supper and he climbs into bed with his swimsuit model girlfriend that has ended up in his life for eternity.

The next morning they are both up early. Danny is out in the barn fueling up the generator and big diesel pickup, and since Kelly is riding along, he loads the ATV to ensure if something happens he can still make it back to their shelter. Soon they find themselves in the cab of the truck, with Chopper running out to join them. Kelly opens the back door and lets the big, black pit bull in the back of the cab. They arrive at the doors and Danny gets out, opening the exit of the shelter. He thinks this is the first time in the past seven months that the shelter will be left unattended.

Out and into the snow cave they drive. It is dark and the bright lights from the truck's light bar are blinding when it reflects from the smooth surface of the icy walls of the cave. They drive a short distance and Kelly says, "I hope they aren't all dead. No offense, but I would like to be able to interact with someone other than you."

"Well, I hope my freaking house on the golf course isn't trashed."

"House? You mean mansion? The place where we went last year, after the horse races, and did it for the first time?" She laughs.

"That would be the one. Yeah, first fuck! Wouldn't it be nice to be able to stay there?"

"Fuck, huh? Is that how you think of making love to me?"

"Not now, but I sure did then."

The truck becomes quiet as they trek through the ice-covered roadway. They reach the intersection of Park Avenue and Highway 7 North. The cave continues for a little ways past this turn and Kelly figures that he must have missed the turn while he was making the tunnel. She is pissed about his comment about what making love meant to him back then, deciding to keep her thoughts to herself.

They travel for about a half an hour and she sees tracks of a car that Danny had pulled out of the roadway and pushed into the wall of the tunnel. The only visible part is the back bumper and taillights. The deathly silence is broken, "Was there anyone in it?"

"No, I checked when I pulled it out of the snow. I hope they made it to the Hot Springs Village shelter, though, because there is no other place between here and there that is safe."

They arrive at another intersection and the tunnel continues straight for a short distance once again. The tunnel

29

continues on the road to the right and they turn here on Desoto Blvd.

Kelly can't contain herself, "All of these places where we are turning seem to go on past the turn for a short ways. Did you miss the road?"

"No, the GPS pretty much told me exactly where the road was, but I needed a big enough area to get this big ass truck turned around if it wasn't the turn-off. I could have ended up in a ditch. If I had gotten in a ditch, I didn't want to be closed in. That was a really bad, bad deal the last time."

"Yeah, your dumb ass about died on me!"

"How did you know about the torch? That was a weird thing for a little blonde-haired model to know?"

"My dad was a welder. I saw him huffing that oxygen several times after him and mom were up late drinking and partying. It would help his headache. He explained to me that it is almost the same as the oxygen they give you in the hospital."

"Well, you taught me something."

"That's not all I have taught you." She has a little chuckle as Danny rolls his eyes.

They finally pull up to the place where the tunnel ends. Danny explains that the entrance to the shelter is within fifty feet of where he stopped. He opens the lid on the big center console and pulls out a pistol. He places it in a holster that is strapped across his chest and concealed by his green flannel shirt. She reaches in the back seat and pets Chopper as he is standing with his rear feet on the back seat and his front paws on the back of the center console. She reaches down beside him and pulls out two black rifles. They are assault rifles. Danny takes one and wedges it in the crack between his seat and the left side of the console. Kelly lays hers with the muzzle to the floor, between her seat and the door.

Danny then picks up a black box that is lying on the floorboard and pushes a button. The tunnel buster generator fires up and it begins to move. Suddenly, nothing can be seen except the interior of the big metal dome across the front of the pickup.

30

He turns the lights off as the generator is heating. The ambient lights in the floorboard cast a blue glow across the inside cab of the pickup.

Kelly asks, "You have been doing it like this every day?"

"Yes, I have, and you know, it is usually pretty peaceful."

Soon the tunnel buster's display shows the temperature to be at eight hundred degrees and a green light lights up on the remote. The big diesel engine revs as Danny puts the truck in low gear and starts to drive it into the wall of snow. The truck begins to move forward at a snail's pace and water is running all down around the outside and pours into the bed of the truck as if it were raining.

About half an hour passes, with Danny clearing a lane and backing up and making it about three wide. As he begins a new pass, they feel the dome hit something solid and they feel large chunks of snow fall on the top of the truck. Danny rapidly backs the truck up for fear they could get stuck, or that an avalanche could crush the pickup. The snow is unstable and he thinks it must be because the heat from the shelter is causing it to collapse. They work at melting the replenishing snow mountain for a while until they see stars above and a large white metal door, which is ornamental and much nicer than the country shelter's door, where the road disappears beneath.

The large metal doors have the same latch as the ones that are at the country shelter. He reaches in the back of the truck and gets his trusty hammer, walks up and the latch springs open with barely a touch. He swings the large door open to reveal a lake with a road that runs past the end, with several mansions along the shoreline. By this time, Kelly had joined him standing in the doorway, looking out on to the peaceful looking scene. The grass is all well-maintained and plush summer green. The water is as blue as the sky and at four am, the interior lights are lit brightly.

They were surprised they weren't greeted by zombies or rabid dogs or something, but it all appeared peaceful, serene, the same as when he left it before the shelter was constructed, except the golf course had been turned into a lake. The temperature beyond the door seemed comparable to the temperature of the country shelter. He pulls the big truck through the door, the loud diesel rumbles and echoes as he pulls in.

Chapter 6
No Place Like Home

The two drive along in this big white truck with a ridiculous looking dome strapped to the front of it and start down a neighborhood street. It is a newly paved surface and the big mud grips growl as he passes a red brick mansion with a large circle drive. It has tall large pillars holding up the arched entryway. A short, gray-haired lady, in an orange and white checkered pantsuit, stands in the doorway as they pass by. She gives them a scowl, as she knows this vehicle has not been at the shelter before and she fears it could be trouble.

Danny decides it's better to survey the area before he begins to try to make friends or reconnect with neighbors. He had several neighbors that he knew back before the snow. He drives for five minutes or so, passing the end of the lake and around a curve to the right to a wooded area, and comes upon a large white privacy fence with another rather large home behind it. Each home sits on what he would assume is a thirty-acre track. This is what his home on the golf course came with when he purchased it back in 2110.

Kelly says, "It looks much different during the daylight hours."

"Yeah, during the night I guess it looked like it was in the middle of the woods. I have neighbors, but around here we don't like to be on top of each other. The income level around this area is not middle class. I think the lowest income that I knew of belonged to a heart surgeon."

"Wow, richie rich."

"Yeah, or was. Doesn't much matter now. Possession is the law. I hope no one is in my house."

"Mansion," Kelly insists.

They continue around this unusually high-class neighborhood until they reach the back side of the lake. They turn on a driveway labeled Chimera Drive. They drive down this narrow wooded road for about five minutes, at a slow pace, until they reach a huge home with a finely manicured lawn, adorned with gray brick and trimmed in vinyl siding. The road turns into a light brown cobblestone driveway near the home. It circles the front and opens to a large area that disappears under three roll up doors at a separate shop to the left of the house, and a garage attached to the side of the home.

He looks over at Kelly. "Well, this is it. The lawn is mowed, think it is vacant?"

Kelly looks back. "Let's go see."

They both climb out of the big truck, with Chopper not far behind, and walk up to the large arched entryway with brick pillars on each side and a red door. He grabs the door handle and Kelly says, "You aren't going to knock?"

Danny responds, "Why, hell no, it is my house!" They walk in and find an immaculately clean foyer that extends at least thirty yards and a ceiling that mimics the interior of a catholic cathedral in Italy, with its height and shape. It isn't long and a lady comes walking out in a French maid's outfit, carrying a feather duster. She is about five-foot-six and all of about one hundred and ten pounds. She has dark hair and brown eyes, with a light complexion. She is a very pretty lady of about thirty years old. Astonished, she runs to Danny and throws her arms around him.

"I thought for sure you found a way to get out of this place."

Danny responds while she is still holding him tightly, "Uh, no, Tilley. I have been staying in a shelter near Hot Springs, at my vacation cabin."

She has her legs slightly spread and is pushing tightly against his leg. Kelly speaks up, "Are you two…uh…close?"

Tilley says, "We're very close."

Danny's face turns a slight shade of red as he slowly tries to pull away from the housekeeper.

Tilley says, "Excuse me, I didn't catch your name," as she peers over at Kelly.

"My name is Kelly. Danny and I have been together for the past six months."

"Odd. Danny has never been with any woman for six months."

"I think it wise for you to figure out your place, uh, Tilley, is it? What is that short for, maid? Matilda?"

"Yes, Matilda and I have worked for Danny for the past eight years. I have kept others out of his home in his absence. We aren't your typical housekeeper and owner. We are more like family."

Danny decides it is time to break this up and let Tilley know that Kelly is his new number one.

"Tilley, Kelly is now my long-time girlfriend. She and I very well could get married, so I believe that you should give some thought to the way things could be here. Could you get Chopper into the backyard and give him some food and water and see about him?"

"I will be in my quarters." She leaves the room, wiping tears from her eyes, with Chopper in tow.

Once she is out of the room, Kelly says, "Damn, I thought the horny bitch was going to jerk your pants down and fuck you right here in front of me."

"Look, I have had her at this property for a very long time. There have been times, well, let's just say that we are close. You should make kind with her and not be too disrespectful, or there could be some issues for us."

Kelly realizes in an instant she is not the only female all of a sudden and the maid could very well be competition. She smiles and says, "I remember where the bedroom is."

Danny stops her and says, "We good? We understand each other?"

"Yes." With an upbeat tone to her voice, she says, "Forget about that, let's get to the bedroom. I am tired and I want to see that big beautiful bed that we made love in."

"You go on up. I will be up after a while."

Kelly pauses and is somewhat concerned about what Danny has in mind, but she has been "IT" for a long time now and figures that she can trust him. "Come up when you're ready and wake me if I am out, please."

She takes off up the large spiraling staircase. Danny walks to the kitchen. The maid's quarters are at the end of the large formal dining area. He walks past a large wet bar on the left, with an attending area behind it, and a fully stocked alcohol storage area complete with a large beautiful mirror, fine wine and bourbon on display. The cabinet has hardwood adorning it, as if it is framed like a picture with a glass front. The bar has wine glasses hanging above it, and on the right is a dining area with a large mahogany table, with real tongue and groove wood on the walls in various patterns. The woodwork is similar to a southern courtroom or a southern plantation mansion in detail.

He reaches the end of the room and walks through a door to find Tilley sitting in the living area at a desk, typing on a computer. He looks over her shoulder as she continues to write and doing her best to ignore him. The screen reads "Diary day 149".

"You are keeping a log?" Danny asks.

"Yes, there is no Internet service since the snow."

"We have Internet service through satellite at the country shelter. Who all is left here?"

"Mrs. Sullivan, Audie, and Steve from next door, Sam Landry from down the street, and old Mr. Johnson that took care of the golf course. I think those are all the ones you would know."

"Mr. Johnson didn't know how to fix the Internet?"

"I asked and he didn't seem real interested in it. He has been to visit. I think if I gave him *some,* he would probably try, but I didn't want to get that started. Poor old bastard probably couldn't even get it up. I still wear my maid outfit and he stares at my breasts and tries to see under my skirt if I bend over when he is here. He makes me feel uneasy when he starts with his overtones. I asked him to leave the last time he came."

"So, you have been here all alone all this time? No one has watered your daisies?"

"Well, I didn't say that. There are a few young guys left here. Bryan and Adam are their names. I don't want to talk about that, though. I am happy you are here now. Kelly," she sighs, "is that a real thing?"

"I don't know. She is a model and fine as hell. She keeps me in check. I kind of like that, honestly. She has always seen about me, even when she didn't really have to or want to. She saved my life once."

"Saved your life? No matter, it sounds like you found yourself another damn maid to me."

"I am happy with the way that you have kept the place. We will leave the topic of Kelly for another time. I haven't seen how she will respond when she gets to know the real me."

Tilley is sitting in an office chair. Danny takes a seat on a white leather sofa off to the right of the desk. She turns the chair toward him and spreads her legs, just enough to reveal that she isn't wearing panties. She gives Danny a nice smile as he realizes she sees him looking at her. He says, "Well, it's not like I have to worry about sinning and I'm not married. We could go lie down if you like." They disappear into the bedroom.

A short time later, Danny comes walking out tucking in his shirt. He goes to the master bathroom and showers before taking off to check his home and his fleet of vehicles that he hadn't thought of in a very long time. He steps into the three-bay garage. The garage door is closed and there are several vehicles sitting in front of him. The floor has a black and white checkerboard pattern. There is a red Ferrari that is directly in front of him on the top of a lift, below it sits a "Gotta Have It Green" GT500 Shelby Mustang. The Mustang is a classic that is over a hundred years old. It was the last year they built the retro Mustang in 2014. Cars of 2119 are built to accept replicated fuels, and many are electric.

37

The Mustang had to have a conversion kit in order to run with the alcohol-based concoction that is produced by modern day replicators. He remembers that it doesn't lack any power, even with the alternative fuel. He used it as his daily driver. He walks past these two and near a wall with a line of worktables and cabinets to his right, to gaze at his pickup truck. It is a brand new, shiny two-tone burgundy top and gray bottom, dually Ford F350. He walks around the back of the enormous truck, inspecting it as if he is expecting to see a dent. He looks at the tag on the front that says Chimera.

He looks back at the entrance to the house to find Kelly. She is wearing one of his long sleeved work shirts that button in the front, and panties. Her long tanned legs and blonde hair make her look much different than the work outfit she wore tending to the chores at the cabin.

"What are you up to?" she asks.

"I am just looking over my toys. I haven't been here in almost a year."

"You have a collection of toys everywhere it seems."

"This is my favorite collection, though. Would you like to take a ride in my Ford GT?"

"Like this?"

"Why not? I can play with your leg as I shift through the gears." He laughs.

"And I will enjoy it if that car has the power that I have heard it does."

"You like going fast?"

"I love to feel the power of a fast car."

It's not long and the rumble of twelve hundred horses are heard throughout the house, radiating from the garage. The beige garage door begins to raise and it is about halfway up when a black, with red racing stripes, sports car comes careening out, smoke on each side from the tires. Black marks form as the sound of the twin turbos power the beast out onto the cobblestone driveway. He spins it sideways, drifting around the curve headed out to the main road, the smell of burned rubber and smoke is in the air.

He runs through the gears up to about fourth gear before he begins to brake. He comes to the end of his driveway and stops to look at his beautiful passenger. She has her fists doubled between her beautiful, tanned bare legs, pressing into the leather, racing bucket seat, with her legs clinched against the outside of her fists. "Are you scared?"

"No, excited!" she replies. Without hesitation, the massive engine is heard at nine thousand RPMs as he dumps the clutch and they burst out onto the roadway.

They make a racetrack out of the roads surrounding the lake. They circle around until they are back at the entrance to his driveway once more. He stops the car and again asks, "Are you scared?"

Fists still clenched tightly and chill bumps on her legs, she says, "No! I want you now!" Once again, the little black sports car tears off like it is on a mission, not slowing down until he is sliding all four tires into the garage. He slaps the garage door button on the visor and as the door closes, he meets her at the front of the car. Laying her back on the hood, they make mad passionate love.

Chapter 7
What Do the Neighbors Think?

They finish their time together and go into the house. They find Tilley in the kitchen near the door as they walk in. She has a scowl for Danny that if looks could kill, Danny would be headed to Hell. Danny looks at her with his eyebrows lowered and as if to say, "If you tell, you're out of here."

As they walk past the maid, Kelly says, "Nosey bitch," in a low tone. Tilley gets an expression like, *Bitch, you just had some sloppy seconds.* They go into the main part of the house and up the stairs. They get to the top of the stairs and Danny says, "This has been awesome and all, but I am exhausted. I have got to go to sleep."

"What should I do?"

"I don't know. Go make nice with my damn housekeeper."

"Bitch needs to make nice with me."

"Whatever." Danny throws the comforter back on the large canopy bed and climbs in.

Kelly sits down at a desk, with a computer, that is in the room.

"What's your password? Danny? Danny!"

"Huh? What password?"

"To this computer."

He thinks for a minute in his slumber almost drunken state of near unconsciousness. *I have important records and transactions from Chimera on there*, he thinks to himself.

"Why?" he asks.

"Because I want to see if they are too damn stupid to get the Internet or if it really is broken."

"Can't you let me sleep? Fuck! The password is, uh well, don't hate me," he mumbles as he slowly gains consciousness. "It is, well, Tilleystitties."

"What? Tilley's titties? You can't have a hyphen, can you?"

"No hyphen, you pain in my motherfucking ass, you! What a bitch you can be! Okay. Tilley, capital T, everything else lowercase-titties all one word. My god, will you let me go to sleep now? Fuck!"

"Okay, it worked, prick. Thank you, and you ain't no damn prince charming yourself!"

She works at trying to get an Internet link without success. It isn't long and she hears voices down in the grand room. She slips on Danny's robe and walks to the edge of the stairs. It is two young men. They are flirting with Tilley and it looks like they are expecting something from her. She doesn't say a word as she hears the three arguing, and Tilley says, "Danny is back in this house now. You little bastards can just go fuck each other for all I care." The door then opens and they are escorted out by the maid. Kelly knows this is not the best news. It seems obvious that Tilley's needs have recently been met.

She walks down the stairs when a bang, bang, bang is heard on the door. She hears Tilley say, "I done told you little…" as she opens the door to find an elderly gentleman in overalls. It is Mr. Johnson. Kelly slowly eases her way back up the stairs to a covert location once more.

Kelly looks down upon the two and he hands Tilley a bag.

"Fresh picked squash and tomatoes for the prettiest lady in our neighborhood."

"Great. I am sure Danny will enjoy them."

"Danny? Is he back? I heard the GT going around the neighborhood like a bat out of hell. I figured you let one of your young fuck buddies drive it."

"Fuck buddies, huh? No, my man is back and he drove it around the block. So if you know what is good for you, I would suggest you quit coming here with bad intentions."

"I just want a little something for my hospitality. Is that too much to ask for? I keep your replicator from being clogged

41

and see about the maintenance around the place. All I ever asked is that we spend some quality time together."

"No, no, and never. You have to get out of here before I go and wake up Danny. Go screw old Mrs. Sullivan. I am sure she is lonely."

Without saying much else, he turns and walks out the door. Kelly is resolved to get down there before much else happens. She reaches the bottom of the steps and Tilley looks up and says, "Damn, I got the fucking visitors today!"

"I am no visitor!" Kelly exclaims.

"Excuse my frustration, and I wasn't speaking of you in particular, but I am used to having Danny here alone. He usually doesn't bring girlfriends here for more than a weekend. I know he is a playboy. That is just Danny, but he has always come home to me."

"Well, you best get used to me. I have been who he comes home to for the past six months and neither of us has any plans of changing that."

"You're just another maid."

"I am no fucking maid! I am a model and if he recommended your low ass to me, I might hire you to clean my condominium."

"Just another maid."

"AWRRRRRRGH. You don't get it, do you?"

Kelly storms out of the room and goes back up the stairs. She enters the room with Danny, being quiet as to not wake him. She slips in under the covers and falls asleep beside him. They sleep for several hours.

Danny gets up and slips on his house shoes to go find coffee. He gets to the grand room and goes right into the kitchen. There, he finds the coffeepot ready to go, he just presses the button and waits. Sitting there with his cup in his hand, in walks Tilley. She is very unhappy about the way Kelly is treating her.

"You know, Kelly thinks that she is it for you."

"Woman, I just woke up. I am not in the mood to listen to you bitch about Kelly. Look, she is about all I have right now, so leave it the fuck alone."

Tilley gets up and heads back to her room. The clock on the coffeepot says three am. He looks outside and it is daylight. "Shit, I guess we need to set the hours on the simulated sunlight for them, too. They are freaking helpless here!" He is about ready to go back to the cabin.

He fills his cup back up and grabs another one for Kelly and heads back up to the bedroom. Kelly is up, with her robe on, when he enters the room.

"I would have gotten that for you, babe," she tells him.

"It's okay, I am not sure that you know where everything is yet, anyway."

"I would have just told our maid to make us some coffee." She smiles.

"Leave her the fuck alone! My god, why do two women have to go at it so hard? I am not in the mood to debate this shit as soon as I wake. It is freaking three am and it is daylight. Does that tell you anything?"

"Yeah, they are stupid?"

"I am from Arkansas and I ain't too thrilled about putting these folks down, but my goodness! There are instructional videos and my *blonde model* girlfriend can set the damn daytime/nighttime routine. Give me a break! They have had it like that for six months? What do the replicator pits look like? Is Hot Springs Village overrun with rodents and snakes?"

"These are your people," she replies.

"I guess. Let's go out on the deck."

They walk out on the second-floor deck. It is a large fine deck that is half-covered, the other half has a retractable awning that is set up as a sun deck. It has composite decking boards, a nice small gas burner embedded into the table, lawn chairs, and a basket of fresh fruit sitting off to one side, away from the burner. They have a seat and it is a little nippy, so Danny lights the flame. It is a rectangle metallic black grate with a flame that dances above it. They both pull their chairs up close to the table and near the heat.

"Where did the fruit come from? Is it real?" she asks Danny.

"Yeah, it's real. Tilley knows I come out here in the mornings and she always has fruit for me to eat."

"She came through our room? That is a little weird. We should lock the door."

"No, she didn't come through our room. There is a set of steps just around the corner there. She always uses that to prepare my deck."

"Well, I didn't know. Hell, from what I get, the bitch might slit my fucking throat while I sleep."

"Tilley is a sweet woman. She would never do anything like that to one of my guests."

"The big guy didn't take her for some reason."

It becomes very silent. Danny grabs a banana and pokes Kelly on the leg with it before he peels it and begins eating. They both have their fill of coffee and fruit. Danny knows he has to go find out what is going on with the maintenance on the shelter. He will have to find Mr. Johnson to see what is being done and why things aren't working.

They go down to the great room to find Tilley watching television.

"Where can I find Mr. Johnson?" asks Danny.

"He stays at the maintenance home by the lake, where the golf course maintenance and clubhouse used to be. They dug up the golf course and made the lake."

"Yeah, they tapped into an underground heat source to help heat the shelter naturally through the lake. Kelly, you coming with me?"

"Yes, I'd rather not hang around here with her."

"Same here." Tilley replies.

"Listen, Tilley, you are going to find you a new home. How does that sound?" Danny explains.

"Seriously, Danny? After all this time? Why?"

"Because this will be my new wife, and if you can't find a way to be respectful to her, then you have got to go."

"I apologize, Danny. I didn't realize it was that serious with ya'll. I will quit, I promise."

"Okay, well, you work for me and I afford you this lifestyle and if you can't handle my situation with my woman, then you must go. Understand?"

"Yes, sir!"

Danny takes off to the garage, with Kelly in tow and she has a grin from ear to ear.

Chapter 8
Paradise Broken

Danny and Kelly climb into the green Mustang. He hits the button to open the garage door. The roar of the 5.8L engine livens up the garage. A few revs of the engine and out of the garage they go. He arrives at Mr. Johnson's home a short time later. It is a nice modest single level home with a porch and a screen door. Danny looks at his clock on the car and it is five am. Then he looks at Kelly.

"Is it not a little early to be pulling up unannounced?" Kelly asks.

He sits there in silence for a moment. "Nah, these old fuckers all get up early."

Danny pushes a button and the cutouts open, making the car a lot louder. He revs the engine and out comes an old, gray-haired man, with his overalls mostly on. He is pulling one of the straps over his shoulder and trying to button them as he steps onto the porch. Danny says, "See, I told you he was up."

"Or you woke him, you asshole."

Without another word, Danny opens the car door and begins to walk to the porch.

"How are you, Mr. Johnson?"

"I was fine. Enjoying my morning coffee in peace, watching the fog roll off of the lake through my front winder until I heard this monstrosity. What brings you to my home this early in the morning?"

"You know who I am?"

"Yeah. I don't know what you want or how the fuck you got to our shelter, but I know who you are."

"Great, I funded all of the shelters around here through Chimera."

"I know. What do you want to do, kick us all out? Start chargin' us rent?"

"No, but I would like for you to quit trying to fuck my maid, for starters, and I need to know about the Internet service. We have been trying to reach ya'll from Hot Springs for six months and no one is responding."

"Well, sir, after about the second week of heavy snow, the Internet and television quit working."

"Did you not know that you have a mast that the dish is mounted on, and it has to be raised above the snow so it can see the satellite?"

"No one said a word to me on how to keep that working."

"They gave you videos on how everything works. Did you at least empty the replicator pits and change the filters?"

"Oh, yeah, they showed me that, but nothing on the dish, uh mask, and my computer quit working after the Internet quit, so I didn't figure I could watch no videos."

"Mast…and you don't need Internet to watch a MPEG. Oh, it doesn't matter now. I need to start getting things in order around here. Are the controls in your home?"

"There is a building specifically for the controls. I go in there to adjust the heat sometimes. It heats through the lake somehow, I do know that."

"Can you take me to the building or tell me where it is?"

"It is the new big building on the beach of the lake. It would be on the inside of the circle at Ronda Pi."

"I know the place."

"Why did they have to make a lake out of the Desoto golf course? They done had a lake that they let freeze," Mr. Johnson asks.

"Tapping into natural heat. I got to go."

"Seems like they coulda done that with the other one."

Danny and Kelly hop back into the little green hot rod and the headers thunder out a sound that makes the old codger step uneasy. Danny revs the engine a time or two as he presses a button on the center console, holding it until the dash reads

"Advanced Trac OFF". He spins backing up and tears out of Mr. Johnson's, on a mission.

They arrive at Ronda Pi and sure enough, a new large building is built there. Danny and Kelly walk through the front door to find a control room. It reminds him of powerhouses that he has seen in some of his manufacturing facilities. There is a door that opens to the back of the facility; they walk in to look. There are pumps and pipes going all over everywhere. Several large motors sit at the back. Danny assumes they are electric generators.

They walk back up to the control room and Danny spots a computer. He looks over at his little blonde model and says, "This looks a little fancier than the one at our little abode."

Kelly says, "It looks like the same software." She sits on the high-back leather desk chair. She clicks and navigates through several different screens.

"Don't fuck up their environmental controls. The cabin is too small for all these old bastards."

"We aren't staying?"

"Thinking we will do whatever we want. We could tunnel to Little Rock. I own that one, too."

"I won't screw it up. This is where you change it from constant light to simulated daytime/nighttime mode." She clicks and the outside light dims.

"What about the dish? I hope it has enough stroke and it ain't freaking stuck like ours was."

She smiles. "I pushed the auto-raise and it is blinking red."

"Well, I'll be, kiss my ass! I ain't climbing out in the cold to fix the damn thing. I bet they don't even have a bucket truck."

"You will if I want you too bad enough." She smiles as she looks at him.

"Why didn't they put an override in here? I got to get up to the roof? I don't even know where the hell it is in this shelter!"

"Wait, the red light started blinking yellow." An alarm comes up on the computer monitor that reads HEATING DISH DOME.

"Does that mean it is going to melt the snow itself?" Kelly asks.

"Could be. Let's give it a little time to see."

It turns red again. The alarm banner reads HEAT CIRCUIT FAIL.

Danny says, "Damn it! Try it again."

It turns yellow again, then starts blinking green. The alarm banner turns yellow and reads MAST RAISING, then turns green and reads NO ACTIVE ALARMS.

Danny pulls his phone out of his pocket and it shows that he has WiFi. He shows Kelly. They both get in the hot rod and tear out of there. They pass several houses, with people standing out looking at the lights. Several golf carts are headed toward Mr. Johnson's house. Danny kind of chuckles and says, "Jew got some splainin' to do, Mr. Johnson," as they turn into Danny's driveway. They come up on two boys that look to be about sixteen and seventeen. Danny stops the car and rolls down his window.

"Where are you two going?"

"We are going up to see Tilley."

"Who are you?"

"I am Bryan and this is Adam."

Kelly speaks up, "Didn't Tilley tell you that she didn't want you there?"

"Yeah, but I spoke to her since and she invited us back."

"It's my fucking house, guys. If you have business there, you need to clear it with me," Danny replies.

"Uh, yes, sir. Who are you?"

"I am Danny Nichols."

"I thought you had left on a ship."

"No. You little pricks, get out of my driveway. Don't come here unless I invite you."

The two slowly begin walking the other way. Danny dumps the clutch and does a burnout as he heads on up to the house. They pull up and the black GT is sitting outside of the first of the three garage doors. Tilley is on her knees with two bottles. She is cleaning the black marks they had left. The rumble of the Mustang slowly quiets down as Danny downshifts and pulls around to back into the garage. Kelly says, "Poor little Miss Tilley having to clean the floor." Danny just cuts his eyes at her as he shifts the lime green muscle car into reverse and the door rises. They both get out and walk over to Tilley. She looks up at Danny with a sad expression.

"Sorry, Tilley, I was kind of excited that I could actually drive that badass thing."

"Well, it would be nice if you got out of the garage before you started leaving black marks."

"Sorry, you want me to help?"

"Kelly could, but I can get it."

Kelly is on the far side where Tilley can't see and draws back her foot like she is going to kick her. Danny walks over to a cabinet and opens a drawer to pull out a white cotton rag. He comes back over and kneels down and starts scrubbing. Kelly shakes her head and heads into the house, mumbling something about, "She is the maid, that is kind of her job."

Danny asks, "So, it has been daylight around here for the past six months?"

"Yeah, it never gets dark. I noticed that while you were gone it got dimmer outside, though. That was unusual."

"We set up the system so that it is on a daytime/nighttime routine. It will keep the days and nights as they normally would be. Your Internet should work now, too."

"That is awesome!"

"Mr. Johnson isn't big on computers. I don't know how anyone can be computer illiterate this day and time."

"He must not have known how to turn that on or he would have changed it."

"I guess I should run around and see how many lights are burned out. Are the replicators working right?"

"He keeps up with the lights pretty good. He likes playing with the bucket truck, I think. The replicator has started getting a little bit salty and some stuff comes out pink."

"The filters probably need to be changed. I will get everything up to snuff before me and Kelly go back to the country."

"You are leaving?"

"Yes, but I am only about an hour away now, so I can come visit anytime I want."

"Maybe without Kelly and lock the shelter door?" She laughs.

"I doubt we'll be locking the door, but maybe without her sometime. You have been to my cabin before. That is where the other shelter is. Maybe you could come there."

"Is there anyone else there? I would love to go there and it just be you and me."

"Nope, no one but me and Kelly. The shelter was going to accommodate several others, but the others that I invited left before the construction was complete."

"Does everything work there?"

"Yes, it all works really good. It will all be in working order before we leave here also. The country shelter has a bunch of land to go hunting and fishing on. There must be a hell of a lot of snow, though, because my satellite dish is extended all the way out. I hope it doesn't get any deeper or I won't have Internet and TV there."

"Can't drive your hot rods around there much, huh?"

"Nope, no hotrods, but I have a few four-wheelers."

They finish cleaning up and polishing out the black marks. He goes in to catch up with Kelly. She is up in the bedroom on his computer.

51

"Is that thing working right?" he asks.

"Yes, it is working great. I checked my email and I heard from some people in Little Rock's shelter. They have a virus outbreak there. There are about five thousand people in the shelter that is downtown. They have had two hundred deaths from it."

"That sucks. Do they have any idea how it started?"

"They have some tunnels opened up, but they think it came from someone within the shelter. They have quarantined it."

"Quarantined? I thought we were all quarantined."

"They have a tunnel buster also. They have I-40 open to Conway and I-67/167 open to North Little Rock's shelter, then out to Jacksonville and Cabot. They talk like everyone gets around up there fairly well, so they aren't as isolated as some."

"I want no part of it if they have some virus that is killing everyone."

"I agree, but it may be nice to be able to go get supplies if we need something."

"We will have to keep that in mind. I wonder about Hot Spring's city shelter. How are they doing?"

"I have checked on them, but I don't think they have a tunnel buster. I don't know where they would go, anyway. The next shelter would be ours and it is not documented on the public's list since it is privately owned. I know some people know about it because it was being built before the snow."

"I guess Dallas, Atlanta, St Louis, and all of the big cities have tunnel busters. They have probably opened up roads all over the country."

"I have read information online and saw it on the television. It took a long time for them to get tunnels opened, though. I think they are just now beginning to trust them. They had some collapses."

"When are you wanting to go home?"

"Home? You mean to our shelter?"

"Yeah. Home."

"Right now wouldn't be too soon for me. I need to see about my garden and I wouldn't mind getting away from your housekeeper."

"We have everything working here. I would like to spend some time with Mr. Johnson in the morning, to make sure he knows how everything works, and we will leave after that. We can come back anytime we want, now that we have a tunnel."

"Sounds great."

Chapter 9
Welcome to the Wild Side

The next morning, Danny and Kelly take the big dually Superduty truck and go and meet up with Mr. Johnson. They take him to the control room on Ronda Pi and show him how to set up and control the satellite dome, the daylight simulation, and other various things. They go around and check all of the pits and they seem to be working properly. Danny shows him the filters for the replicator supply and explains how important it is to keep them clean. He had only changed them once and they were past due. They require cleaning every three weeks and Mr. Johnson thought it was every three months. No one had gotten sick, that they were aware of, and the only issue was the food tasted somewhat salty.

Danny did want to go to the equipment shed to find out what kind of provisions were there, in the event that he needed to do some maintenance here. He wondered if it would be necessary to bring equipment with him from their shelter. Mr. Johnson directs them on where to go in order to get there. They arrive at an enormous building with several large roll up doors and a fair-sized parking area. They pull up to a walkthrough door and Mr. Johnson thumbs through a big key ring to find the proper one.

They get the door open and step in to find a multitude of machines. There are Jeeps, trucks, excavators, bulldozers, bucket trucks, fire trucks, brush trucks, and several varieties of tunnel busters. Danny walks up to the tunnel busters and he spots a double. The orange sticker on the front reads MEGA TUNNEL BUSTER. It has two and a half times the width and height as the one attached to his truck. Danny says, "Holy shit! We could cut a trail with that thing." It has a little bag hanging from it and he reaches in and grabs a thumb drive.

They go back to Mr. Johnson's home and drop him off. There isn't much conversation between the two as they come upon the two young men they had the confrontation with the day before. Danny swerves the big F350 over their way and looks over at Kelly. "Competition?"

Kelly laughs. "If you were away for six months, maybe. But just because? Uh, hell no! Just little boys. That may say something for the quality of maids around these parts." Danny just shakes his head.

Danny says, "You know, we need to get back to the cabin."

"I am ready to get home. I want to cook you up some tenderloin."

"How would you feel about driving the tunnel buster truck back?"

"Why?"

"I want my Mustang at the cabin."

"Let's just drive the Mustang then."

"What if there is a collapse? We wouldn't be able to get back out. We would end up stuck," Danny responds.

"Do you have a trailer?"

"Yeah, that would work, I guess."

They get back to the big house on the lake to find Tilley out in the yard turning up the soil with a shovel. Kelly says, "Crazy bitch."

They climb out of the truck and Danny yells, "What the hell are you doing to my lawn?"

"I thought you would like to have fresh vegetables, like you have at the other shelter."

"That would be nice, Tilley, but I don't want a garden in my front yard!"

"Where then?"

"Make it around the side if you want, but not in the middle of my front yard. Fuck!"

"Okay, but I am doing this for you."

"You don't have to, but if you must, have Mr. Johnson come with the tractor. Tell him that I am asking, and have him disc up a spot between the side and the tree line."

"Will do. You sure he won't want some favor in exchange?" Tilley says.

"We had a clear conversation concerning that. I don't think he will be trying to pull your apron strings anymore."

"Really?"

He parks his truck into the garage and walks around the side to get the tunnel buster Superduty. He backs up to his shop, that is opposite of his garage, and opens the middle door, finding a covered car trailer. He backs up and hooks it up. He pulls out, pointing toward the driveway, opens the back door and directs Kelly as she pulls the pretty little green muscle car into the closed-in trailer. It isn't long and they have Chopper in the back seat and are packed and leaving for the country shelter.

They get out into the tunnels and are on the road for about an hour and arrive back at the country shelter. He gets out to open the big doors and finds the latch is not closed. He walks back to the truck and checks his pistol for ammo and chambers a round.

Kelly says, "Problems?"

Not wanting to spook Kelly, he doesn't tell her the latch wasn't closed back. He thinks that he may not have secured it properly since they were in such a hurry and besides, where could they have come from?

"No, no problem, but we have been away for a while. Wild dogs could have taken over for all we know."

Kelly chambers a round in the black AR that she has pulled from the back seat. Chopper looks on attentively. He pushes the door open and pulls the rig through the door and heads back to the big gray doors, being very meticulous in locking the latch back. They drive the short distance to the cabin and nothing appears out of order. They open the door and Chopper comes out barking and growling with a vengeance running past the garden as he heads to the woods.

56

Kelly says, "What's wrong with Chopper?"

"I have no idea, maybe just glad to be home in his woods. There could be a coon or rabbit that has decided they can run across Chopper's territory and he wants them to know he is home now."

"I hope that's all it is," Kelly replies.

Danny begins to open up the trailer and unload the car. Kelly goes into the cabin and starts settling in. A short while later, he has the car parked at the corner of the yard, just in front of Kelly's garden so that he can sit on the porch and admire it. He decides he needs a driveway to the main road so he can drive it some. He hears Chopper out in the woods growling and fighting with something. Then he hears Chopper yelp. He comes back to the house limping a little and his mouth is bloody. Danny goes over to see what is wrong. He has no injuries other than it appears something has hit him rather hard on his leg, it is sensitive and sore. He doesn't want Danny touching him there. Each time Danny tries to look, the big dog pulls away and moans. "What have you had a hold of, boy? Did a deer get you?"

Danny thinks about the door being unlatched and decides that it is impossible for someone to make the trek from anywhere to the shelter without somehow leaving signs. He didn't see any tracks other than the tracks from the big Ford pickup with the tunnel buster and what his wheeler had left. He decides to take a walk in the woods just to see if he can find a dead animal, as the stench from rotten dead things lingers pretty bad in the closed-in shelter.

He walks down past the garden as he hears a woman's voice. He turns back to the cabin and Kelly is standing on the porch. He can't make out what she is saying and yells, "I'll be back after a few. I can't hear you, dumb bitch." He reaches inside his shirt to feel the handle of his .45 caliber handgun, being reassured that he has protection against whatever may be lurking in the woods. He enters the woods where he saw Chopper come out. It isn't long and he spots a few drops of blood on the ground. He also finds a strip of clothing from what looks like a blue flannel shirt. He is very uneasy after finding this evidence and instantly goes on alert, realizing they may not be alone in the shelter. He decides it is better not to be wandering around out in the woods, with it just being him and Chopper, so he turns and begins the trek back to the cabin.

He arrives back to find Kelly sitting out on the porch, with a deer rifle. He walks to the side of the house and gets a water hose and cleans Chopper up.

"Where did you go?" she asks.

"Didn't you see the blood all over Chopper's mouth?"

"I saw he had gotten into something, but couldn't tell what it was. Looked kind of brown on that black mouth of his."

The jet black dog shakes the water off and goes up the steps, with a pronounced limp, to lie down on the porch. Danny walks up the steps and throws the ripped piece of bloody, slobber soaked, flannel shirt on Kelly's bare leg. She is wearing tight white shorts, a white tee, and a beige top with a collar, that ties in the front. She picks it up as if she were picking up a rat by the tail and looks at it, throwing it back at Danny.

"What is it?"

"It looks like a piece of a shirt sleeve to me."

"Where did that come from?" she asks.

"That was where Chopper was growling and barking."

"Well, that isn't a coon."

"Not an animal at all from what I can tell," he responds.

Kelly is a little alarmed now.

She says, "Do you think they will go to the medical facility?"

"If they find it, they likely will since at least one of them is injured. How cold could we make it in here and your garden survive?"

"We could make it about thirty-three degrees, but if they walked here on foot, they must have cold-weather gear."

"True, I can't imagine where they came from or how they arrived at our shelter. Maybe I should go back and look for a shirt. Could it be that he has one of my old flannels and was playing tug-of-war with a coon or something? I have game cams near some of the pits. I will check them and put them in some other locations."

"I will get your rifle," Kelly responds.

She heads into the cabin and comes back out carrying a black assault weapon and an ammo belt across her shoulder. The tight white shorts and long beautiful tanned legs look awful sexy, giving Danny other thoughts. They climb onto the wheeler and take off down the trail to the first pit. She has her gun with the sling across her back and Danny has his with the sling backward, the rifle hanging across his chest. They get to the first pit and he hands his gun to Kelly and begins to shimmy up a tree. He gets the camera and pulls a compact flash card out of it and climbs back down with it and the camera in his hand. They ride to two other pits and retrieve cameras at each one. They ride past the steaming creeks and out to the medical facility. Danny places one on a tree across the road from the white building. He puts a new card in the camera and flips a switch marked WIRELESS on it. They do the same at the main doors.

When they arrive back at the cabin, Danny puts a camera at the end of the garden. Kelly takes the cards from Danny and goes inside to put them into her computer. Each compact flash card has a terabyte of memory, and they record color video when it is triggered. Kelly begins to scan through it and sees several different animals pass by. There are deer, turkeys, and a bobcat. She tells Danny, "Did you know that we have a bobcat?" He just kind of looks her way, then she comes to a video of a man.

A bushy-tailed animal comes flying out of the pit and lands on him. She realizes it is Danny. She begins to laugh and he comes over to look over her shoulder. She knows he is behind her so she backs up the video.

He says, "See, I told you that crazy little bastard came attacking my ass!"

"It is still funny. A little squirrel kicked your ass. My big, tough man!" She busts out in laughter as they both watch the scene unfold again.

"He got his, though, didn't he?"

It isn't long and they realize that this is going to take quite a while. She asks him if the camera software has some type of an alarm so they know when the motion detector is triggered. He explains that it does and opens the software. They are happy to be getting a signal from all three cameras. The pits were too far away to get the wireless signal when they were there, so they relied on the cards. She continues reviewing the images and videos.

Danny goes out on the front porch with Chopper and drinks a beer to watch the simulated sunset. The lights are still bright at the west end of the shelter, but the ones over the cabin begin to dim, casting long shadows that are somewhat similar to a natural sunset. They both see a deer come out on the side of the garden in front of game cam.

He shouts into the house, "Did the alarm for the garden camera come on?"

"Yes, there is a doe at that one."

"Good, they work. How do you know it is a doe?"

"It doesn't have any antlers."

"Bucks shed their antlers in the spring. It is April, you know."

"There is a deer at that one," she replies sarcastically.

He makes his third trip into the house to fetch a beer and Kelly asks if he wants something to eat. "No, I will drink my supper tonight," he replies.

"Don't give me that shit. You know I would have fixed you something had you asked." Kelly spends hours looking at the video without any evidence of anyone out there.

Danny has had his fill of beer and is ready to lie down. He comes into the house and Kelly is talking to people at the shelter in the city of Hot Springs, asking if there was anyone who had made any tunnels or had left that shelter. Danny tells her not to mention their tunnel buster. They will want them to open a path down to there.

Chapter 10
The Op Track

The two find their way to bed fairly late. They get settled in and all of a sudden the computer alarm begins to sound. Kelly and Danny go look at the computer to find a deer in the garden camera. He minimizes the software and begins to walk back to the bedroom and it beeps again. It is a second camera near the medical facility. He sees lights from vehicles, he takes off running out of the cabin, grabbing his shoulder harness and pistol on the way. He is only wearing his pajama pants, with no shirt, and Chopper right behind him as he gets out to the barn. He jumps on his wheeler and blasts out of the door, heading toward the medical building. Up through the ditch, the roar of the large wheeler is very pronounced. He slows down and kills the lights. He begins to drive on the shoulder of the road, being as discreet as possible until he can just barely see the lights from the vehicles. Chopper is just catching up with him when he stops and shuts the wheeler off. He begins to walk and kind of sneak through the darkness of night to get to the medical building.

He gets a clear view of the front door. They have a pry bar they are trying to force the door open with. He shoots the big .45 caliber pistol toward the ground, away from the group. Chopper begins growling and running toward the criminals. There are three of them and they come running out from under the awning at the front of the white facility.

The three jump into two vehicles that Danny has never seen before. They sound like snowmobile motors and have what appears to be a small bobcat or excavator type tracks, two per side, one above and one below. The passenger area is shaped like a formula one, racecar, which comes out from a silver metallic point and gets larger where the passengers lie down inside of it, with a hatch that closes in the cockpit. It is about twelve feet long, with a white label that has OP TRACK down each side of the blue machine.

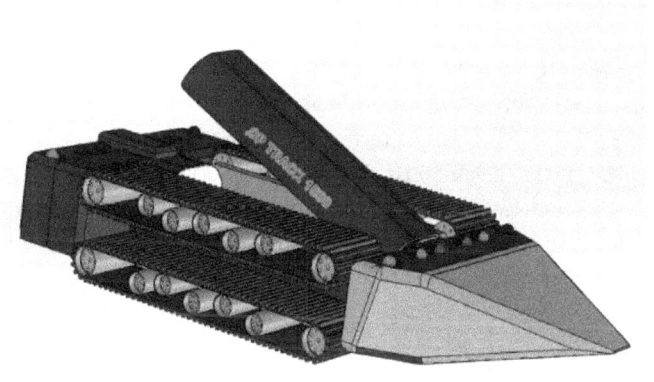

The vehicle is an Op Track and is named for the opposing tracks on each side of it. Danny runs back to the four-wheeler as one zooms past him, with several brightly lit LED lights. The other takes off in the opposite direction down the paved road. They go a short distance and the Op Track makes an 180-degree turn in the road and comes back, with the blinding lights aimed toward Danny. Danny takes the ditch to avoid wrecking and gets a misplaced shot out of his pistol as he begins to consider how many rounds he has with him. The big tires make a low-pitched growl on the asphalt as Danny turns the big four-wheel-drive four-wheeler around in as tight of a radius as it will allow and continues pursuing the tracked vehicles. It isn't a real fast vehicle as Danny gains on it. He knows they will run out of road fairly quickly, as the big doors block the end.

The pair gets to the big doors and the other Op Track is there with the doors open, awaiting their arrival. Danny's wheeler is heard downshifting as he is uncertain of what he will do without cold-weather gear and limited ammo. They reach the other Op Track and the two take off through the doors. Danny reluctantly follows and comes through the doors at nearly full speed, slipping and sliding as the big wheeler hits the ice. He struggles to regain control, but they turn to the right off of the road and into the side of the tunnel, and disappear into the snow. All that remains is a small rectangular entry cavity where they plowed into the snow bank.

Danny stops and looks at what they did. "What the fuck," he yells. He is freezing and doesn't have much time to contemplate the anomaly that he just witnessed. He turns the big wheeler around, slipping and sliding on the frozen road, and heads for home.

He makes his way through the big doors and closes them securely, using the light from the red taillight cast from the wheeler. He walks back to the back rack of the ATV and pulls a bungee cord from it. He puts the cord on the handles of the door, wrapping it around the latch several times until it is tight; securing them from being opened from the outside. He wonders if there could be others in the shelter, but he doesn't believe that he will find them if there are. He is tired and ready to go get some restful sleep.

He pulls up at the front porch of the cabin as Chopper meets up with him, out of breath, and Kelly busting through the front door with her AR pointed at him. He says, "Whoa."

"KaaPOWWWW". She shoots the AR down toward the garden as Danny ducks behind the wheeler.

"It's me, you crazy bitch!"

"I know, you scared the fuck out of me and I wanted to share the love, you dick!"

"I am out there fighting with intruders and you are worried about me scaring you? Women are fucking crazy! You're shooting the damn gun at me for that?" he says as he slowly and reluctantly makes his way around the wheeler, somewhat ducked down as she might take another shot. He then makes his way up to his bed.

Chopper and Kelly follow close behind. "Well, you could have told me what was going on. They could have killed your dumb ass! Couldn't you have used some backup? And I wasn't shooting *at* you or you wouldn't be walking, asshole!"

Danny shaking his head says, "There was no time. Just let me get some freaking sleep, please, and put that damn gun up before you shoot something."

The two get back to sleep and the cameras trigger alarms several times during the night. The first couple of times Danny gets up to see and each time it is deer or coyotes. Danny tells Kelly to keep an eye on the alarms and if there is anything other than animals to let him know.

The next day, they both wake about ten am. Kelly fixes breakfast as Danny sits at the computer looking up "OP TRACK." He finds that it is a purpose built ATV for the deep snow. He and Kelly sit eating at the kitchen table.

Kelly says, "Op Track? Is that what that thing is called?"

"What thing?"

"The thing in the shed that looks like the vehicles they were driving last night?"

"There is one of those in the barn? With the machinery?"

"Yes, there is an orange one that says Yamaha on the front of it and has Op Track down the middle of it."

"I have been in that barn looking at that equipment quite a bit. I have used most of it and I haven't seen no damn Op Track."

"It is sitting behind a big blade looking thing for the excavator, I think," Kelly says.

"Are you sure?" Danny's voice seems to be a little more excited.

He hurries and finishes his replicated sausage, biscuits, and eggs so he can go out and look at what she is talking about. She finishes eating about the same time he does and tells him to go with her out to the barn and she will show him. The two meet up with Chopper on the front porch, looking much more relaxed than he has been since they have been home. He jumps up to follow them. Danny unlocks the walk-through door and they go into the equipment room. They walk to a large spare blade for the dozer and behind it is an Op Track. He admires it for a few minutes before yanking the bag off the hatch handle that contains the memory stick with instructions and manual. He steps back around the dozer blade where Kelly is standing and says, "I love you sometimes!"

Kelly about falls over. She says, "I love you sometimes, too, asshole."

Danny wastes no time getting back to the computer to see how to use it. THE YAMAHA OP TRACK 2000 flashes across the screen. It shows the machine up in Canada where there is about six feet of snow. A man stands beside the vehicle and begins to demonstrate it.

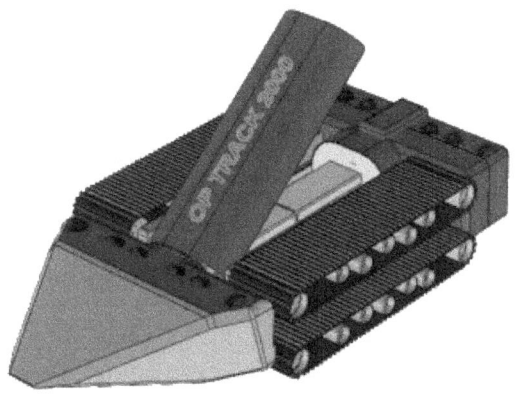

"Welcome to the operating video for the Op Track 2000." The man on the computer screen walks near the machine and points to the two thirty-six inch wide tracks on the right side. "It has two opposing tracks on each side of the vehicle. They turn in opposing directions and this is key for the intent of the vehicle. It can create traction on the top or the bottom tracks. The controller that we will view later in this demonstration will explain how to control the action of these tracks. The machine was built for use within the snow. Yes, folks, that's right, I said within the snow. It can, but it isn't made to travel on snow. It is built to build and travel through its own tunnel within the deep snow. If the bottom two tracks turn faster than the top two, then it will travel in a horizontal direction and create a vertical climb. If they go slower, then it will move in a horizontal direction and begin a vertical descent. If the tracks on the left side move faster than the tracks on the right side, the vehicle will turn to the right and vice versa. It is geared and computer controlled so the tracks are synchronized with variations that are controlled from the cockpit. This machine can do this all while submerged in snow, like a mole."

He walks to the front of the machine and points to the nose. It shows a nosecone that is pointed like the front of a formula one race car, but much more utilitarian looking than for aesthetics. The angle is the same at the top and bottom, extending out past the tracks in front and on each side. The entire machine is orange, with Yamaha graphics, except for the nose and it is a brushed silver metal. The enormous black tracks on each side almost conceal the body. He continues, "The front is heated and serves to melt the snow prior to the tracks penetrating it. This is an important feature when you are traversing through deep snow and it becomes denser, or if you encounter ice. The machine can stall and get stuck by heavy snow or an object that is nearly solid. It also creates a condition that allows you to move much faster in snow that is not extremely dense."

Kelly is standing behind Danny and says, "We could go anywhere with that thing."

Danny replies, "Yeah, and not leave a gigantic path for others to follow."

The man continues as he walks to the side to open a large, rounded, oval-shaped door that rises from the top. The camera pans around to reveal the cockpit to be three padded beds, one in the center and two below, one on each side, with a padded place to put your face when looking downward at the display below. The bed in the center has two joysticks near the front. He continues, "The cockpit is built for comfort and has a GPS system with memory built in, and uses a sonar as well as a radar signature that shows relative distance from the ground and the surface, also the density of the snow that is in front of and behind the vehicle. It is equipped with a 2000cc engine that can produce about two hundred horsepower. The engine is referred to as a 2000cc but is much more compact and powerful than typical engines and operates from diesel." He continues to explain the displays, joystick controls, and how to navigate the screens.

The two finish the video and are hell-bent on giving it a try. They both head out to the barn and begin moving equipment around to retrieve the vehicle.

Kelly says, "Do you think we could go to a department store with this? We could use some canned goods. I would imagine most everything is preserved pretty well because it will be so cold inside, keeping stuff frozen."

"Hell yeah! I can think of a lot of supplies I could use. New guns, more trail cameras, anything we want, and it is free!" He kind of chuckles as he thinks about how he owned so many department stores. Everything had seemed free to him in the past, but he has some excitement with the thought of acquiring new stuff.

They continue digging the little machine out and it isn't long 'til you can hear the rattle of a little diesel engine. He comes backing it out while Kelly watches. Chopper is barking at it and Danny takes it around the yard, kicking up dirt. He gets back up to the cabin and Kelly is still near the barn walking down that way when he emerges with his walkie-talkie.

Kelly yells, "Not this time! I am going!"

She walks up to make sure Danny's mind is right about her intentions and he says, "What if something happens? I get stuck?"

"I guess we'll both die then."

68

Chapter 11
Be Prepared

The two load up in their machine. There is a center bed that has controls on each side. The stations are covered with white leather and it has one station to each side of the center and is very similar to the one in the video. The ones to each side drop down about ten to twelve inches and follow the contour of the body of the machine. A hatch that hinges from the front is raised with small cylinders on each side and matches the shape of the machine when closed. The hatch is tucked down in between the two wide tracks that come up further than it does at the top.

Once inside, they have enough room to look at, and talk to, one another. It is easy for Danny to look down at Kelly on the left side, but she has to turn almost on her side to look up at him in the center station. Danny says, "Man, I am glad I am not claustrophobic."

Kelly says, "This is like lying on a massage table." Danny looks at the colorful screen just below his face as he adjusts his grip on the joysticks. He has one in each hand. On his right, he has a mouse ball to the right side of the joystick and he navigates the screen with the mouse. It isn't long and the rattle of the little diesel engine is roaring. They begin to move forward, with Chopper looking on and barking at this unusual vehicle that just swallowed his masters.

Danny throttles it up and pushes the joysticks forward until they get to the ditch and onto the road. It is surprisingly very quiet inside the machine. They ride along at full throttle until they reach the big doors. They stop and Danny gets out to open them. By this time, Chopper had dropped off his pursuit and returned to the cabin. Danny opens the big doors and climbs over the top of the big track on one side and gets back in facedown into the little Op Track. It is a little cumbersome to get

69

into it this way, but once in, he pulls it through the doorway, only to climb back out again to secure the doors. This time, he pulls a piece of paper out of his pocket, folds it a couple of times, and places it in the crack between the doors so if they are opened, he will see the paper on the ground.

He lies back down into the machine and flips a switch and Kelly has a monitor that comes alive. Each of the two passenger stations has monitors. The cockpit is lit with a blue hue from ambient lighting that is controlled within the display. He clicks through a few screens to find one that shows the tunnel ahead, with dashed lines indicating his current direction of travel. The screen is various shades of blue that seems to indicate the density and temperature of the area in front of and beside the machine. He has the display in snow mode. The machine also has cameras that show the outside.

He begins forward and turns sharply to the right and anticipates burrowing into the snow wall of the cave. *THUD!* The machine stops dead in its tracks, with the nosecone submerged into the snow to the tracks. He pulls back on the joysticks to reverse away from the wall and it is stuck. He looks over at Kelly. She says, "We're stuck already?"

He pushes forward then back on the controls and the machine will not move. He pushes a button to unlatch the hatch and the display reads, OBSTRUCTION. HATCH OPEN NOT POSSIBLE.

Kelly says, "How much gas do we have, *brain surgeon?"*

"Don't give up on me yet." He begins to scroll through the screens as Kelly looks on with her own view of his selections.

He comes to a screen that is marked "NOSECONE TEMPERATURE" at the top. All of the indicators are blue. Near the middle of the screen it reads: enable, tune, off. "Off" has a red banner behind it. He scrolls over to the "On" button and clicks, a green banner illuminates as the red one turns gray. A rectangular bar below it slowly begins to change from a dark blue to a lighter gradiated blue. There are two rows of values shown that display SP, CV, and PV. These values indicate:

- SP Set Point (1250°) [This is the desired value of the nosecone temperature].
- CV Control Value (225°) [This is the actual temperature of the cone].
- PV Process Value (100%) [This is the controller or power output going to the heaters to make them heat to the SP].

Danny looks over at Kelly. "Do you know what is wrong?"

"Hell yes! You didn't have the nosecone heated and it stalled as soon as we went into the snow bank."

"Well, aren't you a bright one?" he smirks.

Kelly says, "Bright enough to know when you are fucking up, and the ride along may not have been one of my best choices."

Danny just kind of chuckles as the PV slowly begins to drop off to 60%, then less and less. The bar at the bottom that was blue is now colored red at the top. The temperature of the CV shows it is now 1200°. He revs the little engine as he changes the screen to show the blue screen with a red nosepiece below it, located in a smaller pop-up selection on the display. He pushes the joysticks forward and they begin to move as he hears Kelly say a prayer and something about why the hell she trusted him for this maiden adventure.

The two travel along, completely submerged in snow as Danny begins to get the hang of it.

"Kelly, would you like to go to the surface?"

"I was thinking a department store. What do you think we will see on the surface? A blue screen?"

"I was thinking the sun!"

"Well, if you think we may see the sun, then yes, I would very much like to see it. I thought it was dim or had burned out. It has been so long since I have had an opportunity to see it."

"No, it isn't burned out and if it isn't cloudy up there, it should be brighter than it was before. The sun is not as hot, but the hydrogen is burning on the outside of it, making it appear brighter. I read up on all of this after it actually happened."

Danny continues as he rolls a thumb wheel on each joystick upward to begin a climb. They climb up through the snow until the display shows a faint horizon of darker blue. The Op Track pops up and is on top of the deep snow. He stops the machine and navigates to a screen that displays the outside air temperature. It shows it to be negative ten degrees Fahrenheit. They both have winter gear in a small cubby at their feet.

Kelly asks, "Is that the outside temperature?"

"That's what it says. I would think it is a little warmer than that, though, because we have been in that ice cream sandwich and the machine is as cold as the snow is. Not sure if that is the air temperature or the temperature of the machine."

"Let's check it out."

Danny pushes the button labeled HATCH OPEN. The entire top of the machine hinges open above them. They immediately feel the strong wind coming into the cockpit. They hurry to grab their white jumpsuits and gloves. Danny climbs out and onto the left track and Kelly stands up on her knees in her seat. The sun is very bright and the wind must be blowing at forty miles an hour. Danny pulls the sides of his white, thick fur-lined pilot's hat down over his ears as his face begins to turn red from the wind.

He yells over the howling wind to Kelly, "You seen enough?"

"Yes, let's get back in there where it is warm!"

They quickly disrobe from the winter gear and climb back into the cabin facedown as Danny presses the HATCH CLOSE button as soon as he can. Their faces are both red from the wind and they are sniffling. The top of the craft comes down

72

and snaps closed. The two settle for a few minutes as Danny turns up the heater and changes the screen to the outside cameras the machine uses when they aren't submerged in snow.

Kelly says, "Much nicer view!"

"No doubt!"

They travel around and see nothing but blinding white snow with an occasional treetop that peeks out of the snow-filled landscape. They drive around and go up to a snowdrift and the machine begins a descent down into a valley. Danny throttles it up and rotates the thumb wheels downward, changing the screen to a depth finder screen that shows the blue images, similar to what they had seen earlier. He turns the craft back toward the shelter and sees an outline of what appears to be a tree. He navigates around it and continues to go downward. He changes the display once more and it shows a street and the outline of different buildings and houses that are along the side. They follow this road as it is the one that brings them back to their shelter. The display has numbers along the bottom that has a label for distance to ground level, height above sea level, and distance to the surface. The distance to ground level shows twelve feet as he makes his way down this street.

They are traveling at a pretty good pace in the dense snow at thirty mph when they briefly see a faint image on the display that looks like an upside down horseshoe or tunnel. Danny exclaims, "Oh shit!" They have come out into the tunnel. They are at the very top of the tunnel and fall ten feet to the surface of the roadway, landing with a *thud*. The engine dies and all of the displays in the cabin are off. The ambient lights are off and it is pitch black dark. He tries to reboot the computer system but everything is dead, he tries the starter and not even a click. They are both shaken up and winded by the collision.

Danny says, "Kelly, are you okay?"

"I feel like I was dropped on my head. What just happened?"

"I think we broke out into the tunnel."

"Asssshole!"

73

"No doubt, but let's see if we can get this hatch open and figure out what kind of shape we are in."

Danny rolls around onto his back and reaches up in the dark cockpit to find a handle. He grabs it and rotates and pulls down. It clicks and he feels the door move. He struggles to bring his knee up to the inside of the door and begins pushing. Suddenly, the hatch springs open. The two struggle to find their cold-weather gear, feeling around in the dark, trying to put on their snowsuits, and shivering. Suddenly, a bright light emerges from Danny. He has a strong LED style flashlight that he keeps in his gear. He shines the light around and realizes they are not that far from the opening to their shelter. He shines it on the vehicle to find one of the bottom tracks appear to be bent, the nosecone is pointed upward, and one of the bottom casters looks like it is broken.

They walk a short distance, slipping around on the frozen road and through the inside of the tunnel, with the bright light reflecting from the walls of the white cave, blinding them occasionally. They reach the doors and Danny begins looking to find the paper is still snugly sitting in the crack of the door.

He rotates the handle and *click*, the lock pops open. They enter the shelter and begin the walk to the cabin. It instantly feels like it is a hundred degrees inside. They begin stripping off their winter gear. They walk down the paved road and are about fifty yards from the door when they hear the sound of a motor running outside in the tunnel.

They both run back to the door and Danny yanks the latch open and pulls the door to reveal two other Op Tracks, and one has a chain hooked onto Danny and Kelly's. Danny fiddles around in his shirt and pocket, feeling for his gun to no avail. He left the cabin without it and they are helpless to stop the group from stealing their vehicle. Danny yells, "I'm killing you bastards!" as they come speeding past the two, with the 2000 skidding along behind them. They look in amazement at what has just happened. Danny slams his cold-weather gear down on the ground. "Those sons a bitches!"

Slightly quieter, he continues, "I hope that motherfucker was busted beyond repair and fucking ruined when we ramped it off onto the damn road!"

A little bruised and sore, the pair makes their way to the cabin. They walk down into the ditch and see a bright green object off in front of their cabin. They continue walking to bring the view of Danny's green Mustang sitting out in front. Chopper comes running over to greet them as they walk into the yard. It is about noon and Danny says, "Well, at least I still got my tunnel buster and Mustang."

Kelly says, "I think there is another one in there."

"What? No way. You better not be shitting me!"

"No, really, I am pretty sure there is another one under a tarp up in the corner, in the dark area."

"They can't be more than twenty grand. Hell, if I had known that I was going to be on this frozen, fornicated fucking place, I would have bought twenty of those damn things."

They don't even stop at the cabin. The two, with Chopper in tow, walk on out past the Mustang and open the side door. They make their way to the corner Kelly was talking about and there is a tarp that has YAMAHA across the top. He pulls back the cover to reveal the big black rubber top track of yet another Op Track.

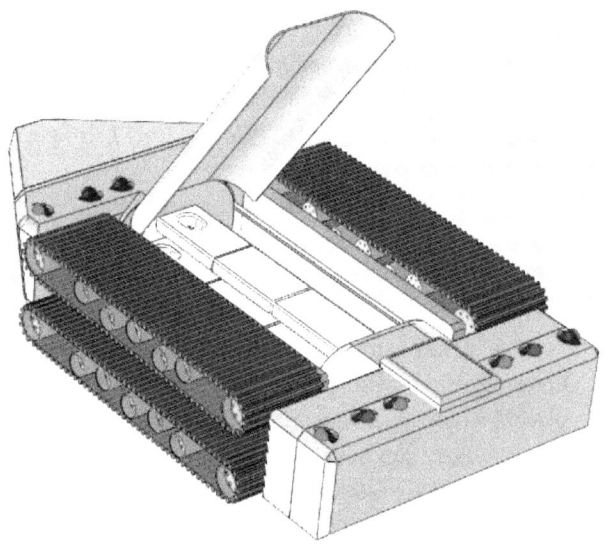

"Hell yeah! 3500cc Maybe I can find those fuckers and catch them with this one."

"If your dumb ass doesn't wreck and break it."

He just gives her a blank stare, as if to be looking through her.

Then he says, "Really? I wish you wouldn't," he pauses, "bitch."

By saying it in this way, he actually is calling Kelly a bitch, but he thinks he can get away with it by saying, "I wish you wouldn't---bitch."

"Hey, that ain't funny."

"About time for some lunch, ain't it, sugar?"

They both head up to the cabin to find something to eat. Danny is very happy that he has another Op Track, as this will undoubtedly be a very quick and easy way to navigate the world he finds himself living in and hopefully get him to some of the stores in the area.

Chapter 12
Recovery

They finish lunch and decide to sit out on the porch for a little while. Danny sits there and discusses going back up to Hot Springs Village. Sitting on the porch, in the nice seventy-degree afternoon, they hear the computer beep. Kelly goes in to find that Danny has mail from WRC. The correspondence is from WRC Commander-in-Chief Charles Phillips.

Dear Daniel Nichols,

I hope this email finds you well. We are currently determining monetary claims and land rights here in Stilligate. We have not had any claim by you. Mr. Ron Lewis has claimed an enormous parcel of land to build numerous factories and has put in a request to take full ownership of your corporation, Chimera. We have full documentation of this man being the acting Chief Financial Officer of your corporation. The doctrine and records indicate that you are the CEO, Chairman of the Board, and full private owner of this corporation, but we have not had any correspondence from you in the past six months.

I remember meeting with you personally with some of the funding efforts during the formulation of the WRC. I know that if you are still alive and well, you have quite a lot at stake. We have had this claim request put in for releasing this corporation that you have built, along with the transferred equivalent Stilligate capital of eighteen billion US dollars in currency, as well as several manufacturing corporations for the past three months. There has been no acknowledgment of your arrival here on the new world, and it would be a shame to see this released inappropriately. If the request goes unopposed in the new world for six Malpeada months, then the transfer request shall be granted.

Please reply to this correspondence at once if you receive this letter, as I have no desire to see someone else acquire what is rightfully yours.

Sincerely,

Charles Phillips WRC Commander-in-Chief

Kelly says, "Uh, Danny, you may want to look at this." Danny comes in and reads the email and says, "No shit? They have land and my money on Goldilocks and fucking Ron is trying to claim it? Fuck that! Oh, that's some bullshit!"

Danny sits down at the desk and begins banging the keys off of the computer. He writes:

Dear Commander Phillips,

I am very much ALIVE and well. A little disappointed that my CFO has not made any efforts to try to contact me. I have the same personal email service as I have always had, however, none of the WRC or Chimera mail servers work anymore here on Earth. I FORMALLY LAY CLAIM to my corporation. Please send the official paperwork that I need to redeem what is mine, sir. I need to find a way to get my dignitary transport to come and get me. Is there any way that could be possible? I assume my pilot, John Glasgow, took the ship without me.

Sincerely,

Daniel C Nichols CEO and PRIVATE OWNER of Chimera Co. Inc.

Danny says, "Now that I have a line in to the empire, maybe those assholes can figure out a way to come and get their fucking boss."

"How would they get you? They can't land a transport without runways."

"They have a great big ass dignitary ship that lands like a helicopter. They can, and from what I can see, they damn well better. I am going to reclaim all that is mine on Goldilocks!"

"You're dreaming. They will never come back for us."

"We'll see. Hell, I paid for at least two or three of those damn ships and half of the shelters around here in Arkansas. I deserve to have them come back for me."

"Are we going to get the new Op Track out?"

"Yeah, let's see if we can find those low life fucks that stole my other one. I bet they didn't get much. I think we ragged that thing out."

They head out to the barn to dig out the new Op Track. It is much larger than the other one and has four compartments for passengers. One center location for the driver, then two on each side that are spaced to the side and a little below each other. About a quarter of the bed lays beneath the center, then the next is arranged in the same way on a lower level on each side, following the outside contour of the body of the machine. They are shaped in somewhat of a triangle from top to bottom. Danny gets a good look at this and says, "I guess this is the damn bus. We can carry four passengers."

He climbs inside of the large vehicle and it cranks for quite a while before the deeper growl and rattle of the bigger Track busts off and starts. The blue lettering down the center of the big white Track says, YAMAHA OPT III. He throttles her up and begins the trek through the barn. He pulls out of the big door, with the tracks just barely clearing on each side, and stops. Kelly sees the hatch pop open and walks out of the barn to him. He climbs out and explains that he wants to go to Hot Springs Village to check on things. Kelly says she would rather stay there for this go round.

Danny asks, "You mind if I bring Tilley back?"

"Go ahead and bring that bitch back. We will have a fucking hunting trip. Two go out, one comes back." She laughs.

Danny doesn't find the humor in that and *click*, the hatch is closed and he cruises up by the Mustang in front of the cabin. He runs in and grabs his gun and a handful of supplies, including what looks like an overnight bag and winter gear. Kelly is about halfway back to the cabin as he makes his second trip out to the Op Track and says, "You aren't planning on staying up there, are you?"

"No, but I want to be prepared for whatever."

"You aren't locking me in here, are you?"

80

"No, but you need to run up there and secure the handle with a bungee cord after I leave."

"How will you get back in then?"

"I will be back here…let's see…it is one o'clock, plan to meet me at the doors at seven o'clock."

"It's a plan. You know I was kidding about bringing Tilley hunting."

"No." He slams the hatch and the loud roar of the big diesel is accompanied by flying grass as he goes across the yard, heading to the ditch.

"Don't be screwing her!" Kelly yells as he is going out of sight.

He travels up the path, knocking small trees and brush down as he goes because the machine is so wide. This machine has a much more sophisticated display. There are two main screens and one on each side, perpendicular to the main. He looks down at the larger screen, then the other two and turns them on. It is as if he has his head at the nose of the machine. The walls of the tunnel are clear, with a blue hue. He travels a few miles and comes upon an orange Op Track. It looks damaged. There is a rectangular impression in the snow where they went in, but his must have gotten hung up when the thieves tried to pull it into the snow without it being powered. It sits on the road abandoned, with the nose buried into the snow at the wall of the tunnel.

Danny pulls up beside it and gets out to view the machine. He ties a rope onto the nose of it and to the back of the large 3500 and begins to return back to his shelter. It is about a half hour by the time he gets back. He pops the hatch and goes up to the doors and turns the handle. He thinks it is stuck, then he remembers. "Damn, Kelly has locked me out. Son of a bitch!" He leaves the machine near the door and returns on his way.

It's not long and he is at the first intersection. He turns to the left. He travels along for a little ways and sees what looks like impressions from the other Op Tracks on the road. He throttles the big machine up and is now traveling about fifty mph. He rounds a curve and sees the back of one of them on the display. He gives the big machine all it has and starts following them.

They realize he is behind them and duck into the side of the tunnel. Danny has the nosecone heated up to about 1400° and is ready for it, submerging his machine into the snow after them. They travel a little ways and he gets close enough to the slowest one to get the nose of his machine against the thief's right rubber track. He nudges up against it, taking all of the cleats off of the top and bottom on the right side, rendering it useless. He pulls a hard right around the stalled vehicle embedded in the snow, and catches the other one. He does the same and they are immobile and have met with their destiny. He makes a circle and slows, thinking about their fate. He thinks about them stealing his machine and trying to run him over and guns it. "Fuck those sorry bastards." Off to Hot Springs Village he goes.

The first Op Track, that is inoperable, guns his and it runs in a circle. He continues to run it in a circle, trying to break free. It seems to be no use as he continues to run back into his own tracks.

Danny continues on and arrives at Hot Springs Village. He enters the doors and starts into the shelter. He turns on the outside cameras and drives until he gets to his driveway. He starts up his driveway and gets almost to his house when he spots two boys walking down the street. He is pissed and swerves the tracked vehicle toward them, making them both jump into the ditch beside the road. He figures he has done enough damage for one day, though, and pulls up to the house and pops the hatch.

Tilley comes out to see what is going on and sees Danny. She runs up and throws her arms around him. He just stands there with no emotion or response to her affection.

He says, "Was that Adam and Bryan leaving my house?"

"Yes, but they didn't come in. They only came by to check on me."

"You sure? So you would be okay with going in and spending a little quality time with me?"

"Yes, there isn't any reason why not."

A short time later, they are in Danny's bedroom. Danny is up sitting at the chair and gets on his computer to check to see if he has heard anything back from Commander Phillips, but nothing yet.

He says, "I told those little cocksuckers to stay away from my house without my permission. I killed two, or maybe three, men on my way here for stealing from me. I would not be fucked up about two more for fucking my woman."

Tilley smiles at the fact that he says that she is his woman.

"They have not been in my bed. Don't you think you could tell if they had?"

"Yes, but still, they keep trying. It isn't like I am worried about going to Hell. I should just go put a fucking bullet in their little cocky ass heads and be done with it."

The room grows silent. He thinks and decides that it is best just to leave the situation alone. Hell, they could have a gun and shoot him for all he really knows. And how would that work out?

"I'm not going to kill your little boyfriends, but I do not want them at my house again! Understand?"

"Understood. You really killed someone?"

"I am sure I did. I cut their tracks down and stranded them in thirty feet of deep snow, in an Op Track like mine."

"They stole from you?"

"Yeah, the bastards took another Op Track I had that was wrecked, and they broke into my country shelter, tried to run me over on a wheeler."

"Well, damn, if given the chance, I would kill them bastards for you."

Danny turns to get on social media to see what is going on in the other shelters. It's always bad news: shootings, violence, rapes, and criminals. *No God, no order*, he thinks to himself. They had a collapse in New York. They believe that they had some incomplete construction causing this. The subways are holding up in many of the major cities. They have had some collapses of their snow tunnel systems. Everything he continues to hear about the larger shelters is very negative.

He turns to look at Tilley and says, "The big cities are crap, you know it."

"I have been on that thing some and I see all of the turmoil going on there."

"Ron was trying to take over Chimera on the new world. I had a communication from the man himself, Commander Phillips."

"Really? What did Ron do?"

"He put in a claim to take ownership of my company and money. I told them to send a transport after me and to hell with him. That company is mine!"

"I completely understand. What did they say when you said you wanted a transport to come after you?"

"It was an email. It takes almost five hours round trip, that is if he answers it when he gets it."

"That is a pipedream, though, huh? How would you get to the surface? How would they land it?"

"Not a pipedream. That Op Track out there has tickets for five to get to the surface. The transport can land like a helicopter. All I need is a pilot and for them to have a desire."

"I bet they come and get you."

"I would think they would after all of the contributions I made to the WRC. We'll see, I suppose. It isn't anything that will happen fast. It is at least six months for them to get here. Then six months back."

"Mr. Franklin was an airline pilot."

"Really? Does he live here in the Village?"

"Yep, he is the last house on the right before you get to the doors on Desoto Boulevard."

"Wow, so if I could find a transport here and figure out if he could pilot it... then we could leave sooner than I thought possible. They are equipped with various styles of controls so that different pilots could fly them. I bet he could handle it. How old is he?"

"He is about fifty, I would guess."

Danny says, "Hell, I imagine he is young enough that he could get there without kicking the bucket on me. That would be a lot quicker than six months waiting for them to get here. But damn, how would I get it out if I could even find it? If it is even here. I fear my pilot already took mine without me."

"I don't know, but will you take me with you?"

"Who would care for my place, Tilley?"

"Seriously?"

"Nah, if I am out of here, you have a seat in my Op Track and my spaceship. You may have to ride with Chopper."

"I can handle that if I can get to the new world."

Danny looks at his watch and says, "Damn, I better go before that ornery ass old lady of mine locks me out."

"Can I come?"

"Not this round, pretty lady, but we will see what we can do the next time I am here."

Danny leaves the house and loads up in the Op Track and down the road he goes. He slows way down as he passes Mr. Franklin's house, studying the display to see if he may be outside. He gets to the doors and off he goes down Desoto.

Chapter 13
Hitching a Ride

Danny arrives back at the country shelter and hitches the big Op Track up to the old bent and twisted machine. He walks up to the door, crossing his fingers, and the latch turns freely in his hand. He breathes a sigh of relief as he walks back to climb into the big 3500. He pulls through the doors and smells smoke. It is odd for Kelly to have a fire, as they replicate just about all of the bio-material that is within the shelter, including wood. He slams the doors back together and drags the old wrecked Op Track up to the cabin.

On the display, he sees a small fire and Kelly sitting beside it in a lawn chair she drug out from the porch. He stops and pops the hatch.

"Look what I found."

Kelly looks back and sees the old Op Track.

"Where did you find it?"

"Along the tunnel. I guess those poor dead bastards couldn't drag it through the solid snow."

"Dead?"

"Well, I didn't go back and check their pulse, but I would say it is a difficult jam to get out of…if they do."

"What did you do?"

"I caught up with them and chased them through the solid snow and used my nosecone to burn their cleats off their tracks."

"Oh, no, so they were stranded in the machine in the snow?"

"Pretty much. Shouldn't be thieves, shouldn't be trespassers, shouldn't screw with my stuff! Not like God gives a shit at this point! What are you doing with a fire going? Isn't that a waste?"

"Yeah, but I figured we could spare a few limbs. I needed this to gather my thoughts. You go up there to screw Tilley?"

"What? Where did that come from? No, I didn't go to do that."

"It just seems strange that I am wanting to go to a store and you want to go without me."

"You could have gone. You didn't want to, remember?"

"Yeah, I guess. It's not like you are worried about sin."

"I was screwing women left and right before you and I met. It isn't sinning that scares me about that. I really don't want to hurt you or her. I will still do what I want, though. I have not made any lifelong commitment to either of you. I didn't go there to do that. We will hit a store in the morning. I have a pilot, I believe."

"A pilot? What does that mean?"

"It means that *if* my transport is still here on Earth and I can find it and figure out a way to clear the snow, we can get out of here!"

"You are going to get us out, aren't you?"

"I am damn sure going to try. Do you want to leave?"

"I honestly don't know. It is pretty peaceful here. There is plenty to eat and the simple life in our shelter is kind of nice, honestly."

"Well, I have to go, or else I lose everything that I have worked all my life for."

"Isn't this like retirement? This is like *Little House on the Prairie*. We can grow a garden, have anything we want to eat, and I guess I have my answer."

Danny says, "Yeah, but I am not done. Maybe God didn't take me for a reason. I believe that I have a calling on Goldilocks."

"Calling, yeah right."

"No, I am serious. I haven't done anything too terrible, well, until now. I never wanted to kill anyone and I think he still has plans for me there."

"Could be, I guess, but it sure feels like we are sinners. It could be that both of us still have work to do."

"I am now worried about the guys in the damn Op Track. I need to know. It weighs on my conscience."

It is now about seven thirty pm and they are both about ready to get inside and settle in for the evening. Danny is very interested in the reply he is waiting for from Commander Charles.

They go in and Danny gets in the shower. When he finishes, he goes into the bedroom with Kelly. Kelly says, "Okay, you screwed her." Then abruptly rolls over, with the blankets securely around her beautiful body.

"Why would you say this in such a certain way?"

"Because the only reason you shower in the evening is if you have gotten dirty. You always shower in the morning."

Danny just ignores her and climbs into bed. Three thirty am rolls around and Danny is still tossing and turning, thinking about the poor bastards freezing to death. He just can't let it go. They haven't really done anything but trespassed, and attempted to take a wrecked Op Track. Damn, is that really a death sentence in 2119? He closes his eyes and manages to get about an hour of sleep. Four thirty is lit on the red LED alarm clock on his nightstand as he throws the burgundy and gray blankets off, snaps on the lamp on his nightstand, lighting up the room, and leans up to begin getting dressed. As he is lacing his boots, he is inadvertently shaking the bed in an annoying fashion.

Kelly says, "What the fuck? You didn't get enough? Got to go hit that nasty whore again? You make me sick!"

"You best just get the fuck off of me. I will take your ass to the town of Hot Springs and drop you off. That bullshit there has run its course now, and if it hasn't, we have, damn it!" he says in an evil sounding voice. "Enough, woman! My god! I can't just leave those poor bastards for dead. I have to go see about them."

He finishes lacing his boots and takes off out to the barn. Chopper jumps up, a little startled that his master is out so early, and follows him. He walks up the path in the yellowish light from the security lighting, reaching the barn and checking the fuel in the 3500. He pulls the Track over to a fuel pump under the side of the barn eve, with a green handle that reads BIODIESEL. It is formulated from the replicator system. He drags the hose across the big black track and into the fuel door to fill the rig up.

He climbs into the machine and drives around the back side of the barn, across the yard to the front of the cabin, near the green Mustang. He sees Kelly standing on the front porch, seemingly waiting on him. He says, "Christsakes, woman. Haven't you bitched at me enough?" He pulls up and pops the hatch, leans up, kneeling on his knees on the operator station.

"What do you want, woman?"

"I kinda feel bad. I want to ride along."

"You sure? I am not listening to any more of your mouth about Tilley."

"I am done with that."

She climbs aboard and off they go. They get near the area where Danny chased the three into the snow to find an abandoned blue Op Track. It has one set of Tracks with smooth cleats and two more without cleats thrown over the top of it. He climbs out into the frigid temperature and walks over to the abandoned Track, no one is inside. He returns to the warm idling 3500, smelling the diesel exhaust, and climbs in.

Kelly says, "No one there, huh? They must have managed to get out of the snow."

Danny replies, "Looks that way. I guess I can sleep with a clear conscience about this."

They return home and climb into bed. Kelly is much more willing to accommodate her man's needs when they are bedding down this time. Danny is too tired to even have a desire, even with his beautiful girlfriend, and explains he has to have some sleep.

Danny wakes about eleven am to the smell of bacon, freshly brewed coffee, and sausage gravy. He walks into the kitchen in his night pants to find Kelly cooking up a nice breakfast for him the old-fashioned way. He thinks to himself that she is over the whole Tilley thing.

"This is nice," he says.

The computer beeps before Kelly can reply. He steps over to the computer desk and finds a response with several attachments from Commander Phillips. It explains the forms attached are what is required to claim his property and assets on Alpha Kantabury I and that his dignitary transport shows to have been fabricated in Arkansas and is sitting in a hangar at Little Rock Air Force Base. Commander Phillips explains that if Danny can find any commercial or military airplane pilot, they could pilot the craft. The email also has an attachment for codes, where keys are located, ownership rights, and instructions on how to pilot the spaceship. Also, the hangar where the ship resides has fingerprint recognition access and has been coded to recognize Danny's fingerprint.

Danny gets up from the computer as his breakfast is ready and sits down at the table.

Kelly asks, "Any word from the man?"

"Yeah, my transport is at Little Rock Air Force Base, just waiting for me."

"Under a million pounds of snow, no doubt."

"I bet there is a way. It is in a hangar and all of the buildings I have seen so far have a gap or a drift near the edge that is thin. Remember the first time we opened up Hot Springs Village? It all just melted away with the big F250."

"Is a hangar as tall as a shelter?"

"I doubt it, but they have to be big to hold a C130. That is what is kept at that base. Hell, they may have snow cleared there for all I know. Post some bikini pics, babe, talk to the airbase for me."

"Just like that, pimp me out, huh?"

"This is your ride to the new world, too."

"I got you. I will see if I can raise some interest at Little Rock Air Force Base."

Kelly gets on the computer and updates her profiles to include some boating pictures taken at an area lake before the snow, and puts interested in men on base in Jacksonville, Arkansas.

Before you know it, she has friends all over the shelter at the base. She starts inquiring about the flight line and if it is clear or snow packed. She finds out that not very many have access to the flight line, but they said that the base had been partially cleared near the main gate and some areas around the entrance.

Danny goes out and jumps on his wheeler. It is time for his trek around the shelter to empty the pits and check on the integrity of the structure. He gets to the first pit and it is unusually full. There is a strong odor as he presses the button. He doesn't hang around as he is excited to find out what Kelly learns about the base. He cruises to the second bin to find it just as full as the first one. He wonders how many ground-dwelling creatures could there possibly be. Are they breeding? Are they coming from caves? How the hell do they come continuously for six months, nonstop? How long will it continue? Months, weeks, or years? He doesn't ponder the thought too long, but it does seem amazing to him that, for now, it seems as though there is an unlimited source of food.

He finishes the last pit and starts his normal trip back by the hot springs when he sees a large dent in one of the outer walls. He pulls over to take a look. It appears that someone has run an Op Track into the shelter. He just doesn't know if it was recent or if it was an old dent that he hadn't noticed before. It looks as though whatever did the damage was hot, as it appears the paint on the panel is burned. He decides it doesn't matter much if they are to get out of there. He jumps on the paved road and comes upon the medical facility.

91

He pulls up in the driveway and wonders if the gang had gotten in. He walks up and sees the damage to the door trim that had happened two days prior. It has deep impressions and pry marks on it. He pulls a key out and unlocks the door. He makes a quick walk through, finding nothing out of place and grabbing a large white bottle of hydrocodone and pouring an unmeasured amount into a smaller bottle. He grabs his scar on his chest from the squirrel and says, "What the hell, it kind of hurts." He sticks the small bottle in his pocket, locks up, and takes off back on his way. It isn't long and he is parking in the yard of the cabin, admiring his tough looking little muscle car.

He heads into the house to find out what his hot lady has found out about the base. She is on social media, just chatting up a storm as Danny walks in.

She cuts her eyes at him and he says, "You have a pilot?"

"One? I have fifteen. I don't know if any are over twelve years old, but they can all fly an F16, according to them. I really didn't think the government left that many pilots behind."

"They want pussy, they will tell you anything to try to get your little rebel flag bikini down. Any requests for naked pics?"

With fire in her eyes, she snarks back, "Any? I think that is all these horny bastards want. Don't they have women up there in that shelter? My god!"

"Ten foot tall and bulletproof behind that keyboard. If they saw you in person, they would probably piss their pants and stutter, trying to work up the courage to ask you your name."

"I know, that is why it always makes me uncomfortable talking to these guys that are probably jacking off while looking at my pictures. I did find out some information that I believe to be true, though. There are some hangars that are cleared. They cleared some for accommodations for the people that live out in the country near there and for fear the main shelter wouldn't house everyone. They also said that not very many people are

92

allowed on the flight line, so I doubt any of them really knows anything."

"Did they give you hangar numbers?"

"No, I will keep trying to keep them focused on what I need to know, rather than sending me naked pics and trying to dry hump the screen."

"If they have a way to clear the shelters, maybe my old buddy, Commander Phillips, could have them clear mine."

"Ask him."

"I want to go to Walmart and the local sporting goods store to see if anything is left. I would like to get some more supplies and maybe some fresh food. Real food."

"Let's go!"

Chapter 14
Bad Men

The two load up in the 3500 and take off to find
Walmart. They make their way out of the doors and go left
down Hwy 7 toward Hot Springs Village. Kelly says, "There is a
Walmart up this way?"

"Yeah, we have passed by it every time we go to the
other shelter." The whistle of the diesel engine and the roar of
the ice road can be faintly heard through the machine from the
wide rubber cleats pounding the ice. They travel at about forty-
five mph for about thirty minutes and Danny says, "It should be
right in here, on the left." They both study the GPS on their
monitors. They see what appears to be a flat area with poles in it
and the GPS lights up, showing that it is the place.

Danny pulls slightly back on the left joystick and Kelly
feels the big Op Track turn to the left. They see a dark blue wall
and the monitors show outlines of their surroundings. Soon they
arrive at the front of the store. Danny stops the vehicle just shy
of the front as he searches for the entrance. He slowly drives
above the sidewalk encased in snow, studying the faint image of
the front of the building until the monitor shows a recess. He
rolls the thumb wheels forward on the joysticks and brings the
machine to ground level as he reaches the entryway. There is a
break in the snow and suddenly the cameras take over and
brilliantly lit LED lights illuminate. They are on a tan
cobblestone tiled concrete floor that is absent of snow. The glass
entryway reflects the light into the camera, making it difficult to
see.

Danny pops the hatch and the two begin to climb out of
the Op Track. Kelly says, 'This is strange. I always dreamt of
coming here and being able to buy anything I want."

"It's all yours today, kiddo, if there is anything left."
They put on their winter gear as it is very cold. Danny pulls the
key and closes the hatch of the 3500. They walk up to the

darkened store and force the automated door open by pushing it to the side. Walking in, Danny remembers the elderly gentleman who used to greet him at the entrance. As they go, they realize the store is untouched. It is as if they had stocked it and everyone left. They both have very bright lights attached by Velcro to their pilot caps. The light is an LED light and an area light that lights everything around them for about fifty yards. They have the area lit very well.

They walk the aisles with their shopping cart. Danny says, "Now, we can only get what we can fit into the Op Track, you know that, right?"

"I know. But we do have a big truck and this isn't very far away from the main tunnel. You can make another tunnel." She smiles like she's found a new puppy.

They walk each aisle, grabbing canned vegetables, cookies, Vienna sausages, and other treats that neither have had for quite some time. They know most have past the expiration date but are hoping the freezing temperature has preserved them, as everything here is rock hard and frozen.

They make their way to the camping gear, lures, and guns. Danny just starts grabbing every weapon that he can get and goes to tools and retrieves a pry bar to open the glass-front cabinets that are locked. As the two are walking back, Kelly says, "Do you feel like you are stealing?"

"A little, I did not own Walmart," he replies. "But all of this is currently being rebuilt far away from here."

"You can only take what will fit in the Op Track, remember?"

"I have an F250. I can come back and get what doesn't fit."

Kelly chuckles. "That was my line. We may need a trailer." They have so many guns and so much ammunition that the cart is bowing down in the front. Danny grabs another that is in the aisle and begins filling it with the best rods and reels that Walmart has on the shelf. They continue on, realizing they will have to come back. They push six carts to the front of the store and are content on coming back with their truck. They pack all of the necessity items like canned goods, etc. into the Op Track and Danny places all of the guns in the vacant passenger stations.

"You freaking big kid, you aren't leaving me any room." She knows they will get hers soon enough and she is just elated they have the opportunity to do this and that she gets new clothes.

Once the Op Track is filled, they leave and they aren't but about a quarter of a mile from the Hot Springs Village shelter. They drive to it with the Op Track unusually loaded. Just before they get there, they see the broken down blue Track the three thieves left. Danny stops.

Kelly says, "What are you doing?"

"They took mine. I am going to take theirs. Mr. Johnson may like it, or even better, I may give it to our pilot, Mr. Franklin. That may be a good ride if we can figure out how to replace the tracks. He probably shit in it when he realized what I did to him, though."

He climbs out and wraps a tow strap to the front of the smaller vehicle and begins dragging it to the front of the shelter. It pulls off to the left side as one side is missing a track altogether. They get to the doors and Kelly gets out and opens them for him to pull through. He pulls in and she closes them. The bare pavement makes the machine bellow out one hell of a racket. It sounds like someone is dragging a car on its top and squealing tires all at the same time as he drives down Desoto Blvd, making a long wide black mark and scrapes on the surface of the nice black roadway.

He turns right to go to Mr. Johnson's house and gets a glimpse of something he doesn't expect to see in the display. It appears to be black marks left from an Op Track.

Kelly says, "Did you go this way when you came yesterday?"

"No, I did not. Who made that?"

Kelly reaches down and grabs two black guns with stocks that look military. She slides back a lever on the right side on each to load a shell in the chamber so they are ready for whatever they may find at Mr. Johnson's. He stops just before the turn and unties the broken down machine. He climbs back aboard and they turn to go follow the tracks toward Mr. Johnson's.

Danny stops well short of the house. He sees another blue Op Track setting in the front of his house. Danny and Kelly walk up slowly and stealthily, as to not be noticed.

The next thing they see is Mr. Johnson coming out of the house, with a man, in a black leather jacket and beard, holding a shotgun at the back of his neck and the old man's shirt to keep him from running away. Two others walk to his side and slightly behind and are similar in appearance. The big man with the shotgun says, "You will tell us who it is that lives at the other shelter and drives a white Op Track, or I will blow your head off, old man."

Mr. Johnson pleads with the man. "I truly don't know anyone with a vehicle like yours. Please, please, I wish I could help you, but honest, I don't know."

Danny runs quickly through a lightly wooded area, with Kelly near his backside, trying his best not to be too loud, and to get close enough to get a shot off at them.

Danny yells at the men, "I own a white Op Track. Are you looking for me, you fucking scum?"

The man pulls the trigger of the twelve gauge shotgun, blowing a large hole through Mr. Johnson's throat. He drops to his knees on the ground, then collapses in a puddle of his own blood. Danny already had aim on the one that shoots. The man is looking up into the woods, but doesn't spot Danny. He shoots the man in the side of the neck and the reaction is almost identical to Mr. Johnson's fate, only he falls to his side as he hits the ground with a *thud*.

The other two take off running for the safety of their Op Track as Kelly gets a shot off and hits one in the side. A pronounced blood trail follows as they run to take cover behind the machine. They begin to return fire with the shotgun they had grabbed from the dead man. The pellets pepper the leaves and trees around the couple as they use the trees for cover. Danny shoots again and by this time, the thieves are hidden behind their tracked vehicle. It is a misplaced round as he sees a small dot appear in the blue paint of the hatch of the machine.

Danny runs along the tree line, around the yard to the backside of the machine, trying to flank them and get a shot off around the vehicle. Just then he sees a head pop up. He stops just shy of the side of the house, watching the man look toward Kelly and quickly zeroes in on the center mass of his brown hair. He places a perfect round right in the middle, parting his hair and skull on the right side, dropping the man where he stands.

The other man leaps into the Op Track and Danny hears it fire up. He and Kelly both unload their rifles on the machine as it comes across the lawn headed to the road. Danny is running back up the yard toward the road, trying to intercept them. Kelly is still very near the road and it looks as though the vehicle could run her down if he turns toward the woods. The .223 rounds don't seem to be enough firepower to penetrate the thick aluminum hull of the machine. He gets closer and closer on the road as Kelly begins stepping into the ditch and it appears that he is within range to turn right and take her out when she pulls out her .40 caliber handgun. Her small hand barely wraps around the grip, but one handed, she fires. The gun's percussion knocks her small arm back with such force she almost hits herself in the face with it. This shot puts a round right in the center of the hatch, creating a large cavity as the hollow point, Golden Saber round penetrates the machine. Idling, it begins an unlikely turn, moving uncontrolled, eventually stopping halfway into the ditch across the road.

The two slowly walk up to the machine and activate the hatch from the outside. They find that Kelly put the round through the back of the criminal's spine and through his stomach. Danny stands there looking back over the yard at the carnage and poor ole Mr. Johnson, who had no part in any of it.

They walk on up to the house and nothing appears to be disturbed. They take off to Danny's home, feeling remorseful for Mr. Johnson and begin thinking of how they will clean up this mess. They arrive and go into the front door to find Tilley with a black eye and cuts and bruises on her face from being beaten. The pink little shirt she is wearing is torn. She slowly walks to Danny, crying uncontrollably. He holds her, as he fears that he knows what has happened.

Kelly looks on with a tear in her eye.

"Did they?"

Tilley looks away from Danny's consoling, empathetic embrace and over at Kelly, with the hurt of a woman enthralled and killed, and nods her head yes.

"They all took turns raping me," she says.

Danny speaks, "They paid for it, but not before they killed Mr. Johnson. Those low life sons a bitches will cause no more havoc. They are all three dead."

"Good," she replies. "Where are they? I want to spit on their dead, lifeless bodies. Nasty, no good bastards!"

Kelly speaks, "I will bring you there if you are serious."

"Fuck yes, I'm serious! Sick bastards have taken from me what is sacred and I prayed to my god with no recourse. I want to spit on the bastards and gut them like a motherfucking deer!"

"Probably a limit to what we really need to do, but I would like to ensure they are the men and we got them all," Kelly replies.

Kelly and Tilley take off into the garage and climb into the big gray and burgundy dually Superduty. They drive down to Mr. Johnson's, passing the disabled Op Track with only one set of tracks as they turn onto his street, leaving Danny to survey the damage that was done at his house because they busted some things and took some of his guns.

They arrive at Mr. Johnson's and Tilley goes to Mr. Johnson and kneels down by his lifeless body and caresses his blood splattered face, looking at the contrast of the red blood spots in his full head of shiny gray hair. She wipes tears from her beautiful, young, scratched cheek in order to see as she remembers the old man's life.

"Poor Mr. Johnson. He did not deserve this."

They walk over to the first one and Tilley coughs up phlegm to spit on him and kicks the body. It rolls from its front its back.

"Yes, that is the leader. Mark, he was the one who hit me. He was asking about Danny. I wouldn't tell him anything and he attacked me. He was an evil man and the others joined in as he ripped my shirt open and forced my skirt down."

The two ladies walk to the other man that is about twenty feet away and he is unrecognizable.

She says, "I am certain that is another because I recognize his clothes. Oh, my god! There is one more." She begins to panic in fear of the other man who must still be out there.

Kelly motions for her to follow, saying, "Over here." They walk across the finely manicured blood-spattered green lawn to the black narrow street to the Op Track that was fairly concealed by the road and sitting partially in the ditch. Tilley spits on this dead body also and pulls out a cigarette lighter and proceeds to catch him on fire as Kelly pulls her away.

"We may not want to destroy this vehicle."

Tilley seems to understand as she stops her efforts and says, "That is all of them. If we cremate these bastards, I want to light the fire!"

"Understood."

The two climb back in the big Ford dually and go back down the road toward their house when they see Bryan and Adam walking down the road. They stop and the pair walks up to the passenger side where Tilley sits.

Bryan says, "Whoa, what happened to you?"

"Those men in the blue machine raped and beat me."

"I will kill the nasty sons a bitches," Bryan states.

"Too late. Danny and Kelly have taken care of that. They are strewn all over Mr. Johnson's yard."

"Who is going to clean up the mess?" asks Adam.

"Would you guys do it? Is that too much to ask of you? Someone has to," Tilly asks.

"We will take care of it for you pretty ladies," Adam speaks up.

"Who will take over Mr. Johnson's place?" asks Bryan.

"It is a little too early to decide that, but I doubt there are a lot of people interested in it," Kelly explains.

"We are on it," the boys say as they take off walking toward Mr. Johnson's house, with purpose.

The two girls arrive back at Danny's and park the big truck in the garage and go in to see what Danny makes of it all. He wants a way to lock the entrance doors and wants everyone's homes secured now that they know outsiders could possibly get there. He wants to go check on all of the neighbors, especially Mr. Franklin, his pilot.

Chapter 15
Memorial

The two boys go to Mr. Johnson's and go inside to find his keys. They pull one large round metal ring off of a hook near his utility room. There are hooks that have several key rings hanging on them. They are on a wall that is off of the kitchen. They make their way to his storage sheds behind the house. They open a large hinged wooden door, that appears to be homemade, to find a large John Deere belly mower tractor and a green trailer sitting beside of it. They hitch up the trailer and proceed to get the bodies. They load Mr. Johnson first and bring him outside of the doors of the shelter and down the road of the tunnel to the place where it dead ends.

They carefully lay him near the wall of the tunnel and turn back to get the other three men. They load all three onto the trailer as if they were loading firewood, with bodies strewn on top of one another and a stream of blood running down the bed of the trailer, dripping off of the back. They get ready to start back on their way and Bryan steps up on the tongue of the trailer and unzips his pants and relieves himself on the three men. Adam looks on and says, "Just as well." Bryan turns and takes a step up the tongue of the trailer toward the tractor and holds onto the back of the seat as Adam drives to bring the dead men out to join Mr. Johnson.

They arrive back and pull out a hose and clean up the blood as best as they can and begin gathering fallen timber from the tree line. It isn't long and they have a full trailer load. They do this twice, making a large pile in the middle of the road near the dead men.

They return to Mr. Johnson's home and park the tractor and trailer back in the shed, as he had it. They find his old trusty pickup truck and drive it up to Danny's home. They arrive to see Danny standing out on the front porch. They fear that they will be unwelcome, as they were the last time. They pull up on the cobblestone circle drive, park, and step out.

Danny says, "Welcome, welcome, boys," as he waves his hand, letting them know that it is all right.

Adam says, "Thank you, sir. We weren't certain that it was okay for us to come or not, but we are both concerned about Tilley."

"I understand and rightly so. You are welcome to go inside and see about your friend."

They waste no time at scurrying past Danny and into the house to see about Tilley. Kelly is in the great room when they enter. She says, "She is in her room."

The pair thank her and go to the kitchen, then to the door to her room. They spend some time consoling her and go back out on the porch to talk to Danny about cremating the bodies.

"Sir," Bryan says, "we have placed the bodies out on the main tunnel where it dead ends. We have never done this before."

"Do you think that I have? I guess soak them with diesel or gasoline and set them ablaze, and hope for the best."

"That is kind of what we were thinking," states Bryan.

Kelly steps out on the porch. She says, "Ya'll built a fire pit in an ice tunnel?"

"Yes, ma'am, we didn't know where else to do it," replies Bryan.

"It just seems that it would melt the snow."

Danny speaks up, "It won't matter, but what I worry about is the snow putting the fire out and having a blockage so the tunnel can't be extended there. Perhaps we should just bury them."

The boys have just done most of a day's work and are surprised that something else is desired now.

"Where do you suggest?" Bryan replies.

"I would bury Mr. Johnson in the backyard at his place and put up a marker. The other trash could be dumped into a spot in the snow, for all I care."

"That sounds like a big job. Is there anyone that could run Mr. Johnson's backhoe?" Bryan says.

"I can run it. I tell you what, you get Mr. Johnson and I will take care of the others. Can you guys get a rope tied to them?" Danny kind of smiles.

"Yes, sir. We will have all of this taken care of shortly. What about the wood we gathered?" Bryan replies.

"Bring the wood back and we shall have a fire and a memorial for Mr. Johnson. Set it up on the backside of his place, and we will invite all of the neighbors."

"Sounds like a better plan than we had. We didn't consider melting the tunnel. Sir, I don't know what we did to make you so upset with us, but whatever it was, we hope to make amends." Adam says.

"Don't be fucking my ladies."

With that, the two seem to understand perfectly clear. They realized Tilley must have told him about their visits, and they now know what has been troubling him. They go and gather up Mr. Johnson in the old pickup and tie a white nylon rope to each of the men's legs and head back. It is mid-afternoon when they get all of the wood set up for a bonfire.

Danny arrives and gets the yellow backhoe out and digs a sizeable hole. He finds fifty-five-gallon contractor bags in one of Mr. Johnson's sheds. He waits 'til the boys show up and they place his now frozen body in two of the bags to try to protect him from being directly buried. They use duct tape to seal the bags together as well as possible and place him in his grave. Danny uses the front bucket and covers it back up with dirt.

He has gone into the workshop and found some two by fours. He nails them in the shape of a cross and uses a cutting torch to singe the sides and to make it look somewhat decorative. He then stencils, "Cecil Johnson," with a second line that reads: "May 8, 2043 *** April 20, 2119", in the wood and uses the torch to outline it for a marker. Once in place, he uses Polyurethane spray to coat the marker and protect it from the elements.

Danny asks the boys if they know everyone in the shelter. He asks that they invite them to the bonfire, grilled food, and a tribute to their fallen community member to start around nine pm. He then returns home.

Sunset comes for their simulated nighttime routine and the interior lighting in the shelter begins to dim as they all begin to gather at Mr. Johnson's. Danny pulls in with a charcoal barbecue grill in the back of the big F350, driving across the beautiful lawn to the backyard, leaving tire impressions as he goes. He pulls the grill out with the help of Bryan and sets it up. He has hot dogs, hamburgers, and all of the fixings. He lays everything out on the tailgate of the truck. He fires up the grill as more guests arrive.

Mr. Franklin is there, Tilley, Adam, Bryan, Kelly, Mrs. Sullivan, Sam Landry, James Smith, Audie Summerville, and Steve Jackson all showed up to pay their respects, most are driving golf carts and others are riding along. This is most of the people that live in the Hot Springs Village shelter.

Danny starts up the grill and tries to get a head count of the number of people that want to eat. Surprisingly, most everyone wants some real meat. He puts the meat on and begins socializing and having a fellowship with the members of his community. It is a warm feeling he gets from the group. He wonders why some of them are not in Heaven. They all are well-to-do people. He begins to inquire. He asks Mr. Franklin about his experience flying and before long, the food is done and everyone is eating. Danny and Adam light the bonfire as darkness falls. Danny grabs a plate and a lawn chair and has a seat next to Mr. Franklin. He asks him to call him David.

"David, so did you kill someone or commit adultery? Why would you be passed over? You seem like a very decent man of morals. You aren't a booze hound, I don't see any tracks on your arms, there aren't any signs that you have been up there trying to climb into bed with Tilley. Why would you be on such bad terms with the big man? If you don't mind my curiosity."

"I will tell you if you will be honest with me about such things." They both swig a nice cold Michelob Light beer. He continues, "You know, I never killed anyone, I never committed adultery, and my wife was taken when God came. I had a dream and God came to me the night of the first big snowfall and I came to the realization that I was left behind. I kind of charged it off to just a dream, but I believe that He spoke to me."

"God did? What did he say?"

"God said, 'Son, you have been a fine man. You have lived your life appropriately, didn't really lie or steal, but all of your life you have cussed me."

"Really, using God's name in vain? Saying GD caused you to miss out?"

"I can't be sure. Who ever really knows about dreams, but this one was special. I was standing among clouds and He wore a white robe and a golden band on his head, and I specifically remember it was very vivid. I believe it was the most realistic dream I ever remember. I just wish that I had been more careful in choosing the way that I have spoken during my life. He is right, though, GD has been top three in my vocabulary my whole life. Who would have thought that this day and age where people are murdering, lying, and making a mockery of their lives that mere words could condemn you to Hell. Now, what about you? What has kept you here?"

"You may think this is crazy, but I don't think it was because I wasn't welcome. I think that I still have things to do. I think it could be the same for you as well. Cussing blocked you? Surely not."

"Cussing, using God's name in vain is one of the Ten Commandments, brother."

"You ever consider that there could be a way out, though? Maybe they left you for a reason to go to Goldilocks even?"

"How on earth could I get to Goldilocks? My wife didn't want to go, so I skipped it. I really thought they were crazy about the whole ice age. Now God has taken her, and here I am alone with my daughter in that great big fancy house."

"I have a transport. You being an airline pilot, I bet you could fly it."

"You give me way too much credit. An airplane and a spaceship are two different things entirely."

"They have controls for a 767, 747, a leer jet, and others."

"Really? How would we get it off the ground? There can't be a runway open anywhere on Earth."

"It has vertical takeoff and landing."

"See, now you are talking helicopter. I sure as hell can't fly that!"

"It is like a drone. It has a gyroscope and almost does that on its own, I believe."

"*Believe* is a big word when you are flying a spacecraft, ole buddy."

Danny says, "I will get you specifications and manuals. Would you be willing? Do you want to go if I get you what you need to fly it like a 767?"

"What the hell. Six months, though? No copilot? If you can convince me that we can get it in the air and back on the ground without killing everyone, I believe I would give it a shot if the controls are as you say."

"Deal! Pack yo bags!" He chuckles.

"I feel like I just made a deal with the devil." Danny just kind of smiles somewhat fiendishly at David.

Danny joins up with Tilley and begins to go around the fire meeting everyone. He meets Mrs. Sullivan, who is a very attractive older lady. She is the heir to the worldwide Sullivan Stores. She inquires about what he and Mr. Franklin were speaking about. Danny is pretty evasive concerning it because he isn't sure who could or should go and who must stay. He has a few drinks and feels compelled to invite everyone, but he knows in his heart that there must be bad people among him.

He meets Sam Landry, who owns a local chain of restaurants that extends down into Texas and Louisiana. They talk about business and that Chimera owned a competing restaurant chain near his. Sam can joke about it now, but they were fierce competitors back in the day and Danny had no idea.

He then comes to Audie. Audie was a local high-class escort service owner. He knew who she was by the circles he was involved in. They begin a conversation.

Danny asks, "You remember me?"

"Everyone remembers you, Mr. Nichols. It seems that you never partook of my service."

"Nah, I don't pay for pussy. It usually comes when I want it. I may have had some of your girls before."

"I may have given you a few girls on the house before."

They continue along this line of talk for a little while until Kelly seems a little tired of hearing about it and grabs his arm. "You want another beer," she asks as she tugs on his arm.

"Yeah, I will take one." The two take a walk to the back of the truck. Kelly explains that she isn't thrilled about hearing of his escapades with other women. He seems to understand and they go back to the fire.

Many aren't saying a word, just having a nice drink and staring into the fire, thinking of different things. Some think of their loved ones leaving like they have died. To them, it is the same thing. They were taken away from them by God and to them it is the same. Others miss their loved ones that are now away on Goldilocks.

Danny has one more fella to speak with that he hasn't met before. He sits down beside of Steve Jackson and inquires about what he does.

Steve replies, "I was a plastic surgeon for the wealthy in this area."

"Work on anyone I know?"

"Probably so, but I rarely talk about customers or what they had done. It is kind of a doctor/patient confidentiality thing."

"I understand."

The conversation was light and quick and the group spent most of the night, up 'til about midnight, just enjoying the rare fire and fellowship. Tilley is the first to announce that she has to get in bed. She had an early morning. The others slowly speak of calling it a night when Danny speaks up and says, "I wanted to have this gathering to celebrate Mr. Johnson's life. We haven't spoke a great deal about him and I wonder how many of us knew him, or if any of us really knew much about him. I have done a little research and here is what I found out about this man who has died in our community. He was seventy-five years old and a veteran of the Marine Corps and was a highly-decorated and respected man. He was our groundskeeper, he was married for thirty-three years to a lady named Linda that died of cancer ten years ago and his first name was Cecil. I would like to say a prayer for this man who has lost his life. We can only hope that somehow he repented and has been forgiven. Could we please bow our heads?

Lord, we realize that we all here have done irrevocable things in your eyes and we are not in your Book of Life, but we ask in your name that you accept this sinner and forgive all of our sins. In Jesus' name we pray, and ask your forgiveness. Amen."

Every single person in attendance says, "Amen."

Chapter 16
Day Tripping

Danny wakes first and looks over the bed, with the simulated sunlight peering through the French doors that lead to the deck. He sees someone on the other side and raises up to see the poor little-tattered maid that had such a rough day the day before. He decides to let them sleep, and to work this one out on their own. He doesn't think it is a bad thing if Kelly would get on board. He chuckles as he pops to his feet to go find coffee.

He makes his way to the kitchen where he finds his coffeepot all ready to go with the flip of a switch. His black ten-year-old house shoes feel so nice, as he knows how chilly the ceramic tile usually is in bare feet. He sits waiting on the coffee and sees a deer pass by the back window of the kitchen. He gets up to look. "Those girls have enough issues right now without me shooting that .30-06 to take down a deer. It sure would be nice to have some more meat, though." His coffee makes a gurgling noise as it finishes.

He pours himself a cup, smelling the aroma of the fresh coffee, thinking about how nice he really has it. He considers if this could be retirement for him and maybe he could just let Ron run things there. He is a little undecided on the choice that he really should make, or if he has a choice at this point. He gets up to go look for the deer. He doesn't see it and it is probably gone.

Looking at the clock, he finds it is six thirty am. He opens the back door and walks out on the deck. He is looking over the new lake that was made and watching the fog roll off of the warmed water. He remembers Mr. Johnson speaking of watching the fog. He sits down on a lawn chair and realizes that Chopper is back at the other shelter alone. He hadn't really planned on staying the night here. He reflects on the previous day and how bad he felt about taking someone's life, then the relief and joy he actually felt when he saw those men drop and draw their last breath. He still feels as though his being left there

110

is all part of the master plan and he will be welcome when the time is right. He believes that he, Kelly, Tilley, and Mr. Franklin have more to do before their time is through.

Tilley comes walking out on the deck, wearing a thin white nightgown, with seemingly nothing underneath.

"Good morning, how are you this morning, pretty lady?"

"Much better than yesterday."

"Glad you woke up before my li'l swimsuit model bitch."

"Oh, no, she asked that I come up to the bedroom. We sat and talked last night for a long time after you crashed. We were both drinking wine. I am not sure that she is okay with me fucking you, but before we were done talking, she asked if I felt safe to go into my room."

"What did you tell her?"

"I told her that I would be fine. I wouldn't sleep, but I would be fine. She then asked if I could sleep if I was near you. I said yes and she invited me into your bed. I started out with you cuddling to me, but she couldn't have that so I was shuffled to the outside and that was that. I slept well."

"No shit? She actually put you into my bed next to me?"

"I was astonished myself. I don't think she is a bad person. She is just possessive."

"I would love to get things to where we could all three sleep together."

"I bet you would. You talk her into it, I am game."

About that time, Kelly turns the door handle and walks out onto the deck. They both greet her and the talk of a threesome somehow leaves the discussion.

Kelly asks, "Tilley, did you sleep well?"

"Much better than I expected. I was surprised that you invited me into your bed like that. I thought you disliked me."

"I don't like the relationship that you have had with Danny. I do like you and feel terrible for what you went through

111

yesterday. Perhaps you would like to return to the country shelter when we go later today."

Danny speaks up, "I need to find out if I have heard any more about Chimera. How would ya'll feel about staying here and letting Ron run the company on the new world?"

Neither girl knows what to say to this, as they both felt that Danny would be hell-bent on getting to the new world. Kelly says, "Is that what you are wanting to do?"

"I don't know. I have come to enjoy this life and lifestyle. I am unsure that the big city life is exactly what I would like at this point. We have access to any store without the need of money, we have all of our basic needs met, two beautiful women to spend time with, and I can hunt and fish all day and night if I like. I have my own little world."

"How long will it last, though? Will the Earth or our ecosystem sustain us into the future? Do we have one year, two years, or fifty years to be able to live off of the replicators?" Kelly asks.

"That is an important question. I am unsure of how many natural resources we have at our disposal. It is my understanding that every shelter was designed to be self-sustaining if the resources are treated properly. In light of all that has happened, we must secure the outer doors on both shelters and find another groundskeeper for this shelter. I can't handle them both."

They decide to go to a local Co-Op type of store called Atwoods. It isn't long and they have the coordinates for the store in the GPS unit and all three are in the Op Track, headed for locks for the outer doors. They pass through the big doors and Kelly obliges Danny by opening and closing them as they pass through. Tilley has never ridden in an Op Track and she is amazed by the display and the way they lie down in the machine. She tells them, "It is like lying on a massage table."

They arrive at the large farm supply store and Danny is searching for the entryway with the camera when they find it. He pulls the Op Track up as close as he can, but this entryway

112

doesn't have an eve like Walmart. He ends up having to bust through the glass doors in order to get the machine in an area where he can open the hatch.

They pop the hatch and Danny and Kelly get out, putting on winter gear. Tilley doesn't have anything more than a light jacket so she stays in the Op Track. Kelly lets her know that she will find her something as she closes the hatch back. Danny and Kelly take off into the store, with their area LED lights abundantly lighting their way. Danny looks back at the idling Op Track and sees white all throughout the front windows of the store and a big mound behind his machine.

They find a section that has a big sign that says Dickies and begin to look through coveralls and heavy coats. They find some that are appropriate to Tilley's size and return to the Op Track. Danny pops the hatch and out she comes. She puts on the winter gear and follows the two. Danny sees so much that he would like to take along with him but knows the Op Track only has room for a handful of items.

He finds barn hasps and takes about eight different varieties. He then makes his way to the fabrication section and finds a nice big welder, but it is too big to ride in the Op Track. He finds a cutting torch kit complete with regulators, an oxygen tank, and a small acetylene tank. He begins to drag them back to the machine when he stops and pulls the heavy metal top off of the oxygen tank. Tilley looks at him as if he is nuts. He cracks the valve slowly and they hear a sharp whisping noise as he inhales the pure oxygen from the tank.

Kelly says, "Hangover?"

Danny replies, "Yeah, it has been a while for that much beer." Tilley asks if it helps with a headache. Danny nods yes and she leans over and takes a big whiff of the gas as Danny opens the valve slowly for her. Kelly kind of smiles as she makes her way over to the bottle of relief that the two are enjoying when Danny says, "You too, huh?" Kelly just nods as she gets a big whiff of the invisible headache reliever that she turned Danny on to not more than a month prior.

113

They load the bottles up into the extra seats in the cockpit of the big Op Track and begin their trek back to the Hot Springs Village shelter. They get there and pull into Danny's home. He assembles the torch kit and places all of the locks into the big dually pickup truck and goes out in search of the boys. He drives around the block, without any sign of them. He pulls in at Mr. Johnson's residence and lo and behold, Adam steps out. He walks up to the window of the big truck to see that it is Danny.

"What's up, Mr. Nichols?"

"Call me Danny, please. I want to feel like you guys are not going to be invaded again when I leave. I want to install some locks on the big doors."

"I thought they already had locks."

"The locks can only be reached from one side or the other. That is no good. If I come here, I want to be able to get in."

"I see. You need some help?"

"That is why I came over. Where is Bryan?"

"He is in the house. I will go get him."

Shortly, the two boys come back out and load up in the passenger side of the truck. Danny goes to the doors and unloads the supplies. He selects an adequate padlock and realizes the hasps are fine and he only needs to create an opening so he can access it. He uses the cutting torch to make an opening large enough to be able to reach the hasp from inside or out. He is now content that he can leave the shelter secured and still be able to gain access when he needs to. He gives the boys a key and asks if Mr. Johnson has a key making machine. They explain that he does. He brings them back to Mr. Johnson's.

The three go out to a shed to find the machine and make fifteen copies of the key, ruining several in the process of learning how it works.

Danny is getting ready to leave with keys for everyone when he asks, "You boys plan to live here now?"

"Yes, sir. We were thinking that we could maybe take over as caretakers of the shelter."

"Ya'll have a lot to learn about how to care for a shelter. What about your parents? Do you guys have a mom and dad that live here?"

"My mom is still here," answers Bryan. "Adam and I have been staying with her. There are several vacant houses that we could claim, but we both really like Mr. Johnson's place and his role."

"All right, well, there are tutorials online about what all you have to do to take care of the place. He should also have the original manual as well. Ya'll need to take this serious if you are going to do this."

"We understand, and it is important that we have your blessing on what we are doing, Mr. Nichols," Bryan explains.

"As long as you don't fuck up the place."

Danny gets in the truck and returns home to get Kelly and hopefully Tilley. He pulls in and parks the big dual-wheeled truck in the garage. He closes the door and the air tight cab of the truck prevents it from closing all of the way, so he opens and slams the door. Kelly looks out the great room window, from the computer, wondering if something is wrong. She and Tilley, a little uneasy, meet up with him as he enters the kitchen.

Kelly asks, "Something wrong?"

"Should there be? Why do you ask?"

"We both heard the door slam hard on the truck."

"It just wouldn't close well. It gets an air pocket in there or something sometimes and isn't easy to close. So, what's going on around here?"

"Nothing much. I think I'm about ready to head for the country shelter and check on Chopper."

"Did we leave him plenty of food and water?"

"Yes, but if not, he knows where the creek is and he is a good hunter. I doubt that dog goes hungry."

"You're probably right. So what about Tilley?"

"What about her?"

115

Tilley has returned to her room by now, as she has found nothing was wrong with Danny.

"I was thinking she could head back to the country cabin with us."

"I was pretty nice last night. I kind of understand what she is going through, but I'm still not real comfortable with you two getting too damn chummy. Last night, if I hadn't pulled her to the outside, I think you would have pulled her panties down. You got kind of carried away with the whole snuggling idea there."

"I am a man. What do you expect? I may have even thought it was you that was next to me."

"She can go, but her ass is on the couch!"

"Great, ya'll get ready."

Kelly goes in to tell Tilley that they would like to have her as a guest at the country cabin. Tilley is really happy as the rule has been no Adam and Bryan. She wasn't sure she could honor that when they are gone, considering all that has happened. It has given her a fear of being alone. She begins to pack. An hour passes and they are all set to head out. Danny opens the cockpit on the Op Track and they all three lie face down into their stations. He looks at Tilley. "It's been a while, everything locked up?"

Tilley replies, "Yes, sir, Mr. Nichols."

The rattle of the diesel engine comes alive and a high-pitched sound radiates from the engine. Blue ambient lighting goes the length of the inside of the machine. Danny lies in the center at the command and everything in there is dimly illuminated with the blue hue. He pushes the joysticks forward and they all feel the power of the tracks as they grab the cobblestone driveway to begin their journey.

Danny gets out of his driveway and almost to the lake when he makes a left onto Mr. Johnson's road. Kelly and Tilley both wonder where he is headed, as the exit is straight ahead past the end of the lake.

He drives for a little while to reach the house and finds the blue Op Track sitting near the front porch, with the hatch removed and the boys standing around it. Danny pulls up beside them and pops the hatch. He struggles as he climbs out of the machine.

He walks over to look at what they have gotten into.

He says, "What are you guys doing?"

Bryan speaks up, "Well, sir, we cleaned all of the blood out of it. It has a drain port like a fishing boat. We thought we would try to replace the hatch with the other machine and see if everything still works. We figure if it doesn't, we may be able to patch it together using the other one you drug in… if you didn't mind."

Danny looks over near the side of the house to find the other blue machine without a hatch or tracks.

"I don't mind. Just don't ruin either of them. I may go and find some parts and you guys will have two. Wasn't there a big dealership around here before the snow? We get free parts these days."

"Yeah, there were a couple of dealerships in town," Bryan says.

"Okay, well, you guys do what you can, but if we need some parts, I will be back around in a couple of days. I will take you to the dealership to find what we need to get them both going."

A big smile goes across both of the boys' faces.

Danny continues, "I am taking Tilley down to the country shelter. Will you guys keep an eye on my place up there? Do you think ya'll will be okay tending to the shelter?"

"Yes, sir, we would be honored to watch after your place. Is Kelly going to be up there or is everyone going?" Adam replies.

Danny wasn't too fond of that question. "Don't you horny little bastards worry about who is going to be fucking home there, you just keep anyone out."

117

"Uh…okay, sir, but if we don't know if anyone is supposed to be there, then how can we be sure if the lights come on and off or if someone comes or goes? We won't go up and mess with Ms. Kelly, hell, she would probably shoot us." Adam responds.

Danny thinks, *Getting shot would probably be worth it*, but realizes he probably overreacted. He is concerned about these testosterone charged young men and does not want them screwing Kelly. If he was of that age, she would probably just have to shoot him to keep him away.

"No, and I didn't mean to be so rude to you guys, but I was nineteen once myself and if there was a Kelly in the neighborhood, I would be tapping that, or at least trying to."

"We get your concerns and she is a beautiful lady, but you have made things clear about your women. We will keep our distance. Breathing is kind of a privilege that is taken all too lightly these days," Bryan responds.

"That is a good understanding to have, young man. Well, we are leaving. Message me on the computer if you have issues."

Bryan hands Danny his phone and asks him to put his email and phone number in it. Danny puts in the information and he climbs back into the big Op Track and away they go. He can't resist showing the boys what his 3500 will do. The diesel engine comes alive, blowing out a large plume of black smoke and the tracks dig into the yard as Danny accelerates across the front lawn and out into the ditch. The big Track comes up off of the ground as he jumps the ditch and onto the road.

Kelly and Tilley are less than impressed as they are jostled around on the inside of the machine. It is padded on each side of the stations, but it is still uncomfortable to their small delicate bodies.

Chapter 17
Three's Company

They get to the gate and Kelly goes climbing out and tells Tilley to come on so can show her how to do this. The two walk to the gate and unlock it. They get it open and Danny pulls the big wide-tracked machine through. They lock up and hop back in.

Danny drives a ways and decides that he will take Tilley to see if she needs some stuff from the store. With a quick jerk of the joysticks, they are off into the wall of the tunnel. He travels alongside the road and is careful of avoiding the occasional power pole and power lines that are left. It isn't long before the outline of the front textured brick of a Walmart store is shown on the display.

Danny pulls the machine up and into the entryway and stops. Kelly looks over at him. "What are we doing?"

Danny replies, "Tilley may need some stuff and I want some of the ammo that I left here." The three get out and Tilley leads them to the female section and she loads up on feminine hygiene products and odds and ends of shampoos, conditioners, and other products. She only has about two bags of items when they make their way back to the machine. She asks if it is too much trouble for her to go back to electronics and grab a computer and maybe a tablet. They accompany her to electronics and all three grab two or three laptops, as well as a few top of the line tablets.

They arrive back at the machine.

Tilley says, "I never considered that the stores would still be packed like this."

Danny replies, "When the end came, it was kind of sudden. The ones that God didn't take, and didn't leave for Goldilocks, were scrambling to find shelter before the snow overcame them. No one has really had any way to reach the stores, so they have been left fully stocked."

119

"We could eat for years from the various stores just in this area," Tilley replies.

"The idea is that our shelters become an ecosystem or a little society on its own. They left us with enough bulbs and natural resources to sustain it for at least our lifetime, but how cool is it that we can get out and explore?"

"It is very cool. I wish we could visit other shelters and see what life is like there."

"We have to be very cautious with what we do. The people out there could be ill, crazy, or just plain criminals, like the ones that showed up on the Op Tracks."

"I still want to explore."

"We'll see, Tilley. We'll see. If everything works out, then we won't be here long."

They are now out in the main tunnel and driving to their shelter. They make the turn onto the road that leads up to the front doors of the shelter and Danny stops just shy of the doors and pops the hatch. They all three just sit there. Kelly says, "I showed you how to open the door for a reason, Tilley."

"Oh," she replies as she kind of scrambles to get out and open the door for the machine to pass through.

As she is unlocking the gates, Danny says, "No need to be so rude." Kelly doesn't say a word, she thought she was being rather polite about it.

They get through the gate and Tilley climbs onboard. Danny drives on up to the cabin. Chopper jumps on the side of the machine, anticipating Kelly and Danny's return. They climb out to find him barking and excited. He missed his owners.

They walk up to the porch while trying to walk and pet ole Chopper. He is giving them some strong sniffs as he smells some things that he doesn't recognize. They get in the house and Kelly comes back out of the door with a plate of food for him. He seems awfully happy to see the food and begins to devour it after a few more sniffs of Kelly's leg.

Tilley walks from the porch and into the mudroom of the little cabin, kind of surprised to find an entryway with boots,

120

waders, fishing poles, and a basic padded bench type of seat to sit on. The floor looks somewhat dirty and it certainly isn't the way she would keep things for her man. As she makes her way into the cabin, she says, "You're certainly no maid," somewhat under her breath. Danny kind of smirks as he heard what she said. Kelly comes out of the bedroom to get more supplies out of the machine and asks what Tilley said, without a response.

Kelly walks out for another load of canned goods and Danny's guns that he just couldn't leave for the next trip and begins carrying them in. The other two begin to make the same trips back and forth. There are game cameras, locks for the gate, guns, ammunition, canned goods, and all kinds of meat.

Tilley asks, "You guys really think this meat is okay?"

Kelly says, "Have you ever froze something and thawed it out after a year? As long as it isn't freezer burnt, then it will be absolutely fine."

They continue to load up the freezers. The deer meat is about depleted that Danny had killed late last season. They had more storage space in the Op Track than anyone had realized.

Once it is all unloaded, Danny gets on the computer to see if he has any communications from Commander Charles Phillips. He finds the following email:

Dear Danny,

I have been reviewing the documents you sent and they all seem to be in order. We will file the necessary ownership papers for Chimera and all monetary items that belonged to you on Earth. We will deny the request from Ron Lewis and complete the transaction, pending your signature when you arrive. I have included documents for you to fill out to appoint a leader in your absence. I assume it will be Ron Lewis and you will take over when you arrive.

On another note: I did some research on your transport ship and it appears that it is incomplete in Jacksonville, on the base. It is sitting in their hangar for quarantine, awaiting fuel rods. The base has an ample supply of fuel rods and I have attached a list of individuals that are still confirmed on Earth

121

and are qualified to charge the transport. This was the last task that was left in the fabrication of your machine.

I regret to inform you that the nearest person, who is still there, is located in Tempe, Arizona. There are other potential qualified individuals in New York, California, and Pennsylvania. The closest safe bet will be Tempe. Ben Calhoun is the man's name. The detailed instructions explain how it is done and it's as simple as suiting up in a protective suit and placing the rods into a chamber. If you have no other means, we can send detailed instructions and you should be able to complete it yourself. I know it is likely near an impossible journey on Earth to travel this distance. If you make an error, it could destroy the base and contaminate the entire area, though. Installing them yourself is not something I recommend, but if you are desperate, it is possible that it is the only way.

We will afford you a remote video link if you desire and opt to do it yourself.

Wish there was better news. I look forward to hearing back from you.

Sincerely,

Charles Phillips WRC Commander-in-Chief

Danny just sits there looking at the screen. "You pricks want to watch me blow myself up on video." He shouts, "That fucking Ron Lewis will not be running my company. He showed his true colors. I am officially firing his ass right here and now. John Thorp, yeah, he was a solid, well-organized plant manager and vice president of the food industry. He will make a good one."

Hearing the shouting and commotion, Kelly and Tilley both come into the dining area where Danny sits talking to himself.

Kelly says, "What's wrong?"

Danny is busy responding to the commander on the PC. He stops and looks up.

"They think I want Ron to run Chimera until I get there."

"Seems like a logical choice. Wasn't he your second-in-command?"

"Yes, but the bastard can't even check on me? Files papers to take my company? Fuck him! He's fired!"

"Aaalrighty then! Who can oversee all that has to be done?"

"John Thorp is my man. He was on one of the early transports, and was always loyal to me. He has some explaining to do as to why he hasn't contacted me, but he will be in charge until I arrive. There is a problem with my transport. The friggin thing doesn't have any gas."

"Gas? They use gas in the transports?"

"Not exactly gas, but fuel rods. It is a form of fuel that the ship runs on. They didn't install them. We have a choice of installing them ourselves, and possibly blowing up all of central Arkansas, or making a trip to Tempe, Arizona, to get a man named Ben Calhoun, who is trained on how to install them."

"How could we get to Tempe with one tank of fuel?"

"I don't know right now. Maybe I could build a trailer that we could carry fuel cans in. I don't know how any of that would work. One thing is for sure, we aren't leaving anytime real soon for Goldilocks."

Kelly leaves the room to attend to putting away the food and setting things out in the mudroom for Danny to take to the barn. Danny goes back to filling out his forms. He completes them and sends them back to Charles, with his intentions concerning Ron Lewis' affiliation with his company. He then sends an email to Ben Calhoun at the contact email Charles listed.

> *Ben,*
>
> *My name is Daniel Nichols. I am interested in soliciting you for your service to install fuel rods into a transport that I have here in Arkansas, at Little Rock Air Force Base. I am interested in knowing if you are capable and willing to allow me to come to Tempe and pick you up within the next couple of weeks, or do you have some method you could use to*

123

get to me in Hot Springs or Jacksonville, Arkansas? In return, I
will make it well worth your while by allowing you to ride along
to the new world with me and my entourage, and you shall not
want for anything on the new world. I can, at this time, offer a
one-time payment of the equivalent of ten million US dollars
once we arrive on the new world.

    Sincerely,
    Daniel Nichols Owner Chimera Inc.

    Danny hits send and goes into the kitchen to see how
Kelly and Tilley are coming along with putting away the
groceries. It seems it is taking them an awfully long time. He
gets toward the back of the kitchen and they are both sitting out
on the deck, talking. *Bonding*, he thinks to himself. This is a
good thing he figures and decides to take his fishing poles and
stuff to the barn, from the mudroom, that Kelly put out for him.

    He makes his way up there and puts his new fishing
poles, fishing lures, and tools up. He makes a couple of trips
back and forth. On his way out the third time, he looks at his
Mustang and notices how dusty it is. He begins to wash and wax
it. Chopper just lies on the porch, watching his master. The car
doesn't take long to finish and he starts thinking that Kelly and
Tilley sure have been out there talking for a while.

    He heads into the house to find they are not on the back
deck. He walks through and into the bedroom to find them both
passed out on the bed. He considers the possibilities as he goes
back out to gather up his locks and a torch so he can fix up the
lock on the outside doors. He gets the four-wheeler and takes off
to tend to the modifications. Chopper runs after him as he dips
down and through the ditch and onto the blacktop. He makes
fairly short work of it and returns to the medical center. He
checks to ensure it is secured and goes for a leisurely ride around
the complex, allowing his mind to wander. He thinks of the man
in Arizona, Goldilocks, the transport, and all of the things that
are going on. It was only a few days ago that life was so simple
and he considers just calling it all off. He could die going all the

way to Arizona in the Op Track. What if he loses a track? How will he get fuel?

Chapter 18
Arizona

He sits at the television now that he finished his joyride and his chores. He's a little distracted with the lovely ladies in his bed and decides to concentrate on how to carry enough fuel to get to Arizona and back. He considers that the man hasn't agreed to do it, and he could be wasting time even considering it.

He decides to build an Op Track trailer. He gets on the computer and looks online to see if he can find one to go by. He brings up "Old World Search Engine," and puts in "Op Track trailer". It turns up several different trailers, but none that can be pulled behind his machine. He then does a search for "Solidworks". He finds a student version available that is several years old and free to download. He begins the download and a tutorial.

Danny now has modeling software that can be used for designing his trailer. His degree, that he never completed, was for engineering. He lacked one semester of completing his Electrical Engineering curriculum and obtaining a Bachelors. He had learned enough, by his measure, and he very well must have. He was the owner of one of the top investment banking companies in the world when the snow came.

He begins to sketch out a model. Before long, he has a trailer capable of carrying about one hundred gallons of fuel. He finds that the design looks very much like an Op Track and begins to consider repurposing the old wrecked one he had recovered. He also begins to do research on the length of his trip and fuel mileage, finding out that it is thirteen hundred miles to Tempe, Arizona. The Op Track gets forty miles to the gallon in snow. He determines an adequate sized fuel tank required to get there and return will be about sixty-five gallons of fuel. He wants one and a half times the fuel that is necessary to allow for pulling the trailer. The Op Track tank holds twenty gallons, so he decides he requires one hundred gallons of fuel. The trailer must hold eighty gallons. He also thinks about what provisions will be necessary to make the long ass trip there and back.

He heads out to the barn to get the wheeler, once again, his old trusty dog, Chopper, follows close behind. He gets the wheeler and drives down to the ditch where he left the wrecked Op Track and ties a tow strap onto it. The big four-wheel drive wheeler grunts and mars the ground beneath its wheels as the old beat up machine begins to move along behind him.

He gets the old machine up to the barn and drags it into the place where Kelly skinned the deer. He begins dismantling it when he recalls an empty fifty-five-gallon drum under the eve beside the barn. He decides that if he compares the cockpit of the Op Track to the fifty-five-gallon drum, he would have a reasonable idea of how much fuel could be stored in the makeshift trailer he is constructing.

He makes his way out to the drum and begins to drag the old rusty white barrel back into the work area. He has the old Track sitting up on jack stands now as he drops the drum beside it. He finds that it is about three-quarters the diameter of the barrel and about one and a half times the length. He decides this is close to fifty-five gallons. This will not do. He has a three-pound shop hammer lying beside the machine and when he realizes this is not viable, it comes wailing by the machine, swapping ends, and collides with the wall, knocking some of Kelly's tools onto the brown bloodstained concrete floor. He cusses as he exits the barn and heads back to the cabin to regroup and consider another way to construct the trailer.

He walks across the green grass of the lawn, that has gotten a little tall for Danny's taste, and goes into the cabin and replicates a beer. He comes back out into the living room to find Kelly and Tilley both sitting on the couch watching him.

Kelly asks, "What are you doing?"

"I guess I am going to cut the fucking lawn if you don't have time."

"You know I always cut it. I enjoy riding the lawn tractor. We haven't exactly been sitting around here watching it grow, you know."

"Don't make a shit. We been back for almost a full day and all you bitches want to do is lie around and bitch about what I am doing, and sleep. This will not fucking do!"

"You best just cool your ass, dickhead! We haven't said the first bad thing to you and in one day, do you honestly think the lawn is at the top of my priority list? What has crawled up your ass?"

"I don't know, I guess you're right. We haven't really been here. I have just been out there putting the locks on the door, and trying to figure out a trailer to pull in order to get us to Arizona and back to get our fuel rods installed. I decided to build a trailer, but then the design I made looked very similar to an Op Track, so I decided to try and use the wrecked one. We need an eighty-gallon tank, plus the tank on the machine in order to make the round trip. The cockpit of the old machine will hold fifty-five gallons if I'm lucky."

"Okay, but that is my fault, how?"

"No, I am just frustrated. I am sorry. Carry on!'

Danny walks out of the cabin with his beer and sits on the porch, thinking of how he may construct this trailer. He decides that he should go to Hot Springs Village to look at the old Op Track he left there. He decides to tell the boys to bring it to him. He heads back into the house and gets on the computer to send them a message. He sends a message explaining to the boys that if they have the shot-up machine running, he needs them to bring the non-tracked, blue one to him.

He finishes that and goes in to replicate another beer when Tilley gets up and replicates him some pretzels. The large warm soft kind that she knows he loves to have with his beer. He is online looking for fuel sources between Arkansas and Arizona, without much luck, when she walks back in with the pretzels and a small bowl of cheddar cheese. He takes the platter with the treats and looks up at Tilley. "How have I made it without you, darling?"

Kelly, obviously unhappy, gets up and goes out the back door. The computer beeps and the boys return a message saying they are waiting on Danny to come and take them to get a track. One of the tracks that was in question is slipping and they don't feel like it will make the trip. They explain that it isn't quite the right size.

Kelly comes back in and says, "Was that the boys that sent you mail?"

"Yeah, they aren't any help. They need help to get theirs going. Li'l young pricks probably just don't know how to tighten the friggin thing."

"How much fuel does the excavator hold?"

"Woman, have you lost your ever-loving mind? There is no damn way we could drive the excavator to Arizona. Come on now?"

"Will you need the excavator to have fuel while we are gone?"

"Uh, let me get this straight. You are proposing that I pull the fuel tank off of a piece of equipment and maybe make some type of trailer of it? Holy shit, girl, you are freaking beautiful and brilliant."

"If you wanted pretzels, all you needed to do was ask."

Danny throws the pretzel platter up on the computer table and is hell-bent on sizing up a tank to use from the excavator, bulldozer, bucket truck, even the Jeep or the Superduty if necessary. He stays out in the workshop until the light begins to go dim outside. Kelly walks up to find a diesel fuel stain on the concrete that is running out of the door. She walks up wanting to know if he is hungry and has a glass of sweet tea for him. He gladly takes the tea as he shuts down the cutting torch and pulls his dark cutting glasses off his face.

He walks over with rusty brown spots all down each leg of his jeans from working with the metal, coughs out some unmentionable bodily fluids, takes a big gulp of tea, slaps Kelly

129

on the ass, and plants a kiss right on her lips. He puts his tongue down her throat. Working with steel always makes the soft touch of a woman's body that much softer. Kelly is a little concerned about the torch and hot burning steel all falling down on the diesel, but doesn't really want to set him off again. So, she just enjoys the attention and asks if he is ready for something to eat. He explains that he is ready and also would like some dessert. He says, "Two desserts would be nice, you know."

"Honestly, who are you kidding? You seriously think that you will be able to keep up with both of us?"

He kind of looks around to see if Tilley may be listening. "Uh, yeah, I think I would do just fine to tell you the truth."

"You like the idea, but I don't. I think it would be absolutely nasty. I am happy with it just being me and you. I don't even want to know about you and her. If that is something that must be, then I don't want to know anything about it. Do *not* include me in your fantasy because I have been a part of that shit before and you know what? It is freaking nasty and you won't last three damn minutes, then me and her will be sitting there twiddling our, uh, thumbs, so just do what you have to do because I can't stop you, but drop this shit with me. Okay?"

"Okay, damn. Do I still get something to eat?"

"Yeah, I will fix you something and I am not mad at you. You are a man with two women living with or near him and I get it, but damn, being realistic, honestly, it sucks."

"I get it, okay? I will be along in a few to eat. Sorry."

Kelly takes back off to the cabin to cook up some steaks. There were frozen Porterhouses that they picked up at Walmart and she fires up the grill on the back deck. She is beating the hell out of them when Tillie walks in. Kelly pauses to look at her.

Tilley begins, "You know, it is every man's fantasy. We could make his come true."

"No, we cannot. Have you ever done that? He won't last long enough for us to get undressed!"

130

"True, but don't you think that with who he is, and all that he does, that he deserves to have us fulfill a fantasy? What would it hurt?"

"It will hurt his pride. It could even set him back on his ambitions. It is hard to believe, with who he is, that he has never done this, but I don't really think he has. If he had, he wouldn't want it so badly. Have you?"

"Yes."

"Was it enjoyable? How long did the guy last?"

"Oh, it was two guys."

Kelly yells, "Whore!" Then begins to beat the steaks again.

Tilley says nothing more and goes out to sit on the porch as the lights are getting near dark. It isn't long and everyone can smell the charcoal and the aroma of the Porterhouse steaks sizzling on the grill. About forty minutes pass and Tilley sees the lights go out in the huge barn and hears the door slam. She sees the outline of Danny, in the darkness, walking down the little knoll and back up the second one to get to the cabin. As he gets closer, she begins to smell diesel fuel and a burned smell of welding. He steps up on the porch and greets Tilley. They both say their hellos and Danny is off into the cabin to see about his supper. Kelly is pulling tinfoil balls out of the oven that have potatoes, onions, seasonings in them, and are filled with butter.

Danny asks, "Almost ready?"

"Almost. I made the tinfoil potatoes for you, too."

Danny reluctantly looks over and discreetly counts the number of tinfoil balls to find there are three. He is somewhat relieved.

"Do we have any pig sauce?"

"Yes, we do. Where did you get that recipe? I want it, we are getting low."

"A family that lived down the road from me while I was growing up gave me that recipe. It is actually North Carolina barbecue sauce, but I really like it on tators."

131

"It is good for that, but it isn't like any barbecue sauce I have ever had."

"Barbecue on the east coast is a little different than ours. Theirs is very vinegary. I like it okay on occasion, but give me some Jack Daniels Old No7 or KC Masterpiece for actual barbecue sauce. They can make a whole hog taste really good with that stuff, though. I guess not everyone likes it, but I do. I believe it is an acquired taste."

"Steaks are done."

Kelly goes out onto the deck and returns with a platter containing three huge Angus, Porterhouse steaks. They all sit down and have a fantastic supper. While they eat, they begin to talk about plans.

Kelly begins, "So, what are we doing about the guy in Arizona?"

"I am working to figure out a way to carry enough fuel on board of the Op Track to be able to make the twenty-six hundred mile journey without having to find fuel."

Danny groans as he gets up from his chair to refill his tea glass. Tilley almost knocks her chair over getting up to see about him. Danny looks at her and says, "I'm okay." He walks to the refrigerator and refills his tea glass. He returns and sits down with yet another groan. It is quite obvious the forty one-year-old man is sore and tired from wrestling with the project in the shop all day.

Kelly, without saying a word, gets up and takes off into the bedroom. Danny just kind of looks over at Tilley like, "Something I said?"

Kelly returns and places an ibuprofen and a hydrocodone beside Danny's tea glass. Without speaking, he snatches them up, with a big gulp of his tea, turning his head toward the ceiling he swallows hard.

"Thank you, Kelly. I hadn't thought of it, but I needed that."

"No doubt. You are stumbling around like an old man. And you want us to give you a fucking heart attack." Tilley smirks.

Tilley and Kelly both laugh, as he knows what she is speaking of. Danny just takes the steak knife and cuts him off another piece of his steak. "Mmmm mmm mm! This is the best supper you have fixed since we have been here, woman! "Who me?" Kelly replies.

Tilley just looks on, as she isn't so thrilled about the exchange. She knows that things are swinging Kelly's way and isn't so upset about that, but he wants to continue to have relations and control over her as well. That is where her issues come from. She finishes and asks to be excused. Danny says, "Did you try that pig sauce on your tators?"

"Yes, I did. It was really good. As a matter of fact, everything was delicious. Kelly, you are a fantastic cook. Your housekeeping skills could use some work, but your culinary skills are second to none."

Kelly says, "Thank you, I think. I think we need to solicit your housekeeping skills."

Tilley says nothing more as she walks out through the living area and through the mudroom to the front porch. It is dark out by now. The light from the security lights make the front yard visible with a yellow hue. Chopper seems to be eager to see someone come out, as he is looking for a steak or a bone. He trots over to her as she sits down on a lawn chair on the front porch. He sniffs her up and down, looking for the food. She pets him and returns inside to find Danny and Kelly having a pleasant conversation. She reaches onto her plate, that is still laying on the table, and grabs the bone from her steak that still has some meat left. Danny says, "He was a little unhappy without you having something for him, wasn't he?"

"Yeah, he wasn't aggressive or anything, but he sure looked disappointed when he realized that I had nothing for him." Tilley grabs a light jacket from the coat rack on her way back outside. She is somewhat surprised that it is a little chilly in

133

the temperature controlled shelter, but figures it could just be her. She gets back outside to find the big black evil-looking pit with what almost appears to be a smile on his face. He gladly snatches the bone from her hand and with one chomp, *crunch*, the bone is in two pieces as the massive jaws of the pit bull bites down on it.

Tilley says, "You really have some strong jaws there, mister." Chopper just looks up at her. He really is enjoying the real bone she has given him and does his best to wag his bobbed tail and continues cracking the bone. His entire tail end moves back and forth. Tilley thinks of the attack that had only happened the day prior. She dismisses her sad thoughts with the fact that they will never hurt anyone again. She wonders how things would have been if she had Chopper there. She is so grateful that Kelly and Danny brought her back here that she is willing to go along with whatever they would like. She is just happy they are who they are and in her life. She has a very warm feeling sitting on their porch, looking out across the dimly lit, slightly overgrown green grass, and garden.

It isn't long and Danny comes out to tell Tilley they are going to bed.

It is about nine o'clock and Danny is tired and would like to feel a soft young woman's body tonight after his manual labor in the shop.

"Where am I sleeping?" she inquires.

Kelly speaks up from the living room, "On the couch!"

Danny says in a low voice, "There is a spare bedroom across the hallway from our room. Make yourself comfortable in there. I may come and visit after a while if you are up to it."

"Come on by if you like. Does the door have a lock?"

Danny just smiles as he nods his head yes. Tilley is a little concerned about Kelly's reaction to finding them together if she wakes while he is in there. She figures that Danny will handle whatever comes to pass, though.

Danny and Kelly go on in to bed and spend some quality time together. Tilley goes into her room about an hour later. She sleeps very well in the nice new bed that seemingly has never been slept on before. It has a bit of a musty smell to it, but not so much that it bothers her. She will want to put some Steri-fab or Febreeze on it and wash the bedding if she sleeps in it again.

The next morning Danny wakes to the aroma of coffee. He reaches over to find Kelly still out. He stealthily climbs out of the bed to find that it is five am and Tilley has made coffee, stripped her bed, and is washing sheets, and has cleaned the living area up. It smells like the scent of Febreeze air freshener.

He grabs a cup of coffee and makes his way into the hallway restroom to find that it has a nice aroma of Lysol bath and shower cleaner. He takes care of his business and considers, "How freaking nice is this? I need to get her in our bathroom to do some cleaning." He thinks to himself, *Two fine bitches, one can clean, one can cook and they are both goddesses in the bedroom. Why do I want to leave this?*

He returns to the kitchen and Tilley is sitting at the table having a cup of coffee. It looks like it is full of sugar and milk. The color of it is a prominent brown.

"You have any coffee with your sweet milk there, pretty lady?"

"Yes, I have milk and sugar in mine. How do you fix yours? I always fix your coffee up and have everything you could want on the side, but I never have coffee with you."

"I like my coffee black and strong."

"I see."

They discuss the sleeping arrangements and Tilley says, "I noticed you didn't visit last night. You lose your nerve?"

"Hell no, your fucking door was locked, you asshole!"

"No way? Really? I did not lock it, Danny, I swear!"

"I am kidding. I just fell right off to sleep after me and Kelly talked for a while."

"What did you two talk about?"

"Fucking."

"Nice..."

They don't have a great deal more conversation, as Tilley thought it rude of him to put things that way. They sit in silence for about five minutes and Danny gets up to find a return email from Arizona.

Chapter 19
Apprised

Danny reads his email.

Dear Mr. Daniels,

I would very much like to come to Arkansas and install the fuel rods in exchange for the favor that you suggested. I have no means of making the trip, but if there is some way you can come to Tempe, I would be happy to return with you. There is only me. All of my family either left on a transport to the new world or left with the good Lord above.

Please let me know your intentions and when you shall arrive and I will let the gatekeeper know that you have come for me. We have outcasts that have caused problems that live in a nearby shelter. Our shelter is pleasant and fully stocked with provisions for the five thousand that are housed here.

How many are at your shelter and how many will be making the trip with us?

Sincerely,

Ben Calhoun, Former Civil Aerospace Fuel Rod Specialist

Danny is relieved to have gotten a reply from him. He thinks of the number of ungodly people he must try to rely on in order to have his mission to the new world. He doesn't exactly stress over his situation but is concerned about everyone being on the up and up about things.

He turns to Tilley. "I wasn't trying to be rude. I was just trying to make a joke."

Sarcastically, she says, "Haha, I didn't know."

"You ready to go back to Hot Springs Village?"

"I like it here."

"No breakfast?"

"I thought Kelly was the cook around here. I wouldn't want to steal her thunder. I could get you some fruit, but I honestly thought she would be up cooking today."

"I got to get to work. I have someone to go get for sure now."

Danny gets up and picks up his coffee. He walks into the bedroom and kisses Kelly, her sleepy eyes look up at him. "I have to get to work on our ride to Arizona. I had a return email," Danny explains.

Kelly, in a sleepy voice, replies, "Please don't get under that heavy equipment without something stable to hold it off of you. Take your walkie-talkie with you, please." She yawns and rolls over, tucking her pillow up next to her, where Danny lays.

He walks over to a corner curio cabinet where two radios are plugged into the wall. He pulls one off and turns it on, laying it on her nightstand. The other he clips on his belt, turning the volume up and adjusting the squelch to a level that screams out a high-pitched static noise. Kelly yells out, "Enough, you fuck head!" Danny kind of chuckles as he turns the knob up once more just to piss her off, and walks through the bedroom door into the hallway. Just then, a glass candle shot glass comes whizzing by his head and crashing into the door to the guestroom. "Dick!"

"All right, bitch! That's enough," he says.

"That *is* enough," she replies as she lays there with her bed-head hair, looking over toward the door, with no sign of him. The expression on her face is one of wanting to kick his ass.

He makes his way down the hallway, with Tilley seemingly ready for shop work. She has on tight white painter's pants and a T-shirt. Danny isn't sure what she is up to.

"What do you have planned?"

"I plan to go mow, or help you."

"We'll leave mowing to Kelly and what if I don't need any help?"

"Oh, you need help, all right. That is big heavy stuff and you can't do it by yourself, safely."

"I believe that I can, but if you want to come keep me company, that is fine. I can think of worse things you could be doing."

Danny gathers up his gun, digs in the kitchen drawer to find a pencil, and a tape measure. He heads on through the living room, with Tilley following, and out into the mudroom they go. Danny sits down and grabs his boots, pulling the left one on he looks over at Tilley putting on an old pair of Kelly's shoes. He says, "Can you weld?"

"Not exactly, but I have held pieces when my dad welded. I am not afraid of the fire."

"Do you know how to read a tape measure?"

"Kinda."

"What is kinda? You know how or you don't."

"I know that big numbers are one inch, two inch, and twelve make a foot, but all the little ones I don't have down."

"Okay, well, just the, uh, big numbers is better than nothing." He chuckles.

They have their shoes laced up and out the front door they go. The light in the shelter is just about correct for sunrise and Tilley sees the sparkle of the Mustang in the yard. "You washed it?"

"I washed and waxed it," Danny replies. They continue on, with Chopper coming around the side of the house looking relaxed, almost as if he expected his master, and following along at a slow comfortable gate. They walk the familiar path up to the barn.

Danny pulls the big door to one side, revealing a large, dimly lit room. Inside, they see the old twisted Op Track sitting up and jack stands with a fifty-five-gallon drum lying alongside the wrecked machine. The machine has the tracks removed from one side and a skid welded along the bottom where they fastened. Tilley looks on as the smell of spent welding rods and torch-cut metal still lingers in the air from the night before. Danny flips a light switch and a flicker begins, then the entire shop fills with bright light. Danny stands there looking over the

139

mess, thinking of the conversation he and Kelly had concerning the fuel tank of the excavator. He stands there with his hands on his hips and says, "Well, hell, without further delay, give the bitch her due."

"Huh," Tilley replies.

"Last night, I built a tongue on the old Op Track, thinking it would accommodate the tank that we will install. Today, I have to pull the tank and see if it will work on the old machine."

He then takes off walking along a pegboard wall, with butcher block top workbenches to his left side. There are tools hanging on hooks as he passes by. A shelf above the bench has various manuals and the bench has a vise toward the very end. The wall is somewhat of a partition between this work area and the storage area behind, where the depot of equipment is stored. He gets to the end of the wall and it opens up into a very large room, as the work area continues on to the end of the barn with two additional large doors for each side.

He walks to the backside of the wall where it is pitch black. Tilley is behind him as he fumbles around for the light switch. The lights flicker and slowly get brighter to reveal an enormous yellow arm of an excavator that makes a triangle with the concrete floor and spans across half of the back room of the building. It is extended out so that it is low enough to fit into the room without hitting the roof. The large tracks are still flat black, with only the very outside edges and inside rollers scuffed with the slightest hint of rust within the scratches. It was shipped here new and has never been out of its resting place, but it did acquire some scratches during transport On the backside of it is an equally impressive piece of machinery. Its large blade extends up near the height of the back of the large excavator. It is a large yellow bulldozer. The condition of it is very similar to the excavator. Danny stands there looking at the machines.

Tilley looks off to the left where the rest of the machinery is stored and there are various garden tractors, one is large and green with a large disc connected to the back. The jeep and large truck with the tunnel buster sits on the outside of several other machines that are lined up as if they were on display. Each one looks as though they have never been used, except the big Superduty that has mud up in the fender wells.

Danny studies the group to try to determine which one will be a donor vehicle and lose its fuel tank today. Kelly suggested the excavator and that isn't a bad idea, but there is the very real possibility that whatever tank is used could be damaged on their twenty-six hundred mile journey. Not to mention the modifications that he feels necessary in order to couple it to the Op Track. He finally decides that the bulldozer would be the best candidate. He slides the large back door open and it isn't long and the bulldozer's starter is energetically whining and trying to start the beast.

Danny cranks and cranks, deciding the machine has likely lost its prime. Tilley is still standing beside the mammoth machine, watching and eager to help. Danny comes climbing out of the cab walking past her and into the work area to a large metal cabinet. It is gray with double doors on the front. He opens the door on the right side to reveal an entire shelf of spray cans in rows on each of the multiple shelves inside. There is one that reads Ether, Starting fluid, he grabs it and starts back through the building to the backside where Tilley has found a five-gallon bucket to sit on. Her small body takes up just a fraction of the large blade behind her, and sits there patiently awaiting his return.

"We will make this ole bitch a crack baby," he tells Tilley as he instructs her to get inside to try to crank it. He lifts a large panel near the front of the yellow monster that has a large pipe protruding out near it. Beneath it, he finds a pipe with an enlarged section, what looks to be a filter behind it. He yells at Tilley, "Try it." About a minute passes without any action and he says, "Did you see how I did that? Do you have the safety bar down near the door?"

He hears a snap inside the big cab and the starter makes a coughing noise once or twice and then engages. He sprays the ether into the filter and the big engine makes a knocking noise that sounds like it is about to bust a gear, or something will come out of the side of it. It gets louder and smoother, then quieter. He sprays the can into the filter as the sound dies off. He does this several times until he allows the big power plant to go silent, making the same loud banging noise as it dies. He climbs down out of the engine bay and steps up on the running board and looks into the cab where Tilley looks out curiously.

He begins to look over the gauges, knobs, and levers, finding nothing that would indicate the fuel is off. He leans in over Tilley's lap and turns the key on. Red lights illuminate and all of the gauges go to 100%, then back down to zero, including the fuel gauge. It has a red light at the bottom.

He looks at Tilley. "Well, I'll be. Kiss my ever loving ass!"

"What?"

"Damn thing has no fuel in it."

"So it is out of gas and we sit here trying to crank it? Why do we need to start it anyway? Aren't we going to remove something off of it? The fuel tank?"

"Yeah, not gas but diesel, and yes, we are actually pulling the fuel tank off."

"You haven't filled my tank in a while, mister!" She grabs Danny's arm and pulls him in close.

"I can think of quite a few better places for that than in the seat of this tractor."

"I can't."

The two spend the next hour letting each other know they have missed each other.

Danny begins putting his shirt back on as Tilley lies in the leather seat naked, with her head on the black leather arm rest on the far side of the seat and her soft white legs wrapped around him as he dresses.

"Will you remember this when you operate this machine?"

"You know I will. If I operate it at all. If we can get this cat from Arizona to install the fuel rods, then we will make some new memories on my cruise ship."

Danny finishes dressing, leaving her to dress on her own. He grabs a blue pail labeled DIESEL on the side and heads out of the large door and to the right, where there is a massive eve that extends several feet wide all the way along one side of the building. Several fifty-five-gallon drums stand there on pallets, and a station that has a pump with three nozzles at the very end. One is labeled Biodiesel, with a green handle.

He places the pail down on the edge of the pallet and pulls off a small cap on the backside. He recalls the time when they had done away with the vent on the fuel cans in an attempt to limit emissions into the atmosphere. "What a stupid fucking thing that was trying to pour fuel out of a can with no vent hole. That hole sucks air, not distributes fumes," he says out loud. He begins filling the fuel can. It isn't long and he has it about half-full and figures it will be enough to start and move the dozer.

He returns to find Tilley looking a little tired. *Wore the bitch out,* he thinks to himself as he brings the can to the fuel neck on the dozer. He pours about half of the fuel in and it isn't long and they have the big machine rattling like the big Superduty does. Tilley scoots over and stands on the far side of the seat as Danny climbs inside and positions the big machine through the doorway and eventually into the door at the back of the work area. He lowers the front blade, lifting the tracks way off the ground and goes and gets some large heavy jack stands and places one to each side, letting the machine down on them.

He is now ready to get down to business and pull the fuel tank out of the new machine.

143

Chapter 20
Making Due

Danny climbs beneath the massive machine and begins pulling metal panels off. It isn't long and Tilley is lying on the cold concrete floor, watching as he unbolts these large metal panels. The first one is loose and one end drops to the floor. Danny sits up and scoots back away from the large panel as he takes the last bolt off. *Crash*! The huge panel shakes the floor as it free falls from the machine and to the floor.

He has a very bright flashlight with a magnetic base. He points the base up and sticks it to the bottom of the machine. He finds a huge black plastic tank behind this panel. There are three metal straps, that are similar to pallet banding straps, holding the tank in place. He climbs out from under the machine and walks over to the pegboard wall, finding a pair of bolt cutters. He grabs them, with a bit of uncertainty on his face, hoping he can find a gap where the strap can be cut. Tilley is still lying, watching as he is gathering tools.

He returns with the bolt cutters and begins trying to angle them on the strap that is flat against the tank. The jaws are just too large and he can't get ahold of the bands. He continues looking to see where the straps are fastened and discovers bolts that make a junction to a second fastener on the far side and near the outside of the machine. This area is deep in the pocket where the tank rests. He can't see any way to get to it, let alone get the cutters in to cut the bolts.

With strong force, he snatches the light off of the machine and begins shining the light up in the hole, looking to find another access panel. From the inside he sees it. It is curved and goes outward above the tracks. "How in the hell does this thing come off?" He starts pulling bolts off the panel until he begins to see light between it and the body of the machine. He goes to the outside and removes the last four bolts. The big panel crashes four times as it bounces off the tracks and collides with the inside of the machine, then eventually to the ground. This hurts Tilley's ears. She gets up and begins to prepare to head back to the cabin. She is thinking that Danny doesn't really want her there, and Kelly must be up by now.

Danny stops her. "Where are you going?"

"I can't take the racket."

Danny walks to the workbench and pulls out a pair of earplugs, handing them to her.

"You sure? You really want me to stay?"

"Of course, I do. How could I have started this thing without you? You have to realize that I am working, though, not focused on you. I have to get the tank off and on the trailer."

"Okay," she responds, feeling like maybe he was just not considering her and wasn't trying to run her out of there.

Danny climbs back under the machine and has good access to the bolts that have the strap holding the tank on. He loosens these retainers, pulls a couple of hoses loose, and pulls the tank out of the housing.

He drags it over to the old Op Track and compares it. It is about a foot taller and about one and a half times as long. *Crap*. The trailer is bigger than the Op Track. It will never make it. It then occurs to him that the 3500 is a much bigger machine than the old one. He also looks over the tracks that he removed, wondering if they would fit Adam and Bryan's machine.

He walks out the back door to find the 3500. He jumps in and pulls around to the front door. The tank looks to be maybe three inches shorter and considerably narrower. He is happy as this looks like, with the right mount, it will work as a trailer.

He gathers a bunch of 1x1 angle iron and begins to construct a sled and frame for the tank, he abandons the notion of using the old Op Track as a frame. He is laying it out and asks Tilley if she would like to go down to the cabin. When he is welding, there is a possibility that he could flash her eyes, making them burn.

She is happy to get away from the nasty mess that he has started now and takes him up on it.

145

She heads up to the cabin to find Kelly on the front porch.

"What is he doing up there?"

"He is building something to carry fuel for the Op Track, I believe," Tilley replies.

"Is he taking a tank off of the excavator?"

"No, I think it is the bulldozer."

"I told him the excavator. If he disables the excavator, I believe we could move it with that big ass bulldozer. I'm not so sure we can move the bulldozer with anything out there."

"It is looking like it is a little late now. He has a big, black, plastic tank on the floor behind the big Op Track and has metal laid out all around it."

"Are you hungry?"

"Actually, I am. I think Danny probably is as well. He asked me about eating before we went up. I didn't tell him there was fruit out on the back deck. I know you enjoy cooking, so I am leaving that to you."

"I appreciate that, Tilley."

"No problem."

"How about some homemade deer sausage, with sausage gravy, biscuits, and an omelet?" Kelly asks.

"That sounds awesome."

Kelly goes off to the kitchen to cook as Tilley sits on the porch, looking over the garden. A doe with a little fawn walks out on the far side. *Kapow!* bellows out from the workshop where Danny is working. Tilley jumps at the sound. She is very upset because she thinks Danny shot at the deer. The deer take off running. She yells out to him, "I am glad you missed!" Danny's head peaks out of the big door, looking up at the porch. He sees Tilley sitting there alone. He is hungry and ready to go find something to eat, even if it is replicated. He wonders what in the hell she is yelling about because he couldn't hear a word with his earplugs in.

He begins the walk across the yard as Tilley sits watching. He makes it to the front porch and Tilley says, "Are you really that heartless?"

"Heartless? What in the hell are you talking about, girl?"

"Didn't you shoot at that doe or her fawn at the end of the garden?"

"Hell no. I didn't even see them. I don't shoot doe this time of year. They are nursing their young, and we need to protect this valuable resource."

"Really? What was that loud bang just before you looked out?"

"I had shut off my cutting torch. It always makes a loud pop if I don't turn off the oxygen first."

"Okay then, I really thought you tried to kill those deer."

"No, if I had shot at that range, one of them would have been lying on the ground."

Just then Kelly steps to the door.

"What's all the hollering and carrying on out here?"

Danny replies, "Tilley thought I was shooting our doe and baby."

"No, we don't kill the ones with little ones until they are old enough to fend for themselves. That is a food source and we take it very seriously. The only way we would do that is if we didn't have a choice."

"I guess I will go replicate me some fucking breakfast if neither of you are going to cook anything."

"I am cooking! Tilley didn't tell you? I have deer sausage, omelets, sausage gravy, and cathead biscuits on now."

"No, we've been too busy worrying about me killing the deer family."

"It will all be ready in about fifteen, maybe twenty, minutes. Don't you smell it?"

"I've been cutting metal and can't smell much of anything really."

147

She returns into the house and comes back out with a nice big steaming cup of coffee and hands it to Danny. He thanks her and she disappears back into the house.

Danny follows her back in and adds some Irish cream to it. He returns to sit down on the love seat lawn chair beside Tilley on the porch. They sit there kind of hoping for a return of the deer when a faint pounding is heard from the north. Danny gets up and walks out into the yard, wondering what the hell the noise is, looking out toward the path that leads to the road. Then he hears it again.

Outside of the front doors are Adam and Bryan. They have the old Op Track up and running, but got most of the way to the shelter and it broke down. They walked the remainder of the way and are cold and in fear of frostbite. They stand outside the door, pounding to get someone to let them in before they freeze to death.

Danny goes in, gets his gun, and comes back out. He hurriedly walks to the shop to retrieve his four-wheeler. Tilley sits on the porch watching the ordeal as Danny comes racing out of the backside of the barn on the big four-wheel drive ATV. He zooms past the front porch, kicking up grass, and appears as a blur as he heads toward the doors of the shelter.

Down through the ditch and up on the road. A low growl is heard as he flies down the road, arriving at the doors. The banging sound is now gone. He slowly walks up to the doors, with the gun pointed at them. He can see the light from their LED lights through the hole he cut for the lock. He has the gun pointed at the hole, safety off, and his finger on the trigger. The boys bang the door again, trying to ensure someone heard them. Danny, being startled, inadvertently shoots the gun, making a large hole in the door well above the lighted lock penetration. It goes dark through the hole and it is deathly silent outside the shelter. Danny yells out, "Who is there?"

"It is me, Bryan, and Adam." His voice becomes very high-pitched and almost like a female, he screams, "Please don't shoot! I think you killed Adam! He fell to the ground when you

148

shot. Oh, my god, my brother, my friend, you killed my best friend!"

Danny starts fumbling with his key to try to get the door open. He is in fear that he may have just shot Adam. He gets the door open to find Bryan knelt down over Adam's lifeless body. Danny grabs the young man by his shoulder, with one hand, and drags him into the shelter. Bryan is following, with tears in his eyes.

Danny begins to look him over and finds the LED headset has a bullet hole right in the center. Adam has a pulse and is breathing heavily. Danny begins slapping the young man. "Wake up, wake up!" Adam begins to come around. Danny finds that he has urinated in his pants and suspects he fainted. Adam opens his eyes.

"Are you okay? Did the bullet hit you?"

"Yea dude; we thought you were dead."

"I, uh, I, umm." Bryan begins to realize that Adam fainted and pissed his pants. "The impact from the bullet hitting the light knocked me out."

"I see. So you are okay? You aren't hurting anywhere, like from being shot?"

"No, just my head. That light sprung around backward and hit me in the back of the head really hard. I guess it was hard enough to knock me out."

The light is only slightly back on the top of his head and it is apparent that it didn't violently move in the way that he explains.

"Yeah, sure…okay. I guess it made your bladder empty, too." Danny kind of chuckles. "Get your chicken shit ass up and come on up to the cabin. What are you two doing here?"

"We were just out trying the Op Track when it broke down. We were near your shelter, so we decided we would try to walk here. Our key didn't work, and we began beating on the door, hoping someone would hear us," Bryan answers.

"How long you goofy fucks been out here?"

"About two hours."

149

"You both have feeling in your hands and feet?"

The boys both answer yes. Danny lets Bryan get on the back of the wheeler but tells Adam he has to walk. He drives slow so as not to leave Adam behind. They pull up in the yard of the cabin and Tilley and Kelly comes out to see what the racket was all about and are wondering about the shot they heard. Tilley asks where they came from.

Danny explains, "They were at the door. They beat on the door as I walked up and it startled me. I accidentally pulled the trigger of the .223. It hit just above Adam's head, busting the LED light he had on, and he passed out, pissing his pants." He finishes by laughing as Adam comes walking up and everyone is looking at his wet jeans.

Adam can't help but have a red face and laugh with them as he says, "In my defense, I had to pee either way. The shot just made me turn loose when it knocked me out."

Danny replies, "Knocked you out, my ass! Go get cleaned up and have Tilley give you an old pair of my jeans. They may be a little big on you, but it will be better than those pissy britches. You boys came just in time to help with my fuel tank trailer. Ya'll hungry?"

They both are very hungry as they haven't had any breakfast. It isn't long and Tilley and Adam return. Adam has jeans on that are rolled up on each ankle, and a belt.

The other three head into the house to find a plate on the table, with a paper towel over it and a bowl with gravy. Kelly had already fixed Danny a plate and he snatches it up and tells the other two they can fight over what is left or replicate something. They both get a plate of food and come back out on the porch.

"'What all do we need to do?" asks Bryan.

"I am building a fuel trailer in case I need to get out further than the fuel tank can handle."

"Wow, I think I would like to learn how to do that," Bryan explains.

They finish eating. The three guys head up to the barn, and Kelly drags out her hoe. She hasn't weeded the garden in several days. Tilley goes out with her and starts pulling the grass out by hand until Kelly explains there is another hoe up in the barn. She takes off toward the barn and Kelly says, "A ho after a hoe," and starts laughing.

She gets up there and asks Danny where the garden tools are and Danny says, "What are you looking for?"

The boys are standing there beside the large gas tank, both have thick leather gloves on and white T-shirts.

"A hoe."

"She is up at the cabin."

The boys both bust out laughing, and Tilley can't help but smirk.

"They are in here."

He takes her around the back of the pegboard wall, where all of the equipment is stored. There is a large rack that has several types of shovels, axes, rakes, and hoes. He pulls one down and hands it to her. She grabs the handle and he pulls her up to him and grabs her waist with his other hand, sliding his hand around to the small of her back, then to her behind, and kisses her.

She says, "Your ho is right here, babe."

He smiles and says, "Get your horny little ass back down to the cabin before I make the guys sit in there and wait for me to get a little dessert after my breakfast." He laughs.

"They can wait."

"No, really, I got to get busy. You are still as fucking sexy as you have ever been, though. My little ho!"

She gets the hoe and heads back to help Kelly.

Chapter 21
Go Time

Kelly and Tilley work the rows one little stalk at a time. They keep chopping the grass until they hear a motor fire up in the shop. A few minutes pass and the 3500 appears, pulling a large black tank behind it.

They get just a glimpse at it as Danny pulls it around the barn to fill it up with fuel so he can see how it is going to pull.

Kelly says, "It looks like we have something."

"I guess that is his fuel tank. Are you going to Arizona with him?"

"I think we both should."

"Why would we want to go if it could be dangerous?"

"To help keep Danny safe. He always works to take care of us, doesn't he?" Kelly questions.

"Well, yeah, but the men should be the protectors. We should send the boys with him."

"Danny doesn't really feel like he can trust the boys yet."

"I trust they will do better at having his back than us."

"Why don't you keep your chicken shit ass home then? Dumb bitch!" Kelly turns back around to start working on the garden again.

Tilley draws the hoe back as Kelly's back is to her and cracks her across the back of the head with the handle. Kelly is dazed and barely standing as Tilley explains, "You will start having some motha-fuckin' respect for me, bitch!"

It is on! Kelly jumps up from the row she is working on, without the hoe, to catch Tilley in the stomach with her shoulder and both arms wrapped around her. She tackles the petite girl to the ground, landing on top of her.

"You piece of shit whore!" Kelly screams as she draws her fist back and punches Tilley in the face. Tilley is screaming loudly as Kelly provides her with a proper ass whooping. She continues with punch after punch to her face and throat. Tilley begins to choke and can't seem to catch her breath as Danny comes running up, pulling Kelly off of her.

Tilley is spitting up blood and continues to gag as she tries to gain her composure, and clearly having issues breathing.

Adam and Bryan look on as Danny says, "I shoulda known this was going to happen. Two women just can't live peacefully under the same roof. This shit happens every damn time! Can't you two get along? What the fuck! Why are you beating the fuck out of my housekeeper?"

"Crazy bitch whacked me in the head with the hoe handle."

"Well, you two have to stop this shit or I'm bringing the both of ya to the Hot Springs town shelter."

"Load my ass up in that Op Track or shut the fuck up about it! I am sick and tired of that threat! If you want that smelly whore and I don't count, then I don't want to count anymore, maybe I should take my ass out of here!"

Danny says, "Just calm down. I don't want you to leave."

"Then you best shut your fucking mouth about it then. I am too good to be threatened by that. I pull my own weight and you did backflips over me until this bitch showed up!"

Danny takes back off for the Op Track, leaving Tilley looking on and Kelly walking toward the cabin. Tilley just sits there with blood on her face, crying. Bryan asks, "Are you okay?"

"I will be. I guess I overreacted, but I am so sick and tired of her attacking me and talking down to me for no reason. Danny used to bring girls like her home for the weekend. She seems to be staying."

"I'm not sure she is a weekend kind of girl," Bryan replies.

"She is to me. Just a hot little whore. Danny's flavor of the week if he had others to choose from, that is what I see."

"She is more than that. She cooks, helps Danny, tends to the
garden, fishes, hunts, and prepares her own meat according to Danny. She is really a hell of a lady."

"Oh, just shut up! That bitch is a flower in full bloom right now. You give her three years and that flower will wilt. She will be thirty pounds overweight if Danny is lucky, it will probably be more. She will be laid up on her lazy ass wanting him to kiss her ass. Right now, though, I guess this is what I get to deal with. I am the one that will always make that man happy!"

Tilley groans as she climbs up off the ground and goes into the cabin to try to smooth things over with Kelly. The boys both look at each other, considering how harsh that was, and head back up to the barn to see how the Op Track is handling the fuel sled.

Tilley gets inside of the cabin and doesn't see Kelly anywhere. She steps out onto the deck to find her sitting, looking out into the woods behind the cabin, where a hill goes up and disappears into a tree line. Four-wheeler tracks remain from years of Danny and others riding up the hill to get to another two-story cabin that didn't make its way into the shelter. A power line extends down to the cabin from poles that have been there for many years. You can see some distribution lines that were clipped up on the hill, providing power to other areas before the snow.

Tilley has a seat in a lawn chair on the other side of the porch. Kelly looks over at her. "Do you want to go again?"

"No, and honestly, you make me feel submissive."

"Whoa. Uhm, hello... You really mean submissive?"

"Yes, you have shown me who is boss. I feel that I should show you some respect. Try to do more to please you."

"I would watch talking like that. I could get the idea that you want to climb in bed with me. I ain't really into any carpet munching, honestly."

"Don't be surprised if I do."

Danny steps out onto the porch. He looks at Tilley. "Are you okay?"

"Yes, my ego is a little bruised and I am a little sore, but I will be fine."

"You crazy bitches don't have any plans of going at it again, do you?"

"Not fighting," Tilley responds.

Kelly looks over at her and thinks, *Bitch wants to go to bed with me?*

"So, you two are good? Kelly, I am going to let the boys take the jeep home. Do I need to send Tilley with them?"

"No, things are really improving with us."

Tilley gets a big smile on her face.

Danny continues, "Tilley, are you afraid now? Do you want to go home with Adam and Bryan? It is getting kind of late in the day."

"No, I think I will be just fine." She flashes her green eyes over at Kelly, with a smile forming across her soft pink lips, thinking about what may come next.

Danny bends over and kisses Kelly as he makes his way back outside. He heads back up to the barn to find the boys standing over his new creation. The big white 3500 has a big black plastic tank with a metal cage around it and a tongue that comes out forming a "V" shape and latches the two together. Danny is ready to bring the unit out onto the snow and see how it works.

"Where's the blue Op Track? Is it just down the road or halfway to Hot Springs Village?"

Adam replies, "We walked nearly a half hour to get here, so it is probably about a mile up the tunnel."

"Let's go see if we can drag that thing back here. Did the motor quit?"

"No, it quit pulling."

The three load up in the 3500, with the fuel trailer on behind it. Kelly and Tilley hear them coming through the yard. They get out to the big ditch with the one-hundred-gallon tank full of fuel weighing it down. It makes a low growl as it pulls the tank through the dry ditch. The skids digging into the weeds as it goes and the big Op Track stands up almost entirely on the back rollers. It comes back down on the solid pavement and each of the men bottoms out the cushions in their stations, taking their breath away for a minute.

They hit the pavement and sparks begin to fly from beneath the tank as they take off toward the doors. Danny stops and Bryan gets out with the key and unlocks the big doors, swinging the one on the right open to allow the machine to pass through. Danny pulls through with the hatch still up. "Lock it?" he yells out at Danny as he passes.

"Always," Danny replies.

Bryan fastens the lock securely and returns to the open hatch. Looking in, Danny is in the operator's station in the middle and Adam is on the left side. He climbs in and Danny presses the *Close Hatch* button and away they go to retrieve the boys' machine.

They head north. The growl of the diesel and the thumping of the tracks can be faintly heard from inside the machine. The display is showing the tunnel ahead on each of the monitors until Danny changes the view. Suddenly, there is a split window on the screen and on the right is a view of the back, showing the diesel tank trailer. It appears to be pulling along very nicely.

They travel for about five minutes and come upon the blue Op Track in the middle of the tunnel. Danny turns the 3500 into the wall and slows way down. He protrudes into the wall, watching the camera and feels the jolt as the trailer follows the big machine into the deep snow. He turns out and drives for some period of time before he makes a big circle in order to come back into the tunnel, in front of the stranded machine.

He pulls back into the tunnel opening and pops the hatch. They all climb out and Danny opens a storage area similar to a car trunk at the back of the cockpit. He pulls out a yellow and white tow strap that has a loop on each end. The three walk to the back of the tank and wrap the strap around the nose of the disabled machine, pulling the slack end through and back up to the 3500's new trailer, affixing the strap to its newly fabricated cage.

Bryan asks, "Think I should get in and try to drive it?"

Danny replies, "I don't think that you could do much to control it without the motor running. I have pulled others and they bob around back there like a jet ski behind a boat."

"You are probably right."

They climb back into the 3500. It is really cold and they are all shivering as they didn't put any cold-weather gear on. They get it back to the shelter and drag it up to the barn. Danny explains that he doesn't have a great deal of time to spend on it and offers to let the boys take his jeep back to the Hot Springs Village shelter.

They head back down to the cabin and Danny has a bit of a sense of urgency as he remembers the fight before they left. He is worried the two women are at it again. It is getting late in the day by this time and the three head into the cabin.

No sign of the girls and Danny thinks, *Crazy bitches may have killed each other*. He walks into the bedroom and finds the two lying arm-in-arm, asleep in the bed. They have the covers over them and he can't tell if they are clothed or not, but he smells the aroma of apples and cinnamon and sees a scented candle burning, and the drapes are pulled. He stands there wondering, *What the fuck went on here?* He kind of shakes his head and goes back to the mudroom where the boys are. *Maybe they just had a long talk and fell asleep*, he thinks to himself.

"They okay?" asks Adam.

"I think they are better than okay. They are asleep."

"Will Tilley want a ride back with us?"

"I truly have no idea what she wants. It would appear that they have made up and are getting along very well."

"You guys go ahead and take the jeep. If Tilley wants to come, I will take care of her later." He kind of smirks.

"Come, huh? Okay, well, uh, no doubt she is well?"

157

"Yes, she looks to be fantastic from what I see."

The boys take off to the barn to get the jeep out. It isn't long and they are driving by the house, tooting the horn. Danny comes out to stop them and escort them to the doors.

"You are coming up there with us?" asks Adam, who is driving the jeep.

"How else will you knuckleheads get the lock open?"

Adam says, "Oh, yeah. Well, can't you just give us a key?"

He just gives them both a blank stare as he walks over to the lime green Mustang. *Vroooooomm pau pau pau*, the muffler sounds off as he brings the little beast to life. He leads them to the doors and lets them out. On the way back, he can't resist taking advantage of the asphalt road and the straightaway that leads past the medical facility. He stops, pressing the brake and pushing a little button just in front of the emergency flashers on the console. He holds this button until "ADVANCED TRAC OFF" illuminates on the instrument cluster. He puts the car in second gear. Without touching the brake, he lights the 19" BF Goodrich T/A Radials up, leaving two black marks that are near one hundred feet long. He reaches fifth gear at one hundred and twenty mph, with the tachometer bumping the red zone when he lets off. He runs down through the gears and does a U-turn on the highway, pulling up slowly to the medical facility parking area. He pulls off to the left and turns the car back to the right. As he dumps the clutch, he begins to turn donuts in the parking lot. "So much damn fun, just one more!" He roasts the tires for one more round and straightens it out for home.

He can't get over what he must have missed with Kelly and Tilley while out rescuing the boys' Op Track. "Those little pricks messed up my only chance with both of them and I will whoop both of their asses."

158

Chapter 22
Arizona Awaits

Danny gets back to the cabin and goes in to find Kelly and Tilley both in the living room. They both seem well.

"So, you two have buried the hatchet?"

Not knowing that Danny had seen them in the bedroom sleeping, Tilley says, "Yeah, I think we can get along okay from now on."

"Indeed," Danny replies.

Kelly speaks up, "What do you mean by that, mister?"

Danny walks to the kitchen and replicates himself a tall Michelob Light, takes a big swig, and chuckles as he walks out of the kitchen and through the mudroom to the Op Track. He starts getting ready for the trip. He fills the tank, checks the oil, and goes over all of the stuff in the manual for preventative maintenance.

He pulls the big Op Track up to the front door and heads in to find out what they have in mind for the trip, and if they both are going to Arizona with him. He wants both of them to go if they can keep from killing each other.

Kelly is sitting at the computer when he gets through the mudroom. She explains, "Ben, your fuel rods guy, emailed you again. He wants to know if you are coming and when."

"That is what I came to talk about. Who wants to go?"

Both of the girls say, "I do."

"Okay, so you two think you can stand being cooped up in the Op Track together for four days?"

"Yeah, I think so," Kelly responds.

"You think that as well, Tilley?"

"Yes, we are working on our friendship."

"Something happen that I should know about?"

They both kind of giggle and Tilley takes off to the guestroom. Kelly wondering what to respond to Ben says, "You want me to answer this guy?"

159

"Yes, ask him if he can be ready in two days."

"You want to leave tomorrow?"

"Yep, we need to get this show on the road. Did you have some plans or something?"

"No, I just didn't realize that we were that close to ready for a four-day trip."

"Ready as we will ever be."

"Okay, I'm asking him now."

A few minutes pass and the computer makes a tone that indicates mail and Kelly says, "He is ready today. He says that he will let the gatekeeper know to expect us on Thursday."

"Fantastic. We shall leave in the morning. I will go tell Tilley."

He walks to the end of the hallway and opens her door. She has on a T-shirt and white panties, sitting at her laptop computer.

"Who are you talking to?"

"My aunt on Goldilocks. We have been emailing back and forth since I have gotten my new laptop."

"You are serious about going to Arizona?"

"Yes. I want to get out of here for a few days."

"You know it could be dangerous. I fear the people there."

Tilley remembers the guys that attacked her and looks away.

"I will not allow anything to happen to you if I can help it. You know that."

"Will we have guns?"

"Of course, we are going to have guns. We will be loaded up like an arsenal."

"Can I have a gun?"

"You aren't holding some grudge toward Kelly that we need to talk about, are you?"

"Nooo. We are good."

"Do you know how to use a gun?"

"My dad taught me how to shoot."

160

"Then yes, we will all have guns. You and Kelly better not shoot each other, though. What is going on with you two? You fist fight this morning and are best friends, maybe even lovers, tonight?"

"Let's just say that we have come to an agreement. She is the dominant woman and I need to respect her spot. But in doing this, she has agreed to respect mine as well."

"I don't really think I understand any of that. Especially coming from Kelly – 'The bitch can't stay for more than a night', but I just want the two women in my life to be happy, healthy, horny, and get along."

"I am happy now. I have been fighting the idea of her being in our life. I actually like her and see a place for all three of us to be best friends, to be honest."

"Hmmm, well, that sounds good to me. It could be better than good. You two been fucking?" He chuckles.

"Why would you ask that?"

"Earlier, you were talking some shit about her being dominant or you being submissive. That is usually sexual talk."

"That is all you men think about is freaking sex, isn't it? We can have a caring relationship without having sex. I am not a lesbian."

"Could you be bi? Bi-curious?"

"Why would you think these things?"

"Why do you keep answering without answering my questions? I haven't heard a straight answer from you yet."

"I have been answering you."

"Whatever!"

Danny leaves the room. He goes into the living area and tells Kelly, "She is in. What have you two been doing?"

"What did she say we have been doing?"

"That is just it, when I ask a direct question, she won't answer. Now you are doing the same damn thing!"

"We have a lot in common and earlier she broke down talking about the men attacking her, and losing her mom and dad. We fell asleep while I consoled her."

161

"No fucking?"

"What? Fucking? Are you freaking serious?"

"Of course, it looked to me... oh hell, okay, just talking, I get it. We need to get to bed so we can get going in the morning."

Tilley sits in the guest room alone and thinks of the afternoon. She and Kelly had quite a bit that they had talked about and she felt much closer to her since then.

The next morning comes early for Danny. He is up around four am. He makes his way to the kitchen to find a bowl of fruit on the dining room table. He turns on his coffee, lets it make about a half a pot before taking a cup, and heads off to the shower. He is careful not to wake up Kelly as he makes his way in the dark through their bedroom to the bathroom. He smells the fresh Lysol bathroom cleaner that he likes so much and the tile, vanity, and shower are all glistening. "Jeez, we need to keep this going." It isn't long and he is dripping wet, toweling off, getting ready for his trip.

He makes his way back to the kitchen and gets his GPS out and begins to look at the path he plans to take. It is around thirteen hundred miles one way. He had already calculated the fuel usage and was a little concerned about food.

He had bought several cases of MREs at one time. He remembers thinking if for some reason he was stuck at the shelter and the replicator broke, he may need some backup. Money was rarely an object for him and he bought about a five-year supply, for two. There were several cases and they should be very easy to find. He couldn't be sure if they had been placed in this shelter or the one at Hot Springs Village. Hell, for all he knew, some dumbass could have donated them to a cause. He begins looking. He searches the pantry, the cabinets in the kitchen, the laundry room, and the hall closet to see if there may be a few stray cases that had been put there. He can't locate them anywhere. He remembers the MREs he had when he was a child. The beanie wienies and little hot dogs were actually pretty tasty. He even remembers some that had a heating pad that you

162

could use to heat up the meal with. He was sure there were all kinds in there. It isn't long and he gives up his search. He decides that he will ask the women. Maybe one of them would know where they are.

He replicates a couple of shots of Bailey's Irish cream. He doctors up his second cup of coffee with a little liquid encouragement. He tastes it and decides that is just not going to be enough for the adventures he faces today. He walks over to the replicator and reaches into a cabinet to pull out a small paper cup to put under the spout and says Malibu rum, shot, no glass. When he places the paper cup under the spout, a clear liquid fills it. He pours about half of it into his coffee and drinks the rest straight. "Damn, what a way to wake up," he says quietly to himself.

A female's voice from the dark front room speaks up and says, "Do you drink this heavily every morning? No pain pills?"

It is Kelly. He didn't see that she wasn't in his bed when he returned from the shower.

"Well, if you would get up with me, you would know, now, wouldn't you?"

"What are you looking for?"

"I was trying to find about ten, maybe twenty, large cases of MREs I bought about two years ago. I am sure I put them at this hunting cabin. Hell, there could be fifty cases, but I remember there were about two that I took out because I wanted them to be available in case we got up here sometime and there wasn't anything to eat."

"What is an MRE?"

"You know, they are military meals. Meal Ready to Eat. They come in a little green or brown pouch usually. You open them and they have a meal in them."

"I don't think I ever had those. I think I saw some boxes with little pouches like you described, though. I put them in the storage room up at the barn. The room is half-full of those things."

163

"Every damn thing I own is in that fucking barn. Hell, I guess I should move up there." He chuckles a little.

"Except for this." He looks in there and sees her in a little pink nightgown, she spreads her smooth tanned legs to reveal blonde hair between them.

"You have a very valid point there, dear. So, they are in the storage room at the barn?"

He wastes no time slipping on his robe and making his way up to the barn to retrieve something portable to eat that they can bring on their trip. Sure enough, there were rows of several boxes marked MRE. He grabs two of them and carries them back to the cabin. He walks back through the living room and doesn't see Kelly sitting on the sofa where she had been moments before. He cuts open a box and pours them out onto the table. There is a large assortment of various kinds. He decides that he will take enough for three people to have three meals a day for six days. That should give them a bit of a variety to eat and have plenty in case they are held up somewhere. He gets into a cabinet and finds a cloth bag. He loads up about fifty-four meals in the bag, then he takes and puts them into the storage box in the Op Track that is sitting in the front yard.

He comes back in and gathers up clothes and goes in to check on Kelly. She isn't in her bed. "Bitch getting her a little morning pussy?"He yanks on Tilley's door and abruptly opens it, thoroughly expecting to find the two in some kind of lover's embrace. He finds Tilley waking to look out to see what is going on. "Up and at 'em! We are getting ready to leave for Arizona," Danny explains.

"Okay, I will be in after a bit," she explains.

He heads back into the kitchen, looking for Kelly. He opens the back door to find her sitting on the porch, staring out into the woods.

"You aren't having second thoughts about our trip, are you?"

"No, I am just relaxing. Just totally ignore my morning offer?"

164

"Sorry, babe, we got time for that later. I am packing."

"Just sitting here wondering why you would pass me by after I put that out there, and thinking about what we have to do today."

"Raincheck for sure, gorgeous lady, but right now, we got to get ready to go."

"You realize if for some reason we break down, it could be death, right?"

"Why do you think that?"

"Will we be buried in the snow the whole way? We can't open the hatch if we are buried. It will be like the guys who you thought you had killed, won't it?"

"No, not really. We won't be buried in the snow for the whole trip. We will start out and travel to the surface. We will actually drive on the surface until we get close to Arizona, then travel down through the snow to get into Tempe."

"I didn't realize. I thought we would be in the snow the entire time."

"Nope, we'll probably still freeze to death if we break down, though. If that makes you feel better about it."

Tilley walks out onto the deck, with a cup of coffee. She says, "Do we have to do this today?"

"Yes, you ladies need to get ready."

Danny heads back into the house and begins gathering ammunition. He places it in the trunk of the Op Track as well. It isn't long and Kelly begins to bring a very large bag out to the Op Track. Danny says, "What the hell is that?"

"Just stuff I need."

"It looks like stuff you don't need. Woman, this is bare necessities. You get three changes of clothes, a small thing of makeup, some winter gear, and one pair of snow boots. The same for Tilley."

"That doesn't seem fair. What all do you have in here, Mr. Danny?"

"Guns, food, ammo! Shit to keep us alive. If you got shit like that to bring along, go get it, but if you want your favorite pillow and blankie, you are shit smooth out of luck if you are going with me."

"Okay."

On her way back in she sees Tilley. She has an overnight bag that she had brought to the cabin. Kelly has a large bag as she passes her and kind of turns her nose in the air, as if Tilley already knew she couldn't bring a bunch of stuff along. But honestly, Tilley didn't have that much anyway.

Tilley gets out the door, finding Danny unhitching the fuel trailer. Tilley asks, "What are you doing? Don't we need that?"

"Yes, but I have to get ole Chopper up to the Hot Springs Village shelter. He may be okay on his own for a day, but four days is pushing it. Big bastard could tear out the replicator."

"Can I ride along? I would like to get some more stuff."

"Damn it, woman, we won't be getting out of here until tomorrow at this rate."

"Sorry, Danny, I can go with what I have, but I don't like wearing same clothes for more than two days."

"Oh, it's okay. I wouldn't want to have to wear the same clothes the whole trip either. I am just getting a little stressed over all we have to do."

Kelly steps out on the porch. "Where are ya'll headed?"

"The other shelter. We have to go drop Chopper off. Do you want to go?"

"Nah, I will stay here. I will get the grass mowed while ya'll are out."

Danny and Tilley both climb in the machine. The diesel engine fires up and a blue light illuminates from beneath the hatch in the darkness of the morning as it closes securely. She sees the bottom tracks start to move and they are on their way.

It isn't long and they find themselves within the tunnel. Danny is lying face down in the middle, studying the path ahead, and Tilley is on his left side, with Chopper sittin' on the right side at the lowest level. He has never been inside of the Op

Track before and seems a little uneasy. Danny has his hands on a joystick, one on each side. They are both looking at a display. Danny assures Chopper that everything is okay, in hopes that he doesn't get too excited. The displays show the horseshoe shaped tunnel ahead and it is illuminated very well by the lights of the machine. They travel for a while and turn left, headed to Hot Springs Village. They come upon the rectangular shaped hole they made in the snow when they went to the Walmart store. They pass on by and it isn't long until they arrive at the other shelter.

Tilley unlocks the doors and Danny pulls through. They head on past the lake and turn right just past the end of it to go to Mr. Johnson's house to find the boys. They pull up into the yard and daybreak has just started, with the lights in the shelter illuminating it slowly on the east side of the shelter.

They see Danny's jeep sitting in the yard as they pull in. Tilley remembers the bloodbath that happened there last week and thinks of poor Mr. Johnson. They don't see any brown or red on the gorgeous green lawn as he pulls into the yard.

Bryan walks out onto the porch, with a rifle in his hand. He puts his hand above his eyes, squinting to try to see who or what it is. He looks like he just woke up. Danny kills the lights on the machine and pops the hatch.

Chopper wastes no time at all coming up and out of the cockpit of the machine. Danny kills the engine and begins climbing out. Bryan yells back into the house, "It's Danny and Chopper."

Adam walks through the door to greet them and Bryan hands him the rifle. He sets it back inside the doorway.

"How you boys doing?"

"We are well. Beginning to learn how to take care of the place, I believe." Bryan replies.

"That is good to hear. I need you guys to do me a favor. We are going out of town for a few days and I would like for you to take care of Chopper for us."

"Sure, Mr. Nichols, that is no problem at all," Bryan says.

"Anything been going on up at my house? You guys been checking on it?"

"Nothing that we know of. We have been by there a few times and nothing has been out of order. What does Chopper eat?" Adam asks.

"You can replicate him just dry Ole Roy recipe dog food and he will be happy. If he gets a taste for something else, he will go hunting."

"Sounds great. We will see about him. Is there anything else you need us to tend to?"

"Not really. Make sure your neighbors are getting along okay, especially Mr. Franklin, and watch for outsiders trying to come in."

"Okay, any particular reason Mr. Franklin needs extra attention?" Bryan asks.

"Not really, just watch out for everyone."

They all say their goodbyes and Danny and Tilley take off to go to their house. He pulls up on his cobblestone driveway, kills it, and pops the hatch. They both go inside of the large mansion. Danny really misses this house and the pampering Tilley always afforded him here. Tilley heads through the large formal dining room to her quarters and comes out with a small cloth bag.

Chapter 23
Road Tripping

The pair finishes their business at Hot Springs Village and return to the country shelter in no time. It is about seven thirty am when they arrive back. The grass looks fantastic and Kelly is ready to go. She comes walking out with four one-gallon jugs of water. Danny figures they can sit these alongside the firearms and asks her to get four more to store on the seats that are vacant on each side, at the very lowest level. Danny gets the fuel trailer hitched back up to the back of the Op Track and they are ready to roll.

They take off and get to the doors. Danny asks does anyone need to go piss as he clicks the hatch to open. Tilley begins climbing out and explains that she went and she is fine. Kelly says, "Bad time to ask, don't you think?"

"You can squat out there on the ground. Hell of a lot better than having frost on the pumpkin after while."

"I went at the cabin, but that is a good question. What will we do if we need to while we are traveling?"

"There is an empty coffee can back there in the trunk."

"Won't that get a little nasty?"

"We can dump it each time, but if you ladies want to, you can climb your hot little asses out in the subzero temperatures on the surface and go. Ice covered tacos," he says, and chuckles.

"The coffee can sounds just fine to me."

Tilley has the doors open and Danny pilots the craft through. She comes climbing in as Danny looks over at her. "They are secured and locked?"

"Yes, sir!"

The hatch is closed and away they go. They travel along for about ten minutes when Danny pulls the craft to the left and they burrow into the wall of the tunnel. The display screens turn a dark blue and shows nothing but the snow intensity and a few power poles that show up in a darker blue. He rolls the thumbwheels back on each joystick and all three can feel the machine climbing. They continue this climb until they see the dark blue turn into a white horizon, with a dividing line that indicates snow and the surface of the snow is in blue and white on the displays.

Tilley hasn't been to the surface and didn't know they would be traveling there. She asks, "We will be traveling along the top of the snow?"

Danny replies, "Yes, we will use much less fuel and there is less of a chance of colliding with anything up here, or putting more strain on the trailer than needs to be."

He then clicks a couple of buttons on the screen. Half of the screen shows the trailer behind them. It looks like it is following very well. It is a sunny day and the bright sunshine is reflecting off the snow covered surface. The camera shows a continuous snow shower building up on the trailer, caused by the tracks of the Op Track.

Danny speaks up, "It looks like our fuel is safe and sound back there."

The display indicates their current speed is fifty mph, it is forty degrees below zero Fahrenheit outside, there is a north wind at thirty knots, and visibility is unlimited. They drive along for about two hours with no issues when the display comes up and has an alarm requesting the machine speed be slowed down. "Hell, I haven't changed the speed in the last hour. It is on cruise for God's sake." Then he sees it.

The wind speed has picked up to about eighty mph. It is a headwind from the west now and he is a little concerned as the sky becomes filled with dark rolling clouds. The machine was not designed for any down force and if it gets much stronger, it could lift the front end off the ground.

"Not our typical weather pattern, I see."

Kelly replies, "I thought maybe that was some glitch."

"I hadn't really thought about it, but I guess it could be. It is a little confused about rather that is the wind or if we are

170

going that fast. I don't know how it tracks our speed. It must be like an airplane or a boat."

Suddenly, the machine begins to shake. The tank behind them looks as if it is coming off the ground as they go over bumps, and the cameras are all showing nothing but a white out blizzard on the outside of the Op Track as Danny changes the view to sonar. All of a sudden, a warning comes up showing the outside temperature has dropped to fifty-five below and the alarm is showing there are issues with ice in the fuel lines.

Danny remembers his training on the machine from the videos and knows there are a few features on the machine that can help with this. He slows the machine and begins to scroll through screens that are showing different controls. He finally gets to one that shows the diesel tank pre-heater. By now, the machine has begun to cut out and sputter. There is a noted silence within the craft. It sounds as though the diesel engine could die. You can almost feel the tension in the craft. To breakdown would be death at fifty-five below zero.

Out of nowhere, a burst of wind comes from the north, tossing the vehicle onto its left side. They are all thrown around the inside of the machine as Danny holds on to the joysticks, hoping to land on the tracks. They stop and the machine is lying on its top. The engine is still sputtering and about to die as Danny throttles it up and gets red errors showing "NO FUEL DELIVERY TO INJECTORS", "RPM INADEQUATE", "ENGINE FAILURE IMMINENT." He rolls the thumbwheels in the opposite direction, as if to climb, and the front of the machine dives within the snow beneath.

He continues this path until they are all holding on for dear life. The girls have their forearms braced against the very front of the cockpit, to keep their heads from hitting. They are essentially standing on their heads. Finally, it begins to rotate around until they are right side up and going east. The engine is still sputtering, but not as bad as before. The alarms have gone away as Danny reduces the throttle and it seems to plane out some. He begins to scroll through the GPS to find if there is anywhere close he can go and let the Op Track heat back up. He spots a small building, which appears to be a carwash, or perhaps a small gas station awning.

He navigates to the small closed-in car wash and pulls in. He scrolls through the menus on the display to find it is ten degrees at this location and no wind present. He pops the hatch and helps Kelly out and into the shelter of the small enclosed area. There is a gash on her forehead. Danny has a bright LED light on his hat that helps to illuminate the inside of this small shelter. He reaches out and places his fingers on her temple and strokes his thumb across her cut, clearing away the blood. It clears away enough for him to spread the area apart to find that it isn't real deep.

The machine dies. He has a fob in his pocket. He pulls it out and cuts power to the machine and the lights go dark. Danny begins to dig in the trunk and finds a first aid kit. He pulls out a small bottle of hydrogen peroxide. He realizes that Tilley is still in the Op Track. He walks back over looking into the cockpit to find her lying face down all the way to the floorboard on the right side of the machine.

"Tilley? Tilley?" he yells.

No response is given. He rushes over to the other side and bends over into the machine, trying to reach her. He jumps up on the tracks and leans inside and into the pilot station and climbs down the other two levels and grabs the back of her shirt. He pulls her lifeless body up and onto the first station and her face is covered with blood and her eyes are closed. He leans over her from the seat above, almost on his head, to try to hear her breathing. It is faint. He shakes her, yelling, "Tilley! Tilley! Wake up for me, please!" He reaches out of the cockpit to the left track in order to grab the first aid kit. He had set it there while tending to Kelly. He fumbles through its content to find some smelling salts. It is in the form of a capsule that he breaks open and waves in front of her nose. She coughs and lets out a big gasp of air as she comes to. He sits her up and she is beginning to regain her composure as he digs through the kit to

172

find a sterile wipe in an alcohol solution. He begins to clean her face.

She screams in agony as he cleans the cuts with the rubbing alcohol. They are from the guns hitting her when the machine flipped. He finds that none of her wounds are deep enough to cause her to lose a great deal of blood and although they could be stitched, it isn't critical.

He turns to find Kelly sitting on the track of the machine, with blood all down her white blouse and she is freezing to death. Danny pulls out her winter gear from the trunk and tells her to put them on. He finds a tube of superglue in the first aid kit and pulls out another alcohol swab, wiping Kelly's cut that is just above her eyebrow. He opens the Super Glue as she pulls away.

"What the fuck do you think you are trying to do to me?" she asks.

"Kelly, do you really think that I would do something to harm you? This was the original intent for Super Glue."

"Bullshit, you are going to freaking poison my ass with that shit! Blood poisoning!"

"No, listen, I know what I'm talking about. Super Glue was originally designed to use in lieu of stitches. I will close it with this and use butterfly bandages to keep it together. It probably won't even scar."

"You are sure? You decide to go with Tilley there and kill my ass?"

"Hell no! I love you, Kelly. Now, let me tend to you. I know what I'm doing."

Tilley hears that and is astonished. Kelly thinks that she must have passed out from all of the blood loss because no one expects Danny to announce his love for either of them.

He finally gets the girls settled down and doctored up. Now, he must diagnose and repair the diesel engine on the Op Track. He clicks the fob in his pocket and the lights illuminate within the cockpit. He leans into the machine and presses the "START ENGINE" button. The little diesel turns over a couple

173

of times and belches out a big plume of smoke and rattles to life. It is still cutting out really bad and rattling like it is going to stall. He lies face forward into the operator's station and begins scrolling through the screens.

He goes back to the one that shows the tank heater and it indicates it is at eighty degrees Fahrenheit. He knows this is excellent, so he continues, almost in disbelief at this point that there is a problem with the fuel freezing. He continues to scroll and finds one that says Tubing Heat. It is off, but it has a help button in the corner of the page. "Turn this function on during extreme temperatures to thaw out the fuel lines, hydraulic lines, and water lines." He quickly goes back to this screen and it indicates the temperature of the zones show ranges from negative twenty degrees to negative thirty degrees. He says, "Ah hah! That's it. The fuel line is froze up, that must be our problem." He turns this heater on and the temperature begins to rise for all of these zones. Soon, the diesel is back purring like a kitten.

Heat begins flowing through the heater on board the machine and Tilley seems to be in much better spirits. Kelly climbs back in, pulling her winter clothes off. She pulls her blood stained blouse off, revealing no bra, and pulls a T-shirt on. Danny says, "Damn, you could cut glass with them things." Referring to Kelly's rock hard frozen nipples. She climbs into Tilley's side of the machine, without much response to Danny's remarks. He thinks it odd that she would climb in crowding that side. Soon, they are all thawed out and ready to begin their trip again.

"So, do we head back to the surface?" Danny asks.

"Hell no!" Kelly exclaims.

"The fuel mileage and speed that we can go on the surface is better than if we try to go in the snow the entire way. Especially if we break down."

"Can you tell when some rogue wind is going to come and blow our little go-cart away?" Kelly replies.

"I can't say for sure, but I think that was an unusual occurrence that may not happen again for a hundred years. I would like to think the weather up there isn't that harsh," Danny states.

"Mother Nature dumped thirty feet of snow on our asses. She has turned into a full blown bitch. You don't think she could fuck us up again up there? Did you hit your head also?"

"I don't think we will make the trip there and back on fuel if we don't go atop the snow."

"If we have to, then okay, but damn, after the storm has kicked mine and Tilley's asses, don't ask us if we want to. That is like asking if we want you to hit us in the head with a baseball bat...again. That is just wrong, dumbass!"

It becomes very quiet as Danny doesn't appreciate her being that rude after he did so much to take care of them. He has done backflips to tend to his women, and this is her response?

"Buckle up, bitch!"

Kelly doesn't say a word as she knows she has pissed him off after he took care of her, and even told her he loved her. That was a first.

"I'm sorry."

"I am serious, both of you better have a strap around your ass when we break the surface, as we could go tumbling around again and this time, I ain't feeling sorry for you."

A few moments later, they are again on top of the snow. The cameras are showing daylight and a white cloudy horizon, with white everywhere.

Danny again flips half of the view of the display to the rear of the machine. In all of the excitement and concern for the girls, he had completely forgotten about his fuel tank. He looks closely and finds that it appears the fuel cap is gone from the tank. There are also dark areas in the snow around the cap. He is sure that he has lost some fuel. He knows that it is detrimental to stay at the top of the snow now to conserve fuel. It would be catastrophic to run out of fuel on this trip.

They have been traveling for about twelve hours now. He knows they will be better off trying to find additional fuel, if it is all gone, than to turn and head back. He took a route that was as the crow flies, or in a straight line, rather than following an interstate. Much of the area beneath him has been undeveloped and would have nothing in the way of a road or fuel stations.

He sets his GPS to alert him when he is within fifty miles of a fuel station, just in case. He scrolls through the display and looks over at his pretty young passengers to see they are both sleeping. The temperature outside shows a mild (by surface standards) ten below and a tailwind of about fifteen knots. He thinks that if this keeps up, he stands a chance to make it on fuel, at least to Tempe. He scrolls again to find his fuel consumption and how much is left. When he reaches the page, it shows that he has another one hundred miles 'til empty and he is operating at a conservative fifty miles per gallon.

The alert he was awaiting comes on and shows a fuel station that is thirty miles north of him, in Albuquerque, New Mexico. He adjusts his direction to head to that truck stop. He drives along for about half an hour, at fifty mph, and is within about five miles of the station as he begins a descent into the snow pack. His intent is to pull in and pray the pumps have some kind of backup power.

He arrives at the huge Flying J truck stop and his display shows ghostly blue outlines of all kinds of trucks around, entombed in the snow. He pulls under the awning to find that part of it has collapsed out near the interstate. He goes closer to the storefront before pulling under the awning. He pulls up to the first pump, pops the hatch to lean out and looks to find that there aren't any lights on the pump at all. Kelly raises up and looks out to see Danny outside of the Track, with his cold-weather gear on and the machine still idling.

Danny has the entire area lit up with his LED headlamp. He walks up to the dark store to find the front sliding door is unlocked but not powered. He pushes on it and gets it open. He walks in looking for some way to turn on a pump. He goes behind the counter, with everything brightly lit from his light, and finds the enable switches for the fuel pumps. He flips one of the switches on and nothing happens. He finds another switch that says "Emergency Generator." He flips this switch to "Enable", and lo and behold, the lights come flickering on. The switch has a green indicator light that illuminates.

He looks out and the lights under the canopy have come on, but the ones near the collapse are dim. He finds pump two, where he is sitting at, and turns it on. "This is freaking awesome!" He knows that many of the truck stops have showers and sleeping areas. He decides they can shower and sleep here tonight if he can find keys to these rooms and everything he needs.

He goes out to find Kelly and Tilley are out of the Op Track. He walks over to pull the nozzle out and put it into the fuel tank of the machine. He says, "Man, this place is a godsend! We get fuel, there is a place to sleep, and we can shower here."

"Really?" Kelly asks.

"It looks that way."

The fuel pump is making a growling noise as Danny pulls the nozzle out to find just a trickle of fuel coming out of it. They smell something that smells like rubber burning. Danny quickly shuts off the pump.

"Damn! I guess the freaking fuel is frozen. It can't be in the ground, though. I bet it is frozen only where it travels through the pump." He goes in to try to find a heater of some type. He searches without any luck, with the exception of a small oxyacetylene torch and hair dryers from the bathroom. He comes back out of the back area of the building to find Kelly and Tilley sitting at a table in the restaurant area of the truck stop, bundled up in their white winter gear. He says, "Well, maybe I can find an outlet and thaw it out with a hair dryer."

He grabs a toolkit that is hanging on a hook on his way out. He gets a socket and ratchet out of the kit and pulls the front off the pump to reveal a U-ground outlet. He plugs the hair dryer into it, setting it so it is pointing at the pipe that is going into the ground.

He heads back in to see about his girls. They are both sitting with a glass of water in front of them and a jug from the Op Track sitting on the table. By now, the heat is on in the store and they are taking off their snow gear.

"Are you ladies okay?"

"Define okay," Kelly responds.

"You're still alive and I haven't crashed the Op Track again so far, right?"

Tilley kind of moans.

It has been about half an hour and he goes back out to find the hair dryer has heated the pipe to a fair temperature. He engages the pump handle and watches as the belt begins to screech and turn inside the pump, rotating the pulley. He pulls the nozzle out a little to find that it is flowing like a waterfall. He is very happy with that and fills the machine with about eighteen gallons of fuel. He then walks back to the tank on the skid and finds there is a big gash in the side. He kicks the side and hears a hollow thump and finds that it is completely empty.

He goes back in and the store heaters have made it very comfortable inside. He begins to pull off his cold-weather gear. He finds the girls have gotten pretty cozy. They have a compact mirror and some baby wipes they are using to clean any blood left on their faces.

"So, ya'll in favor of staying the night here? If we stop at this place on the way back, we can fill back up and won't need the fuel trailer."

"Is the fuel trailer still full of gas?" asks Kelly.

"Diesel is what is in it, but no, it was damaged when we flipped, I guess. It is empty."

Just then a large spark spews from the collapsed end of the awning, spraying sparks that resemble a firework. Then a *whooff* sound is heard. Danny looks out and the spark has ignited fuel at the end of the awning. The wires that were damaged have shorted out. Suddenly, there is a huge fireball on that end of the

178

roof. He yells at the girls to come on as the lights go out in the building.

The three run out and jump into the idling Op Track as Danny flips the "Hatch Closed switch." Explosions are heard outside the machine. The nosecone is cold and he flips the switch to heat it as they all three watch the displays that are focused on that end of the awning. The fire rages, growing towards them. Danny runs the machine against the snow pack and the fire is melting the snow, allowing him to get the machine a little ways away and just far enough away to keep it from the direct line of fire. The nosecone is finally hot enough to go through the snow at a slow pace. He guns the diesel engine to get away from the inferno before it destroys their transportation, and perhaps taking their lives.

Chapter 24
Friendly Shelter of the West

They make their way back to the surface and are well back on the way to the Tempe shelter. A few more hours and they will arrive there. They have a full fuel tank, but their backup tank is ruined. They travel for about an hour and Danny wants to disconnect the trailer, as it is doing nothing but wasting fuel. The girls are pretty much worse for wear and have slept for a little while. Kelly awakes as Danny is stopping.

"Are we stopping?"

"Yes, I am going to ditch the fuel tank. The wind has died down to about thirty miles an hour."

"Why?"

"Because it isn't doing us any good. It has a hole in it."

Danny pops the hatch and bitter cold rushes in, waking Tilley. Kelly now has a thick quilt that she brought along. She slips down to the bottom station with Tilley and they snuggle up close and wrap up tight in the blanket. Danny gets out and sinks up to his knees in the snow pack. He holds on to the top track and crawls along it to avoid sinking into the deep snow. He quickly pulls the pin that latches the sled to the Op Track. The trailer tongue falls to the snow pack. He doesn't have any winter gear on and struggles to get back to the cabin of the machine, shivering, and cranks up the heater.

The girls are glad he is back. Kelly says, "I'm glad you've closed that damn pneumonia hole!"

"I wish one of you would have gotten your lazy asses out there and unlatched that thing." He chuckles.

Kelly says, "Shame about the truck stop. It would have been a nice place to sleep and shower."

"Yeah, well, shit happens. I guess maybe I should have turned the lights off to that section, but I ain't no electro magician."

"You ain't what?" Kelly asks.

180

"I was joking around. You, poor ladies, are too beat and banged up to be in much of a mood for me kidding with you, huh?"

"Pretty much. I really don't want to laugh either, my side really hurts," says Kelly.

"I hope you don't have any broken ribs."

Danny reaches in his pocket and pulls out a pill bottle. He hands it to Kelly.

"What is this?"

"That is for your ribs and to help you feel better."

"There are small white ones, big oval ones, small oval ones, and little bitty pink ones. What will help me?"

"One of everything will make you feel pretty damn good!" Danny chuckles.

"No doubt, but I ain't popping a bunch of pills. What is in there?"

"The best thing for your ribs are the small pink pills and the small round pills. The pink one is oxycodone, for pain, and the small round one is a muscle relaxer. You could try the big oval as well, it won't hurt you. They are ibuprofen."

"How about I just take the ibuprofen and see if that helps?"

"Suit yourself, but give me one of the little pinks, a small round, and a small oval." He chuckles.

"Are you serious? You are just taking this shit to get high, aren't you?"

"Hell no! I have several aches and pains. Ya'll weren't the only ones that were slung across the cabin."

"Yeah sure."

She digs around and hands him what he requests. He leans over on his side and pops them all in his mouth and takes a swig out of the bottle of water he has been drinking.

Tilley speaks up, "Give me the same."

"Seriously?" Kelly replies.

"Hell yes, I hurt. If that helps, then give it to me twice."

Danny speaks up, "It is okay to take one each, but you can't take too many or it can screw with your liver."

"Okay," Tilley responds.

Kelly hands her one each of the same thing that Danny took. "Friggin pill poppers," she says under her breath.

Danny says, "What?"

"Nothing." She decides to help herself to the same little cocktail they had.

They continue on the way and the Op Track is handling much better without the tank behind it, jerking it around. Kelly is beginning to get hungry. They haven't eaten all day. She shimmies around over the seat to reach the trunk and Danny sees her lean up and he guns the throttle, throwing her across the second station and to the foot of the two stations on that side. He kind of chuckles as Kelly comes crawling back up beside Tilley, with tears in her eyes and holding her ribs.

Danny didn't realize that it would hurt her by doing that. He was just being playful. He felt like a complete insensitive moron.

"Kelly, babe, I really am sorry. I was just playing around with you."

"Yeah, well, hardy har har, motherfucker!" She throws a punch as hard as she can into his rib cage on the right side. It actually knocks the breath out of Danny. He is struggling to catch his breath. He says, "I deserved that," catching his breath, trying to speak without panting. "I feel better about throwing your ass around now. What were you doing?"

"I was getting an MRE. I was getting hungry until I had this severe freaking pain in my ribs start back up again. You are right, the pills helped, but now it's hurting again and I lost my appetite."

"This may be a screwed up thing to ask, but could you grab me one?"

"I will, but so help me if you slam on the breaks or gun the engine, I will take this AR and eliminate your sorry ass!"

"Whoa, understood there, li'l tiger lily."

182

She climbs back and grabs a handful of the green packages. The blue ambient light in the cockpit is adequate for her to make out the words on the packages.

"Okay, I have beans and franks, wieners and crackers, and meatloaf with gravy."

"I have always liked the wieners. It has a heater in there, right?"

"Yep, coming right up."

Tilley says, "I would like to try the beans and franks."

"I am not eating this version of meatloaf." She hands off the beans and franks with a heat pack to Tilley. As she begins to climb back, she looks over at Danny and says, "You best not fuck around, asshole. I kid you not, graveyard…fucking…dead! You really did hurt me."

"I understand, baby. Please believe me when I say that I truly didn't mean to."

Just then a tall building begins to come into focus on the monitor and Danny has to make a fairly sharp right turn to avoid colliding with it. Kelly is tossed against the operator's station as she is trying to reach into the trunk. She begins yelling when Tilley speaks up, "There was a building. I saw it. We would have hit it. Please don't kill Danny."

"There better had been 'cause this shit is as fucked up as a soup sandwich."

Kelly has no more to say. She has three MREs to choose from and one of them is the wieners. She tells Danny that she has another wienie packet if he wants it. He explains that he could go for another and this one has chips in it. She opens it and takes the potato chips and brownie out for herself and hands him the heated wienies. She decides she will have a packet of beans and franks.

They finally reach the outskirts of Tempe, Arizona. They have traveled about one thousand, two hundred and fifty miles and have been traveling for almost twenty-four hours. Danny knows that he has to have some sleep and asks the girls, "So, do we want to go to the shelter and see if they have

183

provisions for us for the night, or do we bunk here in the Op Track?"

Kelly speaks up, "It would really be nice if we could find an abandoned hotel or truck stop."

"I don't feel safe with what happened at the truck stop back in New Mexico. There could be fornicated wiring in any structure that is not protected by a shelter. The last thing we need is to burn up while we sleep, or not be able to get out with the Op Track."

"I really didn't think about that. These stations have pretty comfortable pads. I slept really well earlier. These damn pills kind of have me hopped up, though. My ribs are feeling quite a bit better and I really ain't sleepy."

"Too damn bad is all I know to tell you, li'llin. My ass is fixing to get some serious Zzzs! I say we bury this little Track just level with the snow surface to keep any wind from blowing us away. It will let the exhaust get away from us and we just leave this little guy idling. If you're not tired, then you can keep watch for anything that goes south while we sleep."

"Sounds like a plan."

Danny heats the nosecone up and protrudes down into the snow like they discussed. He parks the machine and starts navigating the screens on his display and opens one that shows the configuration of the pad for his station. He adjusts it so that his head is elevated, the arch of his back is slightly curved, and his feet are elevated. It all articulates like a hospital bed. Kelly hears all of the little motors moving his station around and asks, "What is that?"

"That is my station adjusting and getting into position so I can sleep well."

"I didn't know they did that. Why didn't you tell me, prick?"

"Well, you didn't ask, uh, vagina."

"Where is it?"

"Nah, you find it yourself. I am a prick, remember?"

184

Danny then navigates to a screen that says enable/disable station control for station 2, 3, 4, 5. He presses disable for four. That is the one Kelly is lying on.

About half an hour goes by while Danny lays there watching her go through every menu in the display. She finally says, "Where the hell is it?"

Without even noticing, Tilley had already adjusted her bed. Kelly looks over at her as Danny plays opossum and makes a light snoring noise. She says, "Tilley, show me where you adjust that." Tilley brings up the menu where it is located. Kelly looks on the page where Tilley brought it up and there is no button for it.

"You got this freaking bed turned off or something? You ass!"

Danny busts out laughing. Kelly can't help but laugh as well. She is still high as a kite from the pain pills, but she is in very good spirits. "Try it now," Danny tells her.

"Oh, I can't believe you did that! Why are you so mean to me?"

"It is because you are mean to me."

Tilley kind of snickers and says, "You two stopped being funny about ten minutes ago. Isn't it about time you go to sleep?"

Shocked that Tilley actually said that; they both decide they really should get some sleep to prepare for meeting Ben Calhoun tomorrow. Off to sleep they go. Tilley and Danny sleep very well, but Kelly can't sleep. She has her bed exactly the way she likes it. She lies there listening to the low hum of the diesel engine, staring at the blue light casting a shadow on the hatch, and the heat kicking on and off occasionally. She decides to see if she can get a wireless signal on her tablet.

She climbs to the back of the cockpit and finds her little tablet. She lays back down and much to her surprise, it comes up with a wireless signal, complete with access to the Internet. She is very happy about that. She logs onto a social media site to find that she has posts from the Tempe shelter, and all kinds of messages from the boys at Little Rock Air Force Base. Her contacts at the Tempe shelter want to know when she will arrive. She is a little leery of divulging this information, as she has only talked to them online. They seem nice enough, but she fears their motives.

She decides that she will answer them when they are safe and sound at home, or at least en route back home. She hopes their time in Arizona will be short and non-eventful. She enjoys the pleasant surprise of having service away from home. She sends an email to her cousin on Goldilocks and plays a few games with her counterparts that she has gotten to know online. The night kind of drags on until she begins to hear the wind picking up. The vehicle rocks back and forth, even in the dugout they have created.

She lies down in her station and enables the outside camera. It is dark so she enables the night vision. She sees what appears to be tornadoes roaring by over the top of the machine. The display shows deep dark blue images imposed on a white background that appears very similar to large funnels reaching up and into the sky. The blue even has some black areas that she hasn't seen before on the display. She is somewhat fearful as it shakes and shimmies with each passing wall cloud. She realizes that below the surface of the snow they have been protected from these harsh weather patterns and wonders how often these ice-driven tornadoes occur, or if that is even what they are.

She does a search as she hears Danny roll to his side and adjusts his bed slightly. It comes up with the weather after the big snow fall. There are articles concerning the storms that pass through, but little seems to be known about it other than they are the equivalent of F1 through F5 tornadoes. The storms grow massive with little to stop the wind gusts. As she continues her research, she finds they are typically F3 or stronger. She shutters to think that these tornadoes could pull asphalt up off the ground. It would be a shame to have come this far and have the hatch ripped open, or the entire machine be pulled from the cavity that Danny created, and be hurled across the snow.

She lies listening to storm after storm pass until she is uneasy about how violently the machine is shaking. She feels the front of the tracks come up and slam back down. This wakes Danny.

"There are tornadoes," Kelly explains.

"Huh? Tornadoes? What are you talking about?" He feels the Op Track violently shaking as he rolls over and enables his display.

"Holy shit!" He sees the horizon and it indicates that the Op Track is no longer buried. The wind and storms have blown the snow away around the machine, to a point that it has nearly taken the snow cavity away from the machine, exposing it to the harsh weather.

The nosecone is already up to temperature as he begins to move the machine forward slowly and cautiously. He feels the front is very light because of the wind beneath it. They both shutter with concern as they feel the front lift up slightly.

"Damn, I wished you'd woke me up before now."

Without much additional discussion, or hesitation, the diesel engine revs to about 4500 RPM and the big machine moves forward and downward. Soon they can't feel the wind, and it feels as though they are on solid ground.

Danny looks out to find a blue horizon that extends higher than the machine by at least five feet and continues to see the twisters above.

He sits in the dimly lit station, propped up on his elbow, trying to relax so that he can go back to sleep.

"Thank you for saving us. How did you know there were tornadoes?"

"I looked on the night vision screens and I looked it up on the Internet."

Danny rolls over once more to enable his screen and takes a look for himself. There are funnel clouds as far as he can see. It is like a night of the twisters in Arizona.

"I thought it had to be above sixty-five degrees before tornadoes can form."

"Not according to the Internet."

"Internet? How is that possible?"

"I brought my tablet and it has a signal."

"That is awesome. I believe that we are safe now. Please wake me sooner if it begins to get this bad again, my sweets."

Kelly smiles as he rolls back on his back, adjusting his bed to get some more sleep. She plays a few more games. She enjoys online pool and word games. There are others in other shelters that play with her. She decides after a few hours to do additional research about the weather on the surface.

Her additional searches find there are hurricanes that dwarf anything pre-ice age, and occur each day out on the ocean. There are even warm fronts that move through and can melt the snowfall. There were some reports in the Bahamas of a warm front coming through and causing the snow to melt, flooding shelters and dragging them into the water. The shelters ended up at the bottom of the lake, only to freeze over again. She feels a bit remorseful as she is sure they all perished.

She says a prayer for the fallen and decides to get a little sleep prior to the final trek of their journey in the morning. She wakes Tilley and explains about the storms and the need to keep an eye on things to ensure they don't blow away. Tilley is feeling a little better.

"Can I use your tablet?"

"Sure, I have service from a cell tower around here somewhere that is apparently still in operation. Don't run me out of minutes." She smiles.

"Will it run out of minutes?"

"No, I was just kidding. I had an unlimited plan back in the day, but I doubt they will cut you off these days. You never really know, though."

Kelly begins adjusting her bed as Tilley logs into some of her favorite websites. She looks up one of her favorite authors and downloads an old, highly popular book from a classic series called *Imminent Domain*. She thoroughly enjoyed reading the

188

series back years ago. The book was titled "*Finding Goldilocks*." She lies there in the ambient light of the Op Track, reading NJBV's debut book, thinking how accurate a Sci-fi series could be. She realizes that it is almost as if they are living the story that he created so many years ago. She gets about six chapters into the book when she realizes it's six am and Danny wanted to be awake by then.

She climbs around the machine to get to the trunk and finds the hotel-style coffeemaker that she packed especially for him and begins to brew a pot of coffee for her boss.

Danny wakes to the smell of freshly brewed coffee. He slept really well, for a night in a running Op Track. He thought it must be similar to what an eighteen wheeler driver use to experience when the trucks delivered goods. *I bet they didn't have that bed, though*, he thinks to himself as he fumbles around on the console to find the cabin lights. He hears Kelly groan a little when the bright lights come on at the top of the dome. He leans up so he is sitting as upright as he can. He drapes his legs across to the unoccupied station below him on the opposite side from the girls.

"Tilley, I am giving you a raise! Where is my fruit?" he asks as he takes a sip of his fresh brewed coffee.

She climbs back into the trunk and looks through the MREs until she finds one marked preserved peaches. She pulls it out and gives it to him, and another she found marked cherry yogurt.

Danny eats his peaches with a drab green plastic fork. He pokes the fork into the bag, dragging each slice up along the side, and drinks his hot, strong, fresh brewed coffee. He is actually enjoying his morning as he leans over, seeing Kelly with the cover over her head.

"About time you wake up, sleeping beauty. We have to go to the Tempe shelter today and you both need to be fresh and ready for it."

"I will be up in a few minutes. I don't see why we can't do this shit at noon," Kelly replies in a sleepy voice.

189

"You want coffee?" Tilley asks her.

"When I wake up. Do you have any of the chocolate cream that we had at the Hot Springs Village shelter?"

"Yes, I do. I like it in my coffee, too."

Kelly rolls over and leans up on her station, squinting at the bright light from the cabin lights. They brightly light up the white leather interior of the Op Track's hatch.

"I don't think they intended for this thing to be a hotel room."

Danny says, "Much better than some places that I have slept.

Does your bed not adjust?"

"Yeah, asshole, after you enabled it, but it still isn't like being in my own bed."

"You'd bitch if I beat you with a new whip," Danny replies.

Tilley hands her the coffee with the chocolate cream in it. She sits upright, leaning somewhat inward with her knees up and feet on the station pad. The outer dome of the Op Track keeps her from sitting upright. She sips her coffee as the three prepare for the meeting at the shelter.

Chapter 25
The Meeting

It isn't long and they have finished their coffee and are positioned to begin the trek down to the shelter. The cabin light is shut off and they are all lying face down, watching their displays as the machine begins to descend into the snow.

They are clipping along at a pretty good pace when Danny sees a light blue image that looks like an upside down horseshoe. He immediately stops the machine and turns to the right. He knows this is the opening of a tunnel and recalls the damage that was caused to the other Track back in Hot Springs.

Tilley asks, "What is that?"

Kelly speaks up, "That is what happened to the bent and twisted machine that Danny had sitting up at the shop that he tore apart."

"Oh my! So is it a brick wall of a building or something?"

"No, that is an opening to a tunnel someone busted. I suppose the Tempe shelter has a Tunnel Buster." Danny replies.

"I see, so ya'll damaged the other machine by driving into the tunnel?"

Danny is looking into the display, grimacing.

Kelly says, "Hell yeah, by driving into the top and falling the whole way to the ground!"

"Oh, I see, that's not good."

"No, that is why he turned. Now, I bet he will come into the tunnel, but at ground level."

The horseshoe comes into view again, but their approach, this time, puts them at the very bottom of it. In an instant, the outside cameras come on and the Op Track's outside lighting system illuminates the blinding white walls of the tunnel, dominating the display. A smaller window that says GPS with memory comes up on the lower left corner of the display and shows a road. Danny stops and begins to enter an address for the shelter into the device.

A voice comes from the machine and says, "Your destination is twenty miles away. You have selected the shortest route, please use caution as the roads are ice and snow covered." The voice pauses slightly. "These roads are closed and impassable. Please turn around when possible."

Danny begins to follow the arrow on the screen as it displays Highway 60 and soon they see the end of the tunnel. Tilley cringes as they plunge into the end of the wall and continue to follow the road at near full speed.

"Please turn around when possible. Going further is irresponsible and inadvisa..." Danny clicks a button that says Ignore Warnings and the voice begins again after a slight pause. "In two miles turn right onto Interstate 10 – Guadalupe. *If you must.*"

Danny says, "Seriously? Freaking guidance woman giving me shit, too?"

They continue on and the voice continues to direct them and they are again in a tunnel. They pass a couple of small makeshift looking steel   doors covered in rust and aged graffiti. They protrude up from dirty trampled snow and appear to be abandoned buildings and storefronts. These are potentially makeshift shelters.

The tunnel ends with two very large doors that are very similar to the doors on the front of the Arkansas shelters. The snow is very blackened and dirty in front of these doors, from quite a bit of traffic coming in and out of this shelter. It is not at all like the white snow that is around their shelters back home. They pull up and stop. Danny looks at Kelly as she hands him a .45 caliber pistol that he pushes down into a holster on his chest. He doesn't say a word as she hands him another smaller .380 caliber pistol. He rolls over on the top seat and heists his pants leg up to put it into another holster that is there.

"You have your guns? Are you ready for this?"

"Do you want me to come with you?"

"No, you stay here and protect yourself, the Op Track, and Tilley.

Have you learned enough to drive it and get back home if you have to?"

"Yes."

"If they come after this machine, you stop them. Understand?"

Kelly pulls up a black .223 rifle with a rail and all kinds of accessories. She sets three green boxes that say "Remington" in white across the top, on the pad beside her.

"I truly understand. I won't go home without you, though."

Danny pops the hatch and begins to walk to the doors. He pounds on the doors and they unlatch and open just enough for someone to look out.

"Who are you and what is your business here?"

"I am Danny Nichols and I am here to see Ben Calhoun."

"There is no Ben Calhoun here."

"Is this the only shelter in Tempe, Arizona?"

"No, there are others, but this is the only one that is funded and ran by the WRC."

"This is the one he is at. He told me that you would be expecting me."

"Just a minute."

The door slams shut with a loud crash and he hears it lock. Danny stands there for almost fifteen minutes when a thin, slimy looking, slick, greasy haired man, that stinks of B.O., comes walking up from nowhere. He looks back and Kelly has closed the hatch on the Op Track.

"That your machine there?"

"Yeah, that is mine. Who are you?"

"I am John. They don't let me in there. They probably aren't going to let you in. I seen they slammed the door on you."

"What business is it of yours? I suggest you move on."

"You have any food? You need some?"

193

"No, I am just fine. I need to talk to a man in this shelter."

The questionable character walks over to the Op Track and looks it over.

"Some machine you got here, partner. I bet you could go nearly anywhere in that thing."

Danny yells, "Get on! Now! I got business here and you need to go back where you came from. You are causing me stress."

He pulls the big .45 caliber pistol from his chest holster and points it toward the man.

"I have told you for the last time. Now, go on by God!"

The man begins to step strongly in the other direction, looking at the big chrome gun in Danny's hand. He yells back at Danny, "God? You are here with us. What do you know about God?"

Soon he is gone and Danny begins to think that no one is coming to let him in. He goes back to the Op Track. Kelly, attentively watching the camera, pops the hatch and he climbs in.

"Can you get a signal on your tablet? Phone?"

Kelly fumbles around, moving the ammo boxes and laying the gun down to find her tablet.

"No, nothing."

"Lonely fucking feeling, isn't it? Well, damn, I guess maybe we can get back to the surface and try to contact that son of a bitch. The doorman was supposed to be expecting us. I will put the motherfucking rods in my damn self! It would probably be safer than this bullshit."

Kelly and Tilley just look on as he violently slams the controls around. You can hear the big engine rev loudly through the outer walls and they fill the power of the tracks push them toward the back of the machine. Soon their feet are against the padded end of their stations. They have the feeling of going vertical as Danny begins a pronounced climb back to the surface, still pissed off and cussing at them.

194

Soon they break the surface. The Op Track comes off the ground because of the speed they are traveling. They land with a thud and the energetic sound of the engine comes to a slow growl and rattle. Danny begins checking outside conditions to find it is forty below zero and the wind is from the north at sixty mph. He begins burrowing a cavity to protect his machine.

Kelly is already online as he is parking the Track. The monitor shows snow. Danny speaks up, "More snow. That is just what this godforsaken, fucking place needs. More snow."

"I got him."

She is typing on her tablet and she explains, "There was a new man at the door. Not Ben's friend. He wants us to be there at four o'clock this afternoon and he will be at the door with Raul, his friend, and they will meet us."

"You tell that cocksucker to be there with photo ID and his freaking bags packed or we will be putting the fuel rods in ourselves!"

"He says he understands."

Danny brings up the clock on the Op Track and it shows eight thirty-six CST.

"Hey, be sure that prick is talking Central Standard Time, not two hours ahead or behind us."

"He says it is six thirty-six there. Mountain Standard Time."

"Damn! What would you ladies like to do to kill the time?"

Tilley looks over at Kelly and they both snicker. Danny thinks, *Yeah, if I wasn't here, you two would probably go at it, but not with ole Danny, hell no!*

Kelly finishes the conversation with Ben and explains that it should all be good. He will be ready. Danny settles in to go to sleep for a while. Tilley lies just above Kelly and would very much like to go back to her favorite book. Kelly sees her wide awake and hands the tablet up. Tilley gladly takes it and kicks back reading as the other two go back to sleep.

195

It isn't long and the wind is shaking the machine again. Tilley is worried that it may be getting uncovered so she turns over and looks at the display to find it shows eighty mph winds, but the horizon appears to be well above the machine. She looks at the clock and it is about eleven. She thinks she could get some sleep if she could just tear herself away from this book. She decides not to fight it and continues reading *"Imminent Domain: Finding Goldilocks."*

The time goes fast and Tilley, with sleepy tear-filled eyes, wakes Danny as she felt a need to be around other people as the passage in the book just had five thousand people lost in a mishap with the first Armada arriving at Goldilocks.

"Danny, it is three o'clock their time." She has a cup of coffee brewed for him.

Danny wakes up. "What the fuck is wrong with you?" He sees that her eyes are glossy.

"That book. It gets me every time."

"Verne?"

"Yes."

"I know. Don't you dare repeat this, but he gets me, too. Well, time to get up and start getting ready for round two."

Danny fires up the Op Track and begins to descend into the snow as Kelly gets thrown sideways, waking her up.

"Fuck head!" she yells at Danny.

Danny has a big grin on his face as they descend into the tunnel they had traveled earlier in the day. It isn't long and they are parked in front of the large shelter doors. Danny is still loaded down with weapons as he climbs from the machine. He beats on the doors and a Mexican gentleman opens the doors.

"Danny?"

"Yes, I am Danny. I suppose you are Raul?"

In a Mexican accent he replies, "Sí, yes, I am Raul. Ben ask I allow you in to see tha shelter and to go and see him."

"Ben was supposed to be here ready to go. If he isn't, then I am leaving and I will install these rods myself."

196

Raul yells out to a young man walking by in the shelter, "Hey, Poco, go en get Mr. Ben for me."

"Sí, señor," the young boy replies.

It isn't long and another dark complexion man comes walking up. He sticks his hand out and Danny shakes it. They are standing with the door open about two feet. They are all three obviously cold from the twenty-degree temperatures.

Ben says, "Why don't you come in, my friend?"

"I would rather you get your shit and let's go."

"Wait a moment. You are expecting me to take off from my protection and go with you? Just like that? You have to give me some time to decide who you are for sure and that I really trust you to get me there and you will do what you say."

"Listen, I am the sole owner and CEO of Chimera. You can trust me."

"Yeah, like I could trust the mine owner that tried to kill me before the snow."

"Listen, motherfucker. I ain't fucking around here all day. If you are coming, get your shit. If you are not, then I am leaving and putting the rods in myself."

"Okay, okay. I do want to come along. I guess it's going to end up better than being stuck here."

"Okay, let me see your photo ID."

"No, I have none of those."

"You can't prove to me who you are?"

Ben looks over at Raul. "Raul, who am I?"

"You, señor, are Ben Calhoun."

The two kind of laugh.

"Okay, but you know what? The WRC has photo ID records that show your face. If you aren't who you say you are, then I will put a fucking bullet in your face. How do you like that?"

"Go on then. You are an asshole. I don't think I trust you anyway."

Danny says nothing further. He takes off once again to the Op Track. Climbs in, revs the big diesel, and once again they are leaving. They get turned around to find tank trap barricades have been placed in the tunnel in their path. Two men stand one to each side, holding black guns. The three have no idea what to do. They know that a large caliber gun can penetrate the hull of the Op Track. Danny is considering that the nosecone could be damaged, but it could block the rounds. They look at the four camera views in the displays.

The doors both open up behind them, into the shelter. Danny immediately revs the engine loudly and backs the machine into the shelter. Ben and Raul are waiting inside. They back up and are unsure of what is in store for them, as this seems to give Ben and Raul the upper hand on negotiations, if not essentially in control of their destiny.

They clear the doors and they are slammed shut. They all look at the displays as others begin to come around the machine from buildings around this area. Danny says, "Thanks, boys!" He slams the controls to spin the machine around to go forward and begins to navigate the large shelter. Soon they come to gardens growing where homes used to be and then he sees it, the abandoned airport off in the distance down several city streets. This is exactly what he needs. He can take shelter and park the machine in a hangar and determine the next move. They travel for about ten minutes and reach the back wall of the enormous structure. There isn't anyone in sight. They needed this to be able to launch a counterattack, or at least try to establish communications without being captured behind enemy lines.

He stops the Op Track and it is very quiet. Danny says, "Kelly, do you have a signal on your tablet?"

Kelly begins to feel around in the floor of the machine, trying to find her iPad. She pulls it up.

"Yes, I have a faint signal from a wireless network."

"Fantastic! Find out what these crazy bastards are doing."

"It needs a password."

"Kiss my ass! Okay, that isn't impossible." Danny reaches in his pocket and pulls out a thumb drive.

"What is that?" Kelly asks.

"It is a password cracking tool. I never leave home without this and a few PC disabling viruses. You never know when you may need to get into an alarm system of one of these gas stations or hack into say, maybe, a shelter's wireless." He laughs. It doesn't fit into Kelly's tablet so Danny begins to rummage around in the cubby at the rear-end of the cabin. He pulls out a small laptop.

He plugs the thumb drive in and it begins to scan the Ethernet connection. It isn't long and it shows a passcode: HaydensFerry_Frozen_Hell.

"I got it. Try HaydensFerry capital H and capital F all one word, underscore, frozen capital F, underscore, hell capital H."

Kelly types all of that in and suddenly she has service.

"They have a lot stronger signal than we do back in Arkansas to be able to reach it from this remote location."

"The WRC paid for theirs. I paid for ours. I didn't figure I needed Internet up in the woods."

"Bet you wish we had it now."

"Just get in touch with these goofy bastards and find out what the fuck is on their mind. I need positive identification of Ben Calhoun before anyone climbs into the Op Track with us. I am going to start blasting fucking holes in everyone as we leave if they don't begin to cooperate. Damn! This was going to be simple, remember? Just come get this goofy cocksucker."

She begins typing.

"He says he is tired of typing and wants to speak with us directly."

"Is there a way to do that?"

"Yes, we can talk over the Internet on my tablet."

"Get his number and call him then."

A few moments go by with Kelly plucking away at her wireless keyboard. It begins to make a ringing noise, then suddenly an image of Ben is on her screen. She holds it up so that Danny can see. The cabin is brightly lit from the dome light. Danny is lying in the center operator station on the white seat, leaning on his elbow when Kelly points the tablet his way.

"Damn it, Kelly, I thought it would be a phone call, not a video conference. Ben, what is on your mind? What are you people trying to pull here?"

Ben responds from the tablet, "First, my apologies for the neighbors. We had nothing to do with that. Where are you?"

"We found another door. We are back up at the surface."

A voice in the background is heard saying, "Son of a bitch, they found the west entrance."

Danny then pushes a red button on the tablet that reads Disconnect. He lunges back down into the operator station, kills the dome lights, and says, "Hold on, ladies," as he jabs the joysticks forward and races the diesel engine.

Both Kelly and Tilley have now been thrown around the cabin on the right side of Danny.

"What the fuck are you doing?" Kelly asks.

"Didn't you hear that dumb fuck in the background? There is another entrance on the west side."

"Oh, I see."

They go out of the airport and go right, headed toward the end of the shelter once more, only, this time, they are on a mission. Soon, they are on a street named East Sky/Harbor Circle. They drive for a short ways and come to the end of the shelter. Large steel doors block the way in the middle of the street. They stop and Danny gets out to look at the lock. It is a very large padlock that is affixed to the door. He pulls out the large .45 caliber handgun and begins shooting it. He gets about three rounds into it and it is showing signs of fatigue.

There is a large, flat-black, Dodge dually truck that he spots off in the distance, coming around the slight curve from the entrance to the airport. He grimaces as he knows he has been caught. The roar of the tires and the loud roar of the engine lets him know that these men are coming for him. The large truck pulls up with a load of men in the bed all carrying weapons, with ammo belts across their chests.

Danny jumps into the Op Track just before they get there and tries to make an escape, but it is no use. They pull up to the front of the machine and the large crosstie bumper pens the Op Track between the truck and the doors.

Danny and the girls stay there considering a plan. It isn't long and the hatch is popped open from the outside. Danny looks up and sees four men standing on the top track, and beside the machine, pointing rifles at the hatch and in his face.

One of the men says, "Score, we got some women, some hot little mamas, too!"

The large bearded Mexican, who seemed to be in charge, says with a thick accent, "Okay, chew all come out of there."

Danny responds, "Why? What is it that we are doing wrong? Are you the police?"

All three begin laughing. "Policia, there is no policia, thes is the wild wild west and you, amigo, have just stepped into the wrong town."

"Why, what..."

"Shut the fuck up, gringo, and all yous get out of dis damn thing. The mayor will want this moshene. We can go anywhere we want in it. *Fiesta*!"

The guys pull their guns away to make room for the three to climb out. The leader points his gun away from Danny's face as he begins to climb out.

Danny yells, "Now!"

A shot whizzed by his head from Kelly's AR, a bullet penetrates the forehead of their leader. Danny reaches in his holster on his chest and pulls out his .45 and begins shooting. Rounds are being returned as holes are seen being formed in the hatch of the machine. The large metal plate that the tracks are mounted on blocks many of the bullets being fired at them. Danny and Kelly do not let up with the barrage of gunfire from the small machine. Soon, all of the would-be capturers are lying on the ground in their own blood, except for one, who they can see running down the road.

Kelly says, "25-06?"

He says, "You read my mind, lovely lady," as she hands up a long black and wood stock rifle, with a large scope that is at least three inches in diameter. Danny flips up the dust covers and looks down the scope at the man running. Danny steadies himself across the back of the Op Track, to the right of the hatch, and sees the man very clearly through the red lighted crosshairs of the scope. He lines up on the back of his brown hair. He has slowed to a walk now. *KaaaBOOOOM.* A few seconds pass, then his head all but disappears and his lifeless body drops to the ground.

"You won't be telling anyone we got away, will you now, dick?"

He kicks one of the lifeless bodies out of the way as he walks back to the big Dodge pickup and looks in the back at a tank with a handle. It is marked "BIODIESEL."

"Hell, that may be our fuel for the ride home there." He jumps up in the back of the truck and gives it a crank. He hands the nozzle to Kelly and she plugs it into the filler neck of the Op Track.

"Diesel? That smells like cooking oil," Kelly explains.

"That is what they make Biodiesel out of is cooking oil, most of the time if it isn't replicated. It should be fine to run like regular replicated fuel."

It isn't long and the big silver tank of the truck has filled the Op Track, with him working the crank handle back and forth. He walks over to the door and shakes the lock. This time, it turns and he is able to remove it. He pushes open the door to the right to find a welcome sight. A large wall of snow is in front of him.

Chapter 26
The Long Ride Home

He climbs into the machine and they immediately pull up into the safety of the snow. He flips a switch and they are now in sonar mode. He navigates the machine around the outside of the shelter and makes his way to the surface.

"Get that dumb fuck back on the teleconference thing again, Kelly."

It isn't but a few minutes and once again, Ben Calhoun's face is shown on the tablet.

"Why did you send goons after us?"

"Why did you lie about being out of the shelter?"

"Look, I came on good faith that you wanted to come to Arkansas and install our fuel rods. You have blocked my way, not proven your identity, and have been combative about this whole ordeal. Not to mention those bastards coming and trying to capture us."

"The guys that came after you have no affiliation with us. If you would come back to the west doors, I will meet you there with identification."

"No, fuck you! I will install the dam rods myself. I have had enough of this bullshit. We will end up dead fucking around with you bunch of damn crazy ass Mexicans around here!"

"Oh, I am Mexican, but I am aan United States citizen." He pulls out his wallet.

"Yeah, let me see that United States citizenship card, chocho!"

The man begins to put his wallet away. Danny hits the end call button once again and begins to drive the Op Track.

"What are we doing now?"

Freezing cold air is coming into the machine from the bullet holes in the hatch. They have all put on their winter gear as they can't keep the inside of the machine warm.

203

"We are going home."

"Do you want me to try to find a picture of Ben Calhoun?"

"Yeah, email WRC and tell them you would like for them to send you a file image of Ben Calhoun's face."

"Sent," Kelly replies.

No one has heard anything at all from Tilley. She has been lying in the bottom bunk, quiet and scared.

"Are you okay, Tilley?" Kelly asks.

"No. It was like when the bad men came to the Hot Springs Village shelter. I was afraid that they would hurt you and me."

"Danny and I will die before we see that happen."

"I see that. You two are very good friends to have."

They travel along for a few hours and Kelly checks to find an email from Linda Johnson with the WRC. It is a picture of Ben Calhoun. Kelly says, "You are going to want to see this."

Danny looks and the image is of Raul, the man that answered the door the first time.

"Son of a bitch! Why would this guy point me to someone else and not let me know it was him when he answered the door?"

"They are all crazy there," Kelly responds.

"Crazy indeed, but you'd think they would have given me his ID and let him come along if…oh hell, I don't know. Like you said, it was a big waste of fucking time, they are all crazy."

They continue to drive along until the outside wind speed begins to show that the crosswind is getting near one hundred knots. The machine is being pushed sideways as they go.

Danny brings up an image in the corner of the display that shows the nosecone is at fifteen hundred degrees. The roar of the diesel and the tracks thumping can be heard as the wind whistles across the top of the vehicle. The cold air is plainly felt through the bullet holes. They begin a descent into the safety of

204

the snow pack and away from the wind. Their speed slows to about thirty mph.

"I have to go!" Tilley exclaims.

"That's it!" Danny shouts.

"Huh," both Tilley and Kelly respond. "Using the bathroom is a solution?" Kelly asks.

Danny says, "Toilet paper. I am going to stop the Track just shy of the surface and you guys wet some toilet paper and stick up through the holes. It will freeze on the outside and cover those pneumonia holes."

"That may work," Kelly responds.

They have had problems trying to keep the machine warm enough to be comfortable on the inside since they had departed from the Arizona shelter. Soon, they have the toilet paper in place and Tilley has finished her business and they are back en route.

"Email WRC and tell them I want step-by-step instructions on how to charge the ship with the fuel rods. Tell them that Ben Calhoun is some kind of a drug addict thug now or something."

"You sure?"

"You have a better suggestion?"

"We could go to where ever those other guys are at."

"I have my fears of going to an Air Force base. This is like the old zombie movies, only these bastards carry guns and have a little bit of sense."

Soon the cabin is so hot the girls are coming out of their coats. Danny stops the machine and has to use the restroom as well. They are somewhere near Amarillo, Texas, now as he pulls off the large white coat and looks upon his GPS to try to find a suitable filling station. He finds the road they have been following is I-40 and there is a large Pilot truck stop near here. He then checks the fuel level and finds that it isn't too low.

He gets settled once again and begins a descent into the outskirts of Amarillo. They pull into the covered canopy of the truck stop and Kelly pipes up, "Let's try not to blow this stinking place up, please."

Tilley laughs.

"Fuck you," Danny responds. They get the Op Track under the shelter and get suited back up in their winter gear. They climb out and, the front of the headlights are reflecting off of the snow bank that covers the outside of the canopy.

"This one isn't collapsed, so maybe if they have a generator, we could get something decent to eat, some fuel, and maybe even a shower."

"Uh, don't you figure their water is frozen?"

Danny looks back with a grimace on his face. "You're probably right."

They make theirselves right at home as Danny whacks the glass door with a hammer. It doesn't break so he draws back again. Kelly reaches and pulls on it to find it is not locked. He just grits his teeth and follows the beautiful young model into the dark store.

Danny takes off to the left where it says "RESTROOMS." He sits down on the coldest toilet he has ever been on. The lights come on while he is taking care of his business. Heat begins to flow through the vents.

He comes back into the store from the restrooms to find Tilley looking over some beef jerky. She had started the pump and left it to fill the machine. Danny reaches down and grabs all the jerky that is on the hook.

"Here, we got a bargain on these today, FREE!"

Tilley takes them with a smile. "I started the pump to fill the machine with diesel."

"Thank you. Is it full?"

"It should be by now if it isn't frozen."

"It just doesn't feel right to just take this. Do you think they are safe to eat?"

"Yeah, jerky doesn't go bad, especially frozen."

"Did the pump clear and the numbers start moving?"

"Yeah."

206

"We are good then."

The temperature in the store begins to get reasonable and Danny and Tilley find a little dining table and have a seat. They begin to pull off their winter gear. Kelly comes walking back. "Everything come out okay?" Danny asks jokingly.

"Not so much, but I will be okay."

"You aren't getting sick, are you?" Danny asks.

"I don't know. Nerves I think, with all of the stuff that happened back there. You realize that I have now killed at least three men."

"So. They each would have killed us."

"I just never thought that I could take someone's life. I thought about killing Tilley before."

"Huh," Tilley responds, with eyebrows raised.

"Well, you were interfering with my man. I am very territorial and it was just a thought. That has passed, though, and I think of you, as well, I don't know. My maid maybe?"

"Your bitch? Maybe?" Danny says.

Tilley just kind of hangs her head and shakes it slowly while eating her jerky. *No respect*, she thinks to herself. They walk around and enjoy their shelter from the people and the constant fear of the Op Track breaking down and killing them all.

Soon they begin to see wasps. Kelly speaks up, "Odd, I am seeing wasps."

"They can hibernate in cold weather and then come back to life when it gets warm. I was with a buddy of mine at deer camp and we ran out in our pj's because of them."

They start seeing more wasps, and bees. Before they know it, they look out and can't see the Op Track for the swarm of wasps that have taken shelter in the truck stop. They are all swatting at them and start getting stung. Danny runs over to an aisle in the store that has antifreeze and oil to find a row of wasp spray on a shelf in front of a white pegboard partition. He begins to spray it on Kelly. He sprays it on her hair and neck, and in her face. She has another can and is spraying it on his face as she sees large whelps begin to form. Danny is trying to rub his face and tears roll out of his swollen eyes. Tilley has her winter gear back on and has pulled it up over her head, fending them off pretty effectively.

Once they are covered with the wasp spray, they begin to tend to Tilley. Both have whelps all over their hands and faces. Danny grabs the four cans that are left as they brave outside to the Op Track. The wasps seem to be avoiding the repellant that was sprayed directly on them. They get to the machine and Danny begins to spray inside of the machine and yanks the fuel nozzle out, throwing it on the ground.

"Why are they outside?" Kelly asks.

"I don't know, maybe the machine has warmed up the awning enough to allow them to awaken."

It is much warmer outside of the truck stop than any of them expected. Then Danny spots it. There are literally hundreds truck amenity stations that are just lying on the inside of the awning, blowing out hot air. The amenity stations are used to fit into an eighteen wheeler window and provides them with water, heat, air, and entertainment. In 2118 when the snow came, almost all of the larger truck stops had these units for the drivers to use.

"It is all of those heaters lying on the ground over there."

Kelly doesn't even know what all of the window-shaped things are. She is just ready to get away from the wasps, as they have stung her multiple times and her face is swollen in several places.

It isn't long and Danny has the inside of the Op Track cleaned out and they are about ready to go. He climbs in and sees a set of headlights come out of the snow on the rear camera. He focuses on the outside cameras to see what will occur. They all watch as these men get out of their vehicle and begin running around like they are crazy. Danny can't help but laugh because he figures they must have come from the Arizona shelter, trying to catch them. It isn't long and they see the three men on the ground and overcome by the wasps, trying to swat them away.

"Where did these men come from?" Tilley asks.

"I don't know, but I bet it had something to do with the Arizona shelter, don't ya'll?"

"I don't think they meant well for us," Kelly responds.

"I doubt they were trying to help us," Danny says as he hits the gas and plows back into the snowbank, hoping the surface wind has settled down. They continue on and in a few minutes, they are back on the surface. Everyone is refreshed and seem to be in high spirits. Tilley is a bit remorseful about the men that she just watched, on the camera, become overwhelmed. The wind has settled down and the machine is traveling at a really good clip. They are going about fifty mph.

It has become somewhat quiet when Tilley says, "Have we become so calloused that we don't give a good fuck about three men, we know nothing about, get overwhelmed by the wasps, and maybe die? We did nothing to try to help them."

"Everyone we run into in this part of the country is trying to harm us," Kelly replies.

"How do we know they were? They may have just been traveling, like us."

"True, but odds are against it from what we have seen so far. God is gone from here. The devil runs rampant and is pretty much in control. People don't care. They would kill us to take our vehicle, or maybe even for something to eat."

"You don't know that they would."

"We didn't kill those poor bastards!" Danny yells. "Now shut the fuck up about it. Fucking liberals!"

Kelly kind of chuckles as it becomes quiet once again. A few minutes later, the sound of Tilley crying is heard. Danny looks over at Kelly and their eyes meet. Kelly rolls her eyes and says, "Oh well, what could we have done to save them?" They both shrug.

Kelly speaks up, "Okay, bitch! What is it you think we could have done? We are out of wasp spray."

"I don't know," she speaks with a weak whiny voice. She continues, "It just seems like you two…" She sobs and breathes in with a whimper. "It's just you two seemed to find it amusing that these men were attacked without any defense."

"I didn't find it funny. I just felt like they were coming after us. I still feel like they were sent to try to retrieve us. I don't have any remorse about them perishing if that is the case," states Kelly, matter of factly.

"I understand."

"Suck it up, buttercup," Danny says.

They continue their trek on the surface without many more concerns, but their fuel level is beginning to run low as they pass Pleasant Hill, Arkansas. All three see the light come on for low fuel. An automated voice comes over the speakers and says, "Fuel is necessary within fifty miles."

"We better get some fuel in this thing if it is very much further," Kelly replies.

"Oh, my love. We are almost on top of Hot Springs. Hell, I could walk from here."

"We better be getting close or finding another truck stop with a generator."

"We are fine. The tank must not have gotten completely filled." Danny begins to roll the thumbwheels downward to begin the descent through the snow and into the end of their tunnel. A few minutes later, Kelly is unlocking the front doors of the shelter and Danny pulls the machine through.

What a relief the three think as they begin to pull through the ditch and into the trail to the cabin. The machine then sputters and jerks a couple of times, dying at the edge of the yard.

Kelly says, "Plenty of fuel, huh? I sure am glad we were out of the damn snow pack. You could have gotten us killed."

"We are here safe and sound, my dear. Please quit your bitching and start unloading." He pops the hatch on the Op

Track, climbs out, and begins to walk toward the cabin. The shed up on the hill looks untouched, the brilliant green of his lawn, the red unpicked tomatoes, even the plants that he can tell the deer had been into looked good to him. Not to mention the pretty, shiny, green Mustang is a sight for sore eyes.

They all make their way to the cabin and settle in. Tilley is at the replicator and says, "Hamburger, charcoal-grilled with bacon, cheddar cheese, onion, tomato, pickle, jalapeno, mayo, and mustard, crinkle cut French fries and ketchup." It is two pm. They have been traveling for about twenty-five hours. Danny and Kelly climb into the queen size bed in the master bedroom for a long restful sleep.

Tilley sits in the dining room having her cheeseburger. She realizes how fortunate they are to have a food replicator that will provide any food they desire at the command of their voice. It is very similar to the hamburgers she remembers Danny cooking back years ago when he had his Independence Day celebrations.

He had the charcoal grill with smoke rolling out of it and so many people that they would almost close down the street because there wasn't enough parking in his driveway. She daydreams about that for a while. She slept most of the way home, so she really isn't all that tired.

She walks out onto the front porch and expects to see Chopper out there, but then it occurs to her that he is at the Hot Springs Village shelter. She wonders what is next. It sounded like Danny may install the fuel rods himself, and she is concerned that he could die doing this. Even worse, they all could die if they were all there when he installs them.

She decides that it wasn't a problem for her to sleep with them before, so she goes in and cuddles up next to Kelly, and is out as well.

Three am finds Danny climbing out of bed, headed to the kitchen. He finds his coffee ready for brewing. He clicks the switch and starts it and steps out onto the back porch, feeling the cool breeze, wearing only his checkerboard night pants and no shirt. He looks off to the east and thinks of Chopper at the Hot Springs Village shelter. *Those little pricks better be taking good care of my dog*, he thinks to himself. It isn't long and his coffeepot makes a gurgling noise, letting him know it is done. He grabs a large green cup with Remington written in white across it, pours a little water in the bottom to curb the scalding temperature, and pours a nice big cup.

He turns it up to take a drink, realizing his lip is swollen, thanks to the wasps from the truck stop. He knew his face had several stings but had been trying to ignore them. He cautiously gets a sip of his coffee, but it still burns his mouth, so he adds a bit more water and takes off to his bathroom. He turns on the vanity light above the mirror and sees that Kelly has a magnifying mirror on the counter, but then looks in the regular mirror, realizing there was no need to magnify the big whelps on his face.

He opens the medicine cabinet and finds some Neosporin and reaches in his pocket and pulls out a little metal can. He rubs Neosporin on each and takes a hydrocodone, along with an ibuprofen. It begins to numb the pain slightly. He looks into the mirror and remembers the acne he had as a child and how all of these wasps stings resemble the zits he would get. He speaks out loud, "The shit didn't hurt this damn bad, though," in a fairly loud voice. He sees Tilley roll over and look into the bathroom at him, but realizes Kelly didn't move. He knows she is a light sleeper and expected it was her that rolled over.

He remembers reading about too many wasp stings and how they can send a person into anaphylactic shock. He starts becoming concerned about her.

"Tilley, Is Kelly okay over there?"

"Yes, she is just *fine*," she says, with kind of a joking emphasis on fine.

"Nudge her and make sure she is okay. She had some bad stings on her face. I want to know that she is all right."

Tilley begins to shake her and Kelly doesn't move.

"Oh, my god! I don't think she is breathing!"

212

Danny comes running around to the opposite side of the bed and grabs the little beautiful naked model, pulling her up out of the covers, shaking her. Her face is red from all of the stings on it. He shakes her and her eyes open for a moment and then roll toward the back of her head. He fills a faint breath. He runs back to the medicine cabinet, pulling out a bottle of nasal spray. He returns to Kelly and sprays half the bottle up her nose. She coughs and chokes. She leans up, obviously in a bad way, but jumps up out of Danny's grasp and runs to the restroom toilet. She heaves and tries, but nothing will come out. She has very labored breathing but is coming back around.

Danny walks into the bathroom and reaches down to pull her long hair away from the toilet bowl.

"Are you okay, li'llin?"

"I uh." A deep cough comes out of her little kneeling body. "I think I am better. What happened?"

"I don't know. I guess the poison from the wasp stings affected you. You weren't breathing right."

"I felt a little dizzy when I laid down. I did wash the spray off of my face, but maybe you're right and something happened from the stings. Oh, my god, these things hurt!"

"I know, mine does, too."

Tilley comes walking to the bathroom door. She only has one sting on her cheek.

"How did you keep from getting ate up with those things?" Danny asks.

"I still had the winter gear on and I pulled it over my head and Kelly sprayed me with the wasp spray before they really got to me, except that one. The little bastard!"

Kelly speaks up, "Yeah, cry me a damn river over your *one* sting. Can I go back to sleep now?" She stands there with the face of the elephant man.

"No, we are both worried about you now. I want you in the dining room. Let's email Charles Phillips and get instructions on how to install fuel rods," Danny replies.

213

"Seriously? I am about to fucking die here and you want me sending out emails that have already been sent? I feel the love!"

"I can't let you go back to sleep in the shape you were in. Come in here and let me put Neosporin on your stings."

Chapter 27
Wild Thang

Kelly must have fifty stings on her face as she begins to pull out a frying pan to cook them breakfast. It is now about four am. She looks in the refrigerator to find that all of the canned biscuits are now gone. She opens the freezer to find there is less than half a pound of sausage left.

She pulls out the flour, lard, and some baking powder, along with a few other items and begins mixing up some from scratch. Tilley really wants to help her, but she knows when Kelly is in the kitchen, it is best to leave her alone.

It isn't long and Danny comes walking in with a lip pooched out. He walks around for a bit, with somewhat of a mischievous look on his face. Kelly, with her swollen lips, doesn't really even want to speak. Danny pulls out a little tin can and rattles it around. It obviously has some type of medicine in it. He pulls out three pills.

"Okay, I have some Benadryl, oxycodone, and some hydrocodone. What is your pleasure, my love?"

"Why do you carry these around in your pocket?"

"I am an old fucker. I hurt regularly."

"You get high from them, don't you?"

Danny gets an angry look on his face. "I want you to understand that not everyone who uses pain medication abuses them. I do not. I use them when I am attacked by a squirrel, I crash Op Tracks, I work in the shop and can't hardly bend over, but I have never taken a single one to get high. I think that is a bad thing to do and is addictive. They have developed these and doctors prescribe them for a very good reason. Do you think medical professionals distribute these for people to get high? I am sure if I was some kind of addict, then all of the pain pills would be gone by now. I have probably taken a total of ten of them. Now, do you want one? It will help your pain."

215

"Jeez, don't take my head off. I was just messing with you and I don't think that you are an addict. I will take the Benadryl. Give me an oxycodone, I may take it later if it starts hurting bad enough. What I really think we need is an EpiPen, just in case. I think I was close to anaphylactic shock."

"I'm sorry, it's just I had a regular script back before the snow and people always looked down on it. Those people obviously didn't have real problems that caused them pain. I mean, they didn't say a negative word about snorting a line or smoking a joint."

"You are rich. People expect you to have a Dr. Feelgood, anyway."

He ignores her and hands her all three pills, then reaches his finger in his pooched out lip and pulls out a big wad of chewing tobacco. He proceeds to reach toward Kelly's face with it. She dodges to the left, knocking the biscuit mix onto the floor. She runs into the dining room near Tilley.

"What the hell is that?"

"It is chewing tobacco. The tobacco will numb and help pull the poison out of the stings."

"I believe I am becoming fond of the poison. You seriously think that you are going to take that horse shit out of your mouth and put it on my face?"

"It will help you, babe, I promise."

"You use it. I will stick to my Neosporin. Hey, Tilley, look up what is best for wasp stings," Kelly says in a slur, as the stings around her mouth are causing her to not open her mouth as wide as she normally would.

Danny goes to the small cabinet beside the refrigerator and pulls out a broom and dustpan. He begins to clean up the mess that was made from the flour and all that fell to the floor. Tilley is searching on the desktop computer for treatment of wasp stings. She finds an article about tobacco being good for the stings.

"Uh, Kelly, you may want to rethink the tobacco. You can use baking soda, vinegar, and tobacco on the sting to help pull the soreness out. It says here the best thing to do is to use the edge of a credit card to scrape the stinger out, then apply wetted tobacco for a numbing effect."

"Damn! You mean that horse shit really needs to go on my face?"

"Well, it does look like it helps. If you would like to lie down on the couch over here, I will find a card of some type to pull the stingers out with."

"How do I know if the stinger is in it?"

"You and I both will know when I drag this card across it."

Kelly lies down on the couch, facing the ceiling. Tilley turns the overhead ceiling fan's tulip light fixtures on bright and the recessed lighting, that is all around the oak, tongue and groove ceiling, on high. She sits down as Danny heads to the hall closet. He returns with a big LED shop light. He plugs in the two 1500 watt lights and turns both of them on Kelly's face as she scoots over on her back to Tilley's lap. The sectional sofa is to the left of the door and is almond colored and made of leather. It is behind a glass top coffee table on a shiny hardwood floor. The leather couch kind of makes a squeaking noise as they scoot around, getting ready for what looks like major surgery.

Tilley scrapes one and Kelly grunts and groans. She squirms around as Tilley continues, moaning in agony. There are at least fifteen that are swollen enough to have stingers in them. She scrapes at them one by one until Kelly says, "Okay, I give, call me a drug addict. I have to have some relief, ya'll." She reaches in her pocket and pulls out every pill he handed her. Danny has a disappointed look on his face over her comment, but has a glass of water that he hands her. She leans up on her right elbow and takes a swig of the water, swallowing all of the pills.

"Which one was it you took?"

"Hell, I don't know. All of them?"

"I don't usually take the oxycodone, they make me a little high."

217

"I guess I will be a little more than a little high. Fix me a cup of coffee, with a plenty of Irish cream please."

"Kelly, you don't take those very often. You probably..."

He gets a look like she could get up and beat his ass.

"Okay, okay, but if you go acting all ape-shit crazy, I am leaving."

Tilley looks at him as if he is an asshole.

Danny returns to the kitchen, hearing the yelps and the card scraping across Kelly's beautiful face. He speaks into the replicator, "One shot of Wild Turkey 101." He places a coffee cup under the spigot. Then he says, "Two shots of Baileys original Irish cream." The small ceramic cup is about half full. He goes to the cupboard and retrieves a larger cup that is twice the size of a traditional coffee cup and pours the concoction into it and fills it the rest of the way with coffee.

He continues to hear Kelly pant and cry out while Tilley scrapes the stingers out of her face. He walks in as she says, "Okay, this is the last one that is all puffy."

Kelly sits up, holding her face, tears streaming down her cheeks, and rubbing in different areas. She picks up a mirror on the coffee table, "Oh, my god!" She takes the cup from Danny and takes a big gulp. "I look hideous! I feel so awful. How did the damn wasps even get in there?"

"I don't know. I guess the cold came slowly. Maybe that truck stop was heated for longer than anywhere else. It could have been worse. There could have been snakes and alligators in there."

"I don't know if that would have been worse or not. At least they would have had the fucking decency to go ahead and kill my ass!"

"Yeah, well, I don't see that being a better deal. We will heal, and wasp stings rarely leave a scar."

"Do you not have some of that tobacco in a pouch? I don't want the crap in your mouth."

"Yes, and I was only kidding about using it from my mouth."

Danny pulls out a pouch of tobacco and Kelly lays back in a matching leather recliner and places the tobacco around on her stings while Danny lies down on Tilley's lap for his punishment.

It is near six thirty am now and the simulated sun program is beginning to light up the shelter.

Kelly has been sipping on her coffee and the pills are beginning to have an effect on her.

"Danny, where the fuck is my dog, Chopper?" She looks out the window at a rabbit helping himself to the lettuce in her garden.

"He is at the other shelter with the boys, remember?"

Kelly casually walks to the door leading into the mudroom and grabs Danny's shotgun that is leaning up against the molding of the door. She flings the door open and takes off through the mudroom and out on the front porch. BAM click click BANGG click click BANGG!

Danny, lying in Tilley's lap, wasn't paying her much attention and had no idea that she had grabbed the shotgun. He jumps up from the couch, running out to the porch. "Don't you shoot my fricking car!" he yells.

"I may be fucked up, but I ain't stupid! I hit that piece of shit that was eating my damn lettuce."

She begins to walk out to her garden that hasn't been tended to or protected from animals in nearly a week. Most of the lettuce is ate up. She goes looking at her tomatoes and several were rotten on the vine. Animals have pretty much had their way with her beautiful garden. The grass had grown up again, all down each row. She stands there with tears in her eyes and a shotgun in her hand as Danny walks up.

"We can fix it back up." She is inebriated, her face still feels awful, she looks terrible, and has tears in her eyes. Danny comforts her and takes the shotgun as he calmly pulls her face into his large shoulder. The two walk back up to the cabin and walk up the stairs to the porch to find Tilley standing there very quiet, not wanting to interfere as she knows Kelly is really down.

Danny sits her down on the love seat and comforts her.

"Bring me my coffee, please, Tilley?"

"You sure, babe? I think you have had enough of that coffee."

"Well, I have stopped feeling the wasp stings. I actually feel pretty good, to tell you the truth."

Tilley returns with the big mug. "Thank you, Tilley." Kelly is wearing tight white leggings and a long shirt. She pulls away from Danny, pulling her feet up onto the pad on the love seat, almost cuddling up to her mug, taking a big swig of her coffee.

"Are you going to be okay if I leave you out here alone? I really need to let her get these stingers out of my face."

"Yeah, I will be fine."

"You sure?"

Danny and Tilley return into the cabin and continue the difficult task of scraping out the stingers. Danny doesn't have quite the stings that Kelly does. They work at it for a little while, expecting that Kelly has fallen asleep on the porch. Danny leans up and begins kissing Tilley with a long passionate kiss. His hand slips down her shoulder to her breast. Danny's face is hurting, but all of the rest of him is just fine, and a little deprived.

Suddenly, they hear the loud rumble of a diesel engine growling from the barn and metal clanging together as if she is knocking down the door, or running over the Superduty with a tractor.

"Oh shit!" Danny yells as he again jumps up from Tilley.

He runs outside to find Kelly coming down the hill from the barn in the big John Deere tractor with a disc on the back. She has it raised up, but it is in high gear and headed for her garden. Danny goes running out toward the tractor. He soon realizes that she isn't stopping and decides to retreat. He stands near the edge of the yard where the garden begins. It is nearly an acre garden on flat land. The grass in the yard is Bermuda and is as green as a golf course all the way around the garden and up to the barn.

Kelly gets to the garden and stops. She puts the tractor in low gear and drops the disc. The big diesel revs even a little louder as she starts forward. She is hopping up and down across the rows until she turns, swinging the large disc out to the right of the tractor as she maneuvers it to go along with the rows. The tractor groans a little as she makes the turn. Danny looks back and Tilley is standing behind him.

"Crazy fucking bitch! I guess she decided it was time to plow this shit under."

"I can kind of understand where she is coming from. That is a little over the top for this morning, but okay, as long as she doesn't run over your car, the cabin, or us."

Danny looks over at the little green Mustang in the yard. It is about a car's width away from the rows of the garden toward the far end, and away from where she is currently running the disc. He can just imagine the disc swinging wide and hitting his car.

Danny heads into the cabin and returns with his keys. He pulls the car up beside the cabin. He revs the big engine a time or two before getting out. He thinks of how damn hilarious this actually is.

"Well, how 'bout we have a seat on the love seat on the porch and watch this slow-motion train derailment and make sure she doesn't run anything over, pass out, or something."

The two walk up to the cabin and sit there on the love seat, looking out the doorway at her as she makes pass after pass, leaving nothing but plowed dirt in her wake.

Tilley goes into the cabin and returns with the bright light. She rigs it up so she can see Danny's face. They sit there with Danny looking out of the doorway and Tilley sitting in his

221

lap with her legs bent to the side of his lap, picking at Danny's face.

It's not too long and she finishes pulling out the stingers. Danny pulls tobacco out of his jaw and pats it onto his face, nearly covering it. The two sit and decide that Kelly is actually doing a pretty good job with the tractor, even in her inebriated state.

About an hour passes and they see her lift the disc and come pulling up in the beautiful front lawn, leaving tracks and dirt clots from the tread of the tires as she does. The diesel engine is rattling and the brakes are making a clanging noise. She slams on the brakes and drops the disc, *clungg*, onto the grass near the front porch. The big engine starts rattling slower and slower until it finally becomes silent, letting out a belch of smoke from the exhaust on the front hood of the big green machine. The disc made a deep gouge mark about a foot long into the gorgeous lawn.

She comes bouncing off of it.

"I need a refill!"

"You need to chill the fuck out! We just can't have nice things," Danny replies.

"What? Why? You were the one that said I couldn't sleep. Fucking animals and grass want to ruin my garden? I will start the shit over again. If we are truly leaving, then I don't need it anyway. I did not grow it for those low life sons a bitches. That is what we have Chopper for! Good thing he isn't here, I may shoot that damn dog."

"Chopper would never allow that. You know that," Danny replies.

"That's what pisses me off so bad! You shoulda let the boys stay here."

"Really? On your bed?"

"You're right, they would probably have our damn sheets stained."

"I think you could probably nap some now, dumplin'."

"I ain't tired now. Let's go ride the wheeler."

222

"I think we should get back to cooking. How about checking to see if we got a reply from the WRC."

"Nope, I am going riding. If you want to go, I suggest you get your ass on the wheeler."

He looks over at Tilley. "I guess we are going to go riding. Honestly, I need to check the pits anyway. Kelly, if I take you riding, will you settle down a little? No more shooting up the yard and plowing for today?"

"I guess."

Danny walks up to the barn to get the four-wheeler. He takes his time filling it with fuel. He straps a shovel onto the back of it, gathers up some jerky and a few beers out of the fridge in the barn and finds his old ice chest. He gets some ice out of the big deep freeze. He's there for about thirty minutes. He really isn't in a big rush to get out and about and wants to be sure that she really is ready when he returns.

He finally gets it all ready and rides down to the cabin. He leaves it running, expecting to find Kelly with boots and jeans on, all hell-bent for leather. He steps up onto the porch to find both of his little women asleep on the love seat, with Tilley leaned over onto the arm of the seat and Kelly stretched out with her head on Tilley.

"Thank God!" Danny says. "Maybe she will sleep this shit off and settle down. Never have I had a woman that could get that friggin redneck just like that with just a little alcohol."

He considers how she is with the wasp stings. He checks her breathing and goes and jumps on the wheeler. He rides down to the medical facility and goes in to find an EpiPen. He retrieves it and returns back home. He knows now that he is ready if another attack occurs.

He puts the medicine on the counter in the kitchen and sees a notice of new mail on the computer. He finds that he has a reply from the WRC concerning the fuel rods. The instructions are quite thorough; complete with what the temperature of the room must be prior to inserting the containers. He reads and understands that this could be a life or death situation. The email also explains that there are at least four other people in the continental US that are experienced and are competent at installing the fuel rods. Danny doesn't care to do any more traveling and taking a chance on these other shelters after the experience he has had. He has decided that he will install them.

Danny sits and reads the instructions. He considers that this could be the end of LRAFB if he makes an error. The bottom line is, it sounds as if his destiny is how he likes it; up to him. He clicks print and hears the familiar click and sounds of the printer start up to give him a guide that he can take with him.

He goes out and climbs on his wheeler and considers that this could be his final time checking on his pits. It has been two weeks since he has checked them and fears they will be pretty rancid.

He drives past the creek and finds that it is dry. He pulls over to it and is a little concerned that the source could be frozen, keeping it from flowing. The creek also feeds the water into a well they use at the cabin. They have an underground cistern as well, but without fresh water on a regular basis, he must treat it using chemicals. He pulls over to the small ten feet wide creek bed to find that it is bone dry and hasn't had water in it for likely a week.

He drives on and comes to the pond. It is unusually low. He is alarmed, concerned the water sources are being somewhat depleted, but he figures that it won't matter as long as he can get the transport into space soon.

He makes a left and comes to the first pit. It only has a fraction of the animals that he expected. He fears they are thinning out, too. It isn't long and he is at the second and third pits. He finds the same at all of them. He knows, regardless of the final destination, that time is running out on his shelter here.

Chapter 28
Pays to Have Friends

Danny gets back home and checks on his girls. They had gone into the bedroom and were sleeping well. He really wanted to go get Chopper and check on things at the Hot Springs Village shelter. He tries to wake them without success. He tells them he is headed there and will be back later to a response of ZZzzs.

He decides he will take the jeep, but on the way to the barn, he remembers that he lent it to the boys, so he gets his F250. He reaches in his pocket to check for keys and finds that he grabbed the right ones after a little further inspection. The tunnel buster is still attached to the front and he doesn't really want to drive it with that monstrosity on it.

He drops the built- in stands and pulls the pins. He jacks a small lever in the front and soon the tunnel buster is sitting on its own. He backs the big white truck out and pulls down to the cabin. He stops just past the big tractor and between the cabin and the lime green car in the front yard.

Shaking his head at the sight of what the tractor did to his lawn, he walks back into the cabin and replicates a glass of sweet tea. He grabs a pack of post-it notes and leaves the girls a message, telling them that he will be out for a couple of hours.

Back into the big F250 with the engine rattling and some old rock and roll on. *"On with the Show by Motley Crew"* is playing on the stereo. Soon the rattle becomes a roar and he is en route. Up and past the stranded Op Track, which is out of fuel, and to the exit doors. He jumps out and unlocks them and pulls through, noticing the clean snow around the front of his doors. *Clang*! He slams them back and clicks the lock securely.

He pulls out onto the icy tunnel roadway with the bright headlights reflecting back and blinding him as he dims them to reduce the glare. It is about two pm by now and he travels without any issue at about forty mph. Soon, he arrives and enters the Hot Springs Village shelter. He makes the familiar journey to old Mr. Johnson's house, where the boys are staying. He pulls up to find the gray jeep sitting in the front yard. It looks to be in good condition. He is happy that it is still in one piece.

He stops the truck and steps out onto the step below the door as he spots Chopper. He is slobbering and coming at full steam toward his master. The big dog nearly levels Danny as he puts his head against him, panting and whining in happiness to see him.

"I am happy to see you, too, boy!"

Chopper just looks at him with the admiration of a child. Danny says, "Where are them boys at?" He heads on up to the front porch of the gray brick house.

As he steps on the porch, with Chopper in tow, he says, "Hello, anyone home?" He continues on to the front door and knocks. There is no answer. "They surely didn't get off too far without the jeep."

He then hears an engine running. Here comes Bryan, around the side of the house, on the tractor. He has a young lady standing on the hitch behind the seat. It isn't a large tractor. It is orange with a front-end loader. The young girl is very pretty, with dark hair and light skin. They pull up and the tractor kind of bucks and jumps as he kills the engine with the decompression lever. The young lady has a firm grasp on the back of the seat so not to be thrown off.

"Hey, Mr. Nichols! How are you?"

"What are you up to, Bryan? You guys been taking good care of my dog?"

"Yes, sir. He is a great dog, and has been a fantastic guest. He let us know when he wanted out and no squirrels are safe on this side of the shelter." He chuckles and then takes a closer look at Danny.

"What happened to your face?"

"We got into a big bed of wasps on our trip."

"Wow! You would think they would all have froze."

"Not these. Who is your friend here?"

226

"This is Tabatha. She is Mr. Franklin's daughter."

"Well, hi there, young lady. How old are you?"

"Hi, Mr. Nichols. I am seventeen. I have heard quite a bit about you from my dad and these guys. It is nice to finally get to meet you. You sound like quite an accomplished man."

"Thank you."

"He says you have a transport and could be going to the new world."

"I sure do. I don't see too many young people around. It seems that they all either have taken off on a transport or went with God."

"I can't really understand why I didn't go with God. I have given it quite a lot of thought, but I can only think that he left me here for a reason. Maybe to ride to the new world with you guys."

Bryan speaks up, "Adam and I have decided to stay here."

"I don't remember inviting ya'll."

"You haven't, but we felt that since we have become fairly good friends, that you probably would extend the invitation, but we like it here."

"I actually was planning to invite you guys, but I understand about staying here. It really isn't bad here with all of the people gone." He chuckles.

"I really wish that Tabatha would stay." He kind of looks back toward her. "But I have a feeling she isn't really destined to be here," Bryan says.

"You could be right. I feel like Mr. Franklin, Tilley, and Kelly all have more work to do on the new world. Where is Adam?"

"He is around back. We are working on our garden. He is running a tiller."

"Awfully quiet damn tiller, I haven't heard it."

"He may be putting gas in it right now. I heard it quit right before you got here."

227

"I see, I don't have a bunch of time to stay so I better get going. You be careful riding around on the back of that tractor, young lady. If you fall off, you could be hurt badly, especially if they have something hooked on to it. I had a friend that fell under a disc when I was in grade school."

"Yes, sir," Tabatha answers.

Chopper had laid down on the ground beside Danny's feet. He gets up, realizing they are leaving.

"Tell Adam I said hey. Thanks for taking good care of my dog. I will be by tomorrow morning. Hey, would you and Adam care to go with me to put fuel rods in the transport at the Little Rock Air Force Base tomorrow or Thursday?"

"Sure, we will ride along."

"I will plan for it. It will be a long drive in the Op Track."

"We want to help. I can't speak for him for sure, but I will definitely go and I imagine he will, too. Maybe we can go by an Op Track dealer."

"Great. I'm not sure that we will have time to do that. Let's just go ahead and plan for tomorrow about six am."

"Six? Man, you get up early." He pauses, thinking that he may change the time. He kind of looks around and looks at Tabatha. "Okay, six it is," he replies.

Danny climbs back into the big, white, four-door pickup, letting the big jet black dog into the back. He takes his usual stance: hind legs on the back seat and front paws on the console as the two take off back to the cabin.

He arrives at the country shelter and pulls through the front yard, parking up at the barn. Chopper comes bailing out of the back door, running and hiking his leg on everything between the barn and the cabin. He takes off across the barren garden and looks as if to say, "Where are Kelly's plants?" Then he runs up to the big tractor, sneezing and coughing from the smell of the dirt, looking at it as if it seems out of place to him. He sniffs the bucket and hikes his leg on the front tire. Danny yells, "Quit pissing on everything, dumbass. Everyone knows it all belongs to you."

The big dog cows down, with his little, bobbed tail tucked down, trying to tuck it between his legs, and slowly begins to walk to the front porch of the cabin. He is looking for Kelly. With nothing found but Kelly's scent, he slowly walks over to the love seat where she had been sleeping earlier and climbs up. Still sniffing everything on the seat, he finally lies down into a ball shape and kind of snorts, looking up to Danny as if to show some disappointment.

Danny sits down beside him and strokes his back. "Our girls are down and out, boy. It's a good thing you weren't here, that crazy bitch might have run you over with the tractor."

Chopper then notices Danny's face for the first time as the big sad looking face hops up and turns toward him. He is as tall as his master on the seat. He begins to lick at his face and Danny lets him lick at his cheek. It is all beginning to heal now that the stingers are all out and some of it has scabs. He has been told that a dog's saliva has a type of antibiotic and is open to any help he can get with his injury.

He sits with Chopper for quite a while before he decides to check on the girls and see if there is anything entertaining on the satellite TV. He replicates himself a beer, walks back to find Kelly and Tilley cuddled up like lovers again. He returns to the living room and sits down to enjoy some old episodes of a TV series called "*Walker, Texas Ranger*" from back in the nineteen nineties. He and his dog fall asleep in the living room while relaxing and waiting for the girls to wake up.

He wakes up the next morning lying on the floor, with Chopper's butt in his face. He rolls over and it is a little nippy in the cabin. He immediately becomes fully awake. The environmental controls are supposed to keep it between seventy and seventy-five degrees all the time. If it is less than sixty degrees, as he expects, it means there is something wrong. A collapse in the roof, a door open, an issue with the natural heating system. Could the core be getting colder? He jumps to

229

his feet and to the door. He opens it and steps out to the mudroom, then to the porch, finding it a very comfortable seventy-five degrees. He looks at the outside thermometer to find that it is exactly seventy-two degrees.

He scratches his head as it was a false alarm. He stands looking out over the freshly plowed garden, smelling the earth as the light constant breeze blows across it. He breathes a sigh of relief as he hears the outside air conditioning unit come on. Chopper, standing beside him, wonders what is the matter. The big dog looks out the door to see if he can see what has his master's attention.

He walks back in and has a look at the clock to find it is about three thirty am. "Damn, I have got to quit with these screwed up hours." He makes his way down the hallway to find the thermostat. Sure enough, it is turned way down to fifty-five degrees. Rubbing his hands together, he says, "Brrrr!" He begins to click it slowly back up and says, "Hmmm, snuggling temperature?" He clicks it back to fifty-five and heads to the bedroom to find the girls on each side of the bed, with the comforter pulled up tight.

He pulls Tilley's blanket up and begins to crawl over the top of her. He settles in and wraps an arm around each of these beautiful women and pulls one in tight on each side. He sleeps like a baby for the next hour, as do the girls.

Morning comes finding the three waking about the same time. It is about four forty-five am. Kelly moans as she puts her hand on her head. Tilley asks Danny if he is ready for coffee. He is always ready for coffee if he is awake and she goes to the kitchen to start it for him. She returns after about ten minutes, with coffee for him and a glass of water with some Alka Seltzer for Kelly.

They all slowly find their way out of bed and into the living area. Danny turns on the news from Dallas. The news is still the same: people going crazy in the shelters, plagues, hopeless people that feel sorry for themselves. They report on an abandoned truck stop burning to the ground in New Mexico.

230

He doesn't leave it on for long, as it is all pretty depressing. He is thankful he didn't end up in one of the highly populated shelters and fears if others knew how good they have it in Hot Springs, more would come and try to move in on them. Kelly sits there holding her head.

"That was more than just Irish cream in my coffee, wasn't it?"

"You took a bunch of pills, girl. And, uh, I gave you a little shot of Wild Turkey, but I didn't know you were going to go ape-shit crazy! My god!"

"I could have told you that I can't hold my liquor. Why do you think I always just stick to a glass of wine, or maybe a couple of beers."

The Alka Seltzer seems to be helping. She gets up and walks to the front door. She looks through the mudroom at the small window in the door to the outside, seeing her plowed under garden in the light of the security lights.

"What the fuck? What happened to my garden?"

She begins to remember the tractor like it was a dream.

"You plowed it under."

She looks back, with the wasp stings still fairly prevalent and beginning to form scabs on her face, and makes a very mean look toward Danny.

"I plowed it under? And you let me?"

"There was no *letting you* do anything. Hell, I went out to see about you and you about ran my ass over."

"I was pretty upset that I haven't had time to tend to it and the animals had gotten to some of it, but I wasn't ready to throw in the towel."

"I guess, by god, you were! Or at least, you were yesterday, little lady."

She doesn't say anymore. She takes off out the door to look over the damage.

Danny looks over at Tilley as Kelly leaves the mudroom.

231

"Did it look to you like I stood a chance at stopping her drunk ass?"

"Not really. I was kind of fearful that she may take down the cabin with that big tractor, to be honest."

"I feel like apologizing, but I am not sure that I did anything wrong. I didn't know she was bipolar on alcohol."

"Now we do. We should keep that one in mind and any hard alcohol out of her hands."

"No doubt."

Danny gets on the computer and finds a message from Bryan. He wants to know what time they are leaving for Jacksonville/LRAFB. Danny says out loud, "I told you guys six, but let's see who all is going on this trip north." He really would rather the girls stay home, but he knows that they will have his back regardless of what goes on, and he isn't so sure about the boys. He replies telling them to be ready at six am, like he had said yesterday. It could be later, but it won't hurt them to be ready.

"Tilley, do you want to go to the air base with me today while I install the fuel rods? It could be dangerous if something goes wrong."

"I will if you need me to."

"Do you want to? I will not ask you to go unless you want to be there."

"I really feel a need to spend some time at Hot Springs Village. I haven't been there in over a week," Tilley says.

"But you will come along if I need you to?"

"Of course, Danny. I am not afraid. You will keep me safe."

"If I can. You may need to come along to help keep me safe, honestly. I just need someone to have my back. At times like this, when we prepare something that is a ticket out of here and other people are involved, it could get crazy. I want to believe that the boys have good intentions, but you never know until the time comes that they could take advantage of a situation."

232

"Oh, the boys, Bryan and Adam, are going up there?" Tilley asks.

"Yeah, I asked them yesterday when I went and got Chopper."

"I wondered where Chopper came from."

"I went while you two were sleeping. I guess ya'll never missed me."

"I have a bunch of stuff at the other shelter and would like some time to decide what goes and what stays."

"I completely understand."

Danny takes off outside to catch up with his poor little swollen faced, hung-over model. He walks up to her as she stands with a cup of coffee, looking over the plowed field with the light from the security light.

"I am going to the air base today."

"Oh really? You didn't bother to tell me until now?"

"I wanted to tell you yesterday when I got back home from getting Chopper, but you weren't available." He kind of snickers.

"'Cause you got me all drunked up!"

"Doesn't matter now, I need to know if you want to come along."

"Is Tilley going?"

"She would rather go up to the other shelter and spend some time, but the boys are going."

"Figures," she replies with a grimace. "You expecting trouble?"

"Not expecting, but I need someone I know has my back, just in case."

"I understand. Yes, I want to come along."

"Great! Start getting ready. How is your head?"

"Not the best, but better."

The two head back into the house and begin to prepare provisions for a trip. It's not long and they have everything in bags, laid out in the mudroom, ready to be loaded into the Op Track.

233

Danny heads out with the four-wheeler and a five-gallon jug of fuel to put diesel in the stranded Op Track. He comes idling by the front of the cabin to see Kelly and Tilley sitting in lawn chairs on the dimly lit green and damaged front lawn. He stops to get Kelly so she can drive the stranded Op Track back to the cabin. They get fuel in it. It has an auto priming switch that makes it bleed the diesel much easier than the equipment does. She pilots it back to the cabin and they load up. It isn't long and they are arriving at the other shelter. It is now about five forty am and it is still dark in the shelter. They drive slowly to try to keep from waking everyone.

They pull in at the boys' house and Adam comes out to greet them. They are all three climbing out of the machine, looking a little worse for wear, with the wasp stings and the long journey they just finished the day prior.

"You guys look a little rough," Adam says.

"Yeah, well, you will have that on apocalyptic Earth. Hell, I am surprised it isn't worse than it is without God to rely on," Danny explains.

"Have you not read the good book at all? This is not the absence of God, this is the time of tribulations, I feel sure. You can still repent your sins and ask forgiveness. All is not lost."

"I guess I missed that part. I am no theologian, but I do know that we were all left here Hell bound. He chose his flock, unless some of our work is not complete."

"Not complete? As in, we weren't supposed to be left here for the next seven years?"

"I think God has a plan. I think there are a chosen group that should be going to Goldilocks. You, very well, could be one of them, Adam."

Bryan walks out on the front porch, tucking in his shirt, with Tabatha following close behind. Both of them have bed hair and Danny knows what they have been up to.

Bryan addresses them, "What's this talk about God? He left us. I think we will probably just stay here. If we go against His will, there is no telling how that will end. I may turn into

234

ashes when we leave here. We are happy to help you guys get going, though."

"We need to get going. Tilley, are you okay with taking the jeep up to the house? You got your key and everything?"

Tilley says, "I am good if you guys are ready. Tabatha, what are you wanting to do?"

"I will head back over to Dad's. Tilley, could you drop me off on your way?"

"Sure."

Danny says, "You guys have some diesel around here? I should have filled the damn thing before we left our shelter, but the girls were all ready and I didn't think about it. I don't think that five gallons will get us there and back."

Adam responds, "Yeah, we have a biodiesel pump from the replicator in the back."

"Awesome, that will work. I am not sure any of us are ready for another stop at a truck stop."

Kelly gives him a look as he climbs into the pilot's seat and begins to navigate the yard to find their pump. They get the tank full and it isn't long and the boys are loaded up on the left and Kelly on the right. They come out into the tunnel and Bryan opens the doors. Danny goes right on the main road, in lieu of his typical left that brings him to the country shelter.

After a short distance, he comes to the end of the tunnel and brings up the display for the nosecone temperature. It shows it to be at twelve hundred degrees. He passes into the snow with the familiar blue haze forming on the monitors. They then feel the machine begin to climb as he is headed to the surface.

"You boys hang on because I don't know what the weather is like up here. We had a storm blow up that had ice tornadoes on our trip to Arizona."

"No shit?" Bryan says.

"I ended up digging the Track into the snow and we waited it out. It did blow us around pretty good before we realized what was happening, though."

"Sounds pretty crazy," Adam replies.

235

"Scary is the word," Kelly tells them.

They get to the surface to find a wind speed of sixty mph. Bryan, setting on the higher of the two stations, looks up at the bullet holes in the hatch, with toilet paper shoved in them, and points it out to Adam. Adam just shakes his head and shrugs his shoulders. They both think there must be a storm in progress, but Danny lets them know that the strong wind is normal for this day and time. They travel along at a pretty good rate without much resistance. They are going about fifty mph and this is better time than they have usually been able to make on the surface. The roar of the big diesel engine and the occasional rattle coming from the linkage and drive wheels of the tracks can be heard as they make their way north to Jacksonville's Little Rock Air Force Base.

Chapter 29
Fueling a Transport

The four drive along on the thirty-foot-high snow pack and are above everything they come to. Danny begins slowing the machine as they see an image on the display that appears to be a ledge or a drop off. He turns the machine to the right to avoid the obstacle. He soon realizes that it is the Benton, Arkansas, shelter. Each shelter has an uneven area due to the top is much higher and depending upon their rainfall settings, it can be warmer than the ground. In an Op Track, Danny has become wise to staying on the lookout for these obstacles.

"Have you spoken to any of your boyfriends at the air base lately?" Danny asks Kelly.

"I did and there is a sergeant at the base, who has been contacted by Commander Charles, and he is to meet us at hangar 9710 when we tell him we have arrived. Should I contact him? What time do you anticipate our arrival?"

"Have you spoken with him today? Does he know our business? Do you think he can be trusted?"

"No one knows we are coming. He was contacted by Charles Phillips with information on us. He is a black man and is First Sergeant Charlie Carter. He only knows that we are to have full access to anything we wish, and he is to meet us at the hangar and show us around."

"That sounds encouraging. Does he know what is in that hangar?"

"I assume he does."

Danny becomes quiet and the sun comes out and puts a bright reflection onto the snow through the outside cameras. They have now navigated around the Benton shelter and are coming up on the Little Rock shelter. They see tall buildings off in the distance towering up through the snow and the impression from the shelter far off to the left. It covers the river and appears to encompass the Broadway bridge. The tall buildings look as if they are frozen in time. At another time and this could make for a very beautiful picture, with the sun gleaming off the large buildings and the impression of the roadways and river all appearing as ice. Danny and Kelly both recall going through this area many times before the snow.

As they get closer, the large buildings look like they are missing a few window panes in different areas. They see smoke coming out of some of them.

Kelly says, "Unfortunate bastards."

"They may have escaped the plague that is going through the population in the Little Rock shelter. They may not be as unfortunate as you believe. That Bank of America building could be a nice place to live, given their choices, if you think about it."

"They can have it. I will take Danny Town, population two, and sometimes three."

They pass by this area and soon top a slow ascending hill. The landscape looks pretty flat and unobstructed for the path to the base from here on out.

"Can you contact Sergeant Carter for me, Kelly? We will be there within an hour and I would very much like to arrive to install the fuel rods, devise a plan for getting this thing in the air, and go!

Kelly begins typing on her tablet.

"Can you actually text with him on that thing?"

"Yeah, I have a wireless signal and sent a message asking if he is available to meet at hangar 9710. He says they will be expecting us at the main gate."

"Cool."

Bryan speaks up, "This guy doesn't even know we are coming?"

Danny replies, "Oh, he knows and he knows that it is this week, but he doesn't know when exactly. He is expecting us, don't worry about that."

Kelly speaks up, "He is available and will be ready. He said there is not a hangar 9710, though."

"That is impossible. I specifically recall the email from Commander Phillips saying that was the number."

"I have a map. If the number has changed or something, then we can identify the building by the map he sent to us."

"That should work, I guess."

Another fifteen minutes pass and they come to a huge mountain of snow off to the east of them and a snow canyon that would rival the Grand Canyon to the west side. Danny stops the Op Track, trying to decide how to enter the secured facility.

He begins to turn parallel to the recess in the horizon. It isn't long and the displays all go blue as they once again switch from the outside cameras to the sonar assisted view. They descend a ways until they reach the ground. They continue traveling and watching the onboard GPS unit until they find themselves just north of the town of Jacksonville. There is an old stoplight that Danny recalls at an intersection that he can faintly make out through the displays. Suddenly, they are in a tunnel that has been busted in the snow and their cameras are once again active. They are driving down a divided roadway to the front gate of the Air Force base. The snow tunnel here extends from the outside edge of the median of the roadway on one side all the way to the other opposite lanes. Danny wonders how big of a tunnel buster they had that could bust this big of a tunnel. They had to have removed trees that stood in the median and along the side of the road to make the tunnel. He fears that it could collapse because it has such a wide span.

They begin to see daylight at the end and there appears to be an opening. They come out of the end of the tunnel. A large mountain of snow is on each side of the opening where it was cleared. They find themselves on a cleared dry road as they exit the tunnel. The sun is once again shining down on them. Directly in front of them they see a guard shack and two roads, one leading out of the base and one going into it. To their right is a large airplane mounted on a concrete pad and a sign that says LITTLE ROCK AIR FORCE BASE.

Each road has a large steel barrier that protrudes up from the asphalt. The barriers are blue with a yellow striped steel member along the top. They actually see guards inside of the shack and are a little relieved, as they weren't entirely sure what gate of the base was considered the main gate, or if it would actually be manned. When Danny was young, he had friends that lived on base and he attended a few air shows on occasion, but he was not real familiar with it.

Kelly speaks up and says, "This must be the main gate."

"Of course," Danny replies.

Two tall young men with an insignia of MP on their white and gray camo winter gear exit the building and walk out to the Op Track, carrying M16 machine guns slung from a strap. They hold them undoubtedly at the ready for whatever this unusual looking machine may have in store. One has light colored hair and the other dark brown or black. The pair seems somewhat surprised that they have this Op Track sitting at the gate, and look over the wide black tracks on the top and bottom and on each side. Danny pops the hatch as the two look at the machine in awe. He climbs out and walks toward the back of the machine to get his winter gear.

"Hello," Danny says to the two soldiers.

"Hello, sir. Is this an Op Track?" the dark haired soldier asks.

"Yes, this is my Op Track. My name is Danny Nichols. It is my understanding that you men are expecting me and my crew of three."

"Yes, First Sergeant Charlie Carter radioed in your anticipated arrival. He said we are to grant you four passes to have access to the flight line in order to look at your civilian property that is stored in a hangar there. Sir, would you mind my asking what happened to your face?"

"I was stung by wasps. We visited a truck stop and apparently they woke up when we turned on the heat."

"That looks painful."

240

"It sounds like you guys have the information. Do you get a lot of visitors?"

"No, sir. Maybe one a week, and we have to test them for the virus, as Little Rock's shelter has a nasty sickness that we don't want spreading through our base."

"Are there a great number of people left here on the base?"

"We have about two thousand military members and their families here."

"A far cry for the norm?"

"Yes, sir! Could I get your passengers to come inside and blow into our meter? This is a simple test and each of you surely would want to know if you have the virus."

"No problem at all."

Danny goes to the Op Track. "Everyone out!"

Kelly responds, "What's up?"

"We all have to be tested for the virus before we can go on base."

They all climb out and head in. One by one they blow into what looks like a breathalyzer and it shows green for everyone. They confirm everyone's ID by their driver's license. The airmen mention something about Kelly's stings as well. They go back out and stand beside the machine.

A few minutes pass and the light haired soldier comes out and hands each one a pass with their picture on it. They climb back into the Op Track. He asks Danny if he knows where the flight line is. Danny explains that he has a GPS with memory and unless something has changed significantly, he should be fine. The young soldier explains that they have the only civilian, deep snow capable vehicle in the area and they should be aware that others would surely take it if they had the chance. Danny thanks him for the tip and the hospitality.

Danny climbs aboard, the large heavy metal gate drops into the asphalt, and they are off. They drive down black, well-kept streets until they get to the outside of the flight line. They can see the runways ahead. They follow the GPS until they are essentially on the airfield. They stop and Kelly has her tablet open showing a map of the field. They are supposed to meet First Sergeant Carter at the last building on the left before the airfield entrance. They see a blue Air Force truck sitting out front of one of the buildings and pull in near it.

Danny climbs out and begins walking up to the entrance. It is a beige colored building that sits on a hill that goes down toward the back. The entrance has a heavy blue door with COMMAND CONTROL across it. He prepares to walk up the steps to a conservative concrete porch as the door opens. A large black man about forty years of age, short black, military hair cut, wearing fatigues and donning insignias accurate for his rank, steps out of the door to meet him.

"First Sergeant Charlie Carter?"

"Yeah, you got me. I guess you must be Danny Nichols."

"The one and only. Kelly said that you don't have a hangar 9710."

"That was something that was odd. I am pretty sure that hangar is our number 10321. She said she had a map that showed the hangar. Could you show it to me?"

By this time, Kelly and the boys had all climbed out of the machine. Kelly is walking over to the two men, carrying her tablet to show them the map image.

The first sergeant says, "Yep, that is 10321. I have been in there. That big ship belongs to you?"

"Yep, that is my transport."

"You planning on taking any passengers when you take off to go to the new world?"

"Very few, to be honest."

"What happened to your face, man? It looks like something got a hold of you and tore your ass up, damn!"

"Wasps, it's a long story. Be careful of frozen buildings, they can be gathered there."

"I will be sure and do that. Shit looks painful, man, damn!"

242

"Yeah, it sucks."

"Let me get you, fine people, out to this place. I have quite a bit of stuff to tend to today. You will be okay in there by yourselves?"

"Yeah, and honestly, we kind of prefer it that way."

They all load back up and take the short drive out and down the airfield to hangar 10321, following the big blue Air Force truck. It is not a hangar, but eight hangars altogether. One continuous enormous opening made up of several doors that must stretch for six hundred feet. The top of the hangar looks like a skyscraper as they pull up to the front of the huge building. It reminds Danny of a shelter or one of the old zeppelin hangars that he saw in history books.

There is a walk through door on the right side of the big doors and the sergeant pulls up to the left of it and Danny pulls the Op Track up to the right of his pickup, being careful not to hit the truck with the wide tracks. Danny is out and walks up to Sgt. Carter at the door as Kelly and the boys are climbing out of the machine. The sergeant unlocks the door by placing his finger on a keypad beside the knob, stepping inside placing his finger on a second keypad, silencing a chirping noise that is assumed to be an alarm system. He digs around in his pocket and hands Danny a key.

"For this door?" Danny asks.

"Yes, sir. This is your hangar I am told. The key will override the keypad if there is a power outage or some issue. That happens on a regular basis this day and time."

He reaches over past Danny and presses the ARM button on the alarm and it begins to chirp again.

"Put yo finger on the keypad," he tells Danny.

Danny puts his right index finger on it and the chirping ceases once again.

"Looks to me like you all are good. I will be around. If you finish before I get back, just have Kelly text me and I will come by and do a security check on the facility."

"Thanks. I appreciate the respect and the assistance."

243

"My pleasure, what a cool ATV you have there. Is that one of them Op Tracks?" he asks as he looks out the open door.

"Yeah, that is an Op Track. They will go just about everywhere."

"We were supposed to be getting a shipment before the ice. I guess there wasn't quite enough time. We have some vehicles that will go, but they are huge. They take too much fuel to go in them much. Well, you guys take care. I will be around."

Kelly and the boys walk in the door as the first sergeant is leaving. Danny is looking out across this massive room and sees the outline of an extremely large craft sitting in the dark. He steps forward and a motion detector turns on lights throughout the room to reveal an enormous dignitary transport. He is relieved, the sergeant didn't point out where the light switch was. It just barely fits into the four wide by four deep hangar. They were modified to accommodate fueling of the transports.

Danny looks in awe at the ship that will take them to Goldilocks. Bryan and Adam look like they have seen a ghost. After some time looking at the ship, Danny goes to the east end to find the door and the fuel rods' storage area. He pulls out a piece of paper that has the instructions on how to install the fuel rods. He calls everyone together as he walks over to lock the front door.

"I am going to charge this thing with fuel rods. You all need to stand here by the door while I do this. You are not to allow anyone access, not even the first sergeant, until I complete this task. I don't want anyone walking around, you do not need to ask me questions about what I am doing, or interfere in any way during this time. If something happens and these canisters I am carrying are dropped, we will melt the snow from here to Hot Springs Village, maybe to the town of Hot Springs."

"Really?" Bryan replies.

"Understood," says Kelly.

Danny looks down at the paper to ensure he knows exactly what needs to be done.

1. *Prepare the temperature of the room.*

    a. *The ideal temperature is 65 degrees Fahrenheit, however, it must not be below 40 or above 125.*

    b. There was heat that has kept the hangar at a temperature of near seventy, so the first item is covered.

2. *Locate the charging cavity in the Dignitary Transport.*

    a. *This will be located beneath the left wing near the very back. It is an oval-shaped area with four circular cavities.*

    b. *Remove the composite cover and save, then remove and discard the clear plastic dust cover.*

He goes to the spacecraft to find the charging cavity. He unscrews several thumb screws and pulls off a composite 3D printed outer cover and sets it near a trash can, then pulls off a soft plastic dust cover and pitches it into the trash can.

3. *Locate and put on all of the PPE provided in the storage locker that is to the right of the fuel rods' storage room door.*

    a. *This should include a Nomex jumpsuit.*

    b. *Nomex gloves.*

    c. *Conductive covers with a brass bracelet to attach to each ankle for static electricity dissipation.*

He walks over to the fuel rods' storage room and finds a cabinet marked PPE. He pulls out a white jumpsuit, gloves, and covers for his shoes. He pulls his boots off and puts on the white suit. He pulls the strings tight in order to pull the headgear down fairly tight over his head. He has concerns about it obstructing his field of vision. He turns his head side to side, looking toward Kelly, then back toward the ship. He puts his shoes back on and covers them using the baggy footwear covers provided. He pulls his pant leg up to reveal his hairy ankle and snaps a brass colored bracelet around each ankle. He then puts on gloves.

4. *Go into the fuel rod storage room.*

   a. *This room is located on the east end of the hangar and should be adjacent to your transport.*

   b. *Enter this room by scanning your fingerprint.*

   c. *This was recently programmed to recognize your fingerprint.*

   d. *Rub your hand across the brass grounding bar at the right of the door before entering.*

He goes to the door that is marked with hazard radioactive signs. He pulls his right glove off and places his finger onto a reader. A light above the door turns green and a high-pitched click is heard. A small gap is seen at the edge of the door. He puts his glove back on and pulls the door, opening it. He steps through, finding a vertically mounted brass bar to his right. He grasps the bar and runs his hand down it. He then stops while his hand is still on the bar and says, "Lord, if you have a mind of taking me, please give me a heart attack now. There is no good reason to take all of these other people along with me." He continues to pause as if he is sincerely awaiting chest pains.

5. *Locate the storage pods for each block of four fuel rods.*

   a. *Four rods will be necessary to charge the dignitary transport.*

   b. *Find the rods located at storage compartment G13.*

   c. *Enter code LRAFB_DTP1121.*

(No mention of prayer and wishing for death).

He releases the bar and walks to a cabinet with a clear front that is similar to a vending machine. It has a keypad to the right side. He pushes G13. The pad lights up and displays "ENTER VALIDATION CODE." He looks back at his paper and presses L, R, A, F, B, _, D, T, P, 1,1,2,1.

6. *Very carefully pull the rods in their glass container from the storage compartment.*

A whiny sound of a small servo motor is heard. He sees a platform raise from the bottom to location G13 and stop. The canister resting at this location begins traversing forward onto this servo-driven mechanism. Once the canister rests on this platform, it moves to the right where there is an opening so you can reach in and pull the canister out.

7. *Very carefully take this canister to the transport and locate the charging cavity.*

He removes the container from the machine and very cautiously walks to the open door. Using his knee, he shoves the door open and walks through to see Kelly and the boys standing near the front door, with a fair amount of concern on their faces because they know the danger of carrying this canister, as he begins the walk across the hangar to the spacecraft. He thinks to himself, *I am actually doing this.*

8. *Place the end of the fuel rod container that is marked in red into the recess of the charging cavity.*

   a. *The bottom of the charging cavity will rise up to the storage container, releasing a lock for each one.*

   b. *This device will also unlock the fuel rods from the storage container and gently lower them into the charging cavity.*

c. *When this device is fully lowered and seated properly into the transport, a door will traverse from the left that will seal the fuel rods and release the storage container.*

d. *Be sure to hold on to the glass storage container when this occurs. When it releases, it will drop to the floor.*

e. *This is harmless and poses no serious threat if it happens to find its way to the concrete floor.*

He gets to the spacecraft to find the cavity he had opened earlier. He stops and looks back over the piece of paper that has the instructions, then looks at the canister to locate the red end. He puts it into the recessed area, but it doesn't feel as though it went in properly. He feels the holder become firmly attached to the charging cavity and he relaxes a little as it must have seated properly. A few minutes pass and he sees the rods begin to lower into the cavity. Soon, there is only a transparent glass housing sticking out of the side as an inner composite door begins to travel across from the left side. It makes its way all the way to the right and *CRASH*! The glass container releases and falls to the floor. Danny tries to catch it. He immediately hears Adam cry out as if someone stuck a knife in his ribs. He looks over and he is in a fetal position on the floor. Bryan has a terrified look on his face, looking as if he may cry, and Kelly looks at him like, "Well, you fucking killing us?"

"It's okay. It's okay, it was only the container. The rods are safely in the transport."

9. *Once this is released a green LED will illuminate all the way around the oval shaped cavity.*

248

a. *You must now reinstall the composite cover by placing it back over the cavity and installing ten thumb screws to ensure the integrity of the hull of the ship. These screws should be hand tightened.*

A green light illuminates all the way around the oval cavity where he placed the rods. He walks over near the trash can on the floor and picks up an oval shaped black cover and places it over the cavity. He tightens all of the screws and breathes a big sigh of relief.

Danny begins pulling the string for his headgear loose and walking over to Kelly and the boys.

"That glass breaking really scared the fuck out of you boys, huh?"

Adam answers and is back to his feet by now, "Yes, sir. I knew you said that if something went wrong that it would melt the snow all the way to Hot Springs. Uh, Hot Springs is a long way away and, sir, that is *a lot* of snow!"

"That was just the canister. Can you guys sweep that up? I don't need no flat tire on my rocket ship." He kind of snickers as the boys go over to the wing of the spacecraft and begin looking for a broom.

Kelly takes the instructions from his hand, while looking it over, she says, "You did that shit on purpose, didn't you? It says right here to be careful or the canister will fall to the floor. You are such a dick!"

Danny walks away laughing. "Nah, now why would I make such a mess intentionally? Let's take a look at the new digs!"

They both walk up near the nose of the spacecraft and don't see any way to open it. They see an office on the opposite side of the hangar from the storage room and take off walking over there to see if there are some instructions or something.

They step inside of this modest office to find the lights have a motion sensor that turns on when they step in. A standard issue metallic gray military desk is to the left as they step through the door. A packet consisting of a large padded manila envelope has a label that says "DTP 1121." Danny looks back out at the large ship to see number "DTP 1121" on the side of it.

He reaches around inside to find a fob, papers that show everything checked off except for the fuel rods, and certificates of origin.

He says, "I guess this is our logbooks and stuff. Hopefully, this is a key to the door. The craft must be DTP 1121."

He reaches down and grabs a pen from the desk and puts a check mark, date, and signs on the field labeled: Fuel Rods Successfully Installed and Tested.

The two walk back out to the spaceship with the packet to find the boys wandering around, looking at the big triangular engines.

Kelly pushes the button on the fob and nothing happens. She looks closely and there are three buttons: Lights, Alarm, and Door. She pushes the "Door" button again. She double clicks it.

"Damn, just our luck, it doesn't fricken work!"

"Let me see that."

Danny looks at the back and the battery cover has a clear piece of plastic sticking out. He pulls that out and pushes the button and *voila,* the side of the spaceship clicks and a door rotates outward from the top, hinging down to the floor, making a staircase into the fuselage.

Chapter 30
The Departing

The four tour the ship. They walk up the steps to find a door to the left marked "Cockpit", a door straight ahead marked "Dining Area", and one to the right marked "Living Quarters". The hallway is lined with fine woodwork and a sizeable gold plaque that is engraved with Captain John Glasgow - Pilot, Jerry Daniels - Copilot, Daniel Nichols - CEO of Chimera, Owner. The floor is covered in ceramic tile that is in Chimera's company colors. It is lime green with a dark emerald green inlay. This hallway has paintings of Chimera's factory sites in Germany, Arkansas, and Mississippi.

They walk on through the hallway to find a large metal door. They pull it back to reveal a wooden walkway that is similar to a cruise ship deck. It is complete with a rail and a white colored wall behind it.

Danny speaks up and says, "I believe a hologram will be projected of the ocean when the ship is up and commissioned. Kelly, you may have to help us out with getting that part up and running."

"I will tend to the technical stuff as long as our maid is cleaning."

Danny just kind of gives her a scoff.

They walk along the deck and pass various glass-front rooms that have a hallway between many of them.

They walk nearly half the way to the end of the long rail and make a left between two of the glass rooms. They walk down this hallway for a little while until they come to another hallway that is perpendicular to this one, forming a four-way intersection. The fine wood wall has a golden plaque that says, "Suites 1-10 to the left and 11-20 to the right."

"That must be the crew's living quarters. We have fancier suites up top I believe."

They go straight to find themselves on a mezzanine that has a handrail and what appears to be a walking/running path. Below is a grand room that has a pool, a food bar on one end and an alcohol bar on the other. There are palm trees and the windows are round and look white, like a projector screen. The floor in this grand area is partially covered with what looks like indoor/outdoor carpet and adorned with the company colors and marble that is also in lime green with a dark emerald green inlay.

They walk around the large walking path, with a light green colored rubber finish, to find a grand staircase at the end that leads down to the grand room. They walk through this area and back up the stairs that are very similar at the front of the room.

They are now in a dining area. They walk past the tables and to the left to find they are back in the foyer where they entered the ship. The light from the fluorescent lamps that illuminate the hangar can be seen.

Kelly says, "Damn, do we have to go back to the shelter? This is nice!"

"I knew you would like it. I feel like this will be like a six-month vacation for us."

"No doubt."

Adam says, "It is a shame that we can't go."

Danny says, "Who says you guys can't go? If I invite you, then you can. Both of you and your little girlfriend can ride along."

"It isn't that. I feel that I am supposed to remain here to tend to things in the shelters," states Adam.

"The country shelter is showing signs of failure. The fresh water supply shows signs of issues, and if it continues, you will have to use the cistern under the building. Don't get me wrong, by using the rainwater runoff, it will sustain you forever probably, but it is a sign of bad things to come. The pits were thin the last time I checked them, as well. This tells me that time is running out for the natural flow of animals in the area. Again, there is an abundance of wildlife in the shelter, and you can grow food. It can be sustained for many, many years. I am guessing at least seven."

"We appreciate your offer. I think Tabatha is likely going with her dad, but we feel compelled to stay here with hopes of having a simple life."

Danny looks over at Bryan and says, "You feel the same way? You don't have to follow him, you know."

"Yeah, I honestly do. I think the simple life is the way for both of us."

They get ready to step out and *pow*, total darkness. The lights haven't had any movement in over an hour and has timed-out, shutting off. Danny leans out of the door opening, waving his arms and suddenly the lights come back on.

They make their way out of the ship and to the exit door. Danny presses the button that says, "ARM" on the alarm system, it begins to chirp as they make their way out of the exit door. He turns and locks it.

They all climb into the Op Track and make their way to the front gate. They stop to return their badges and the same two guards are there. They explain the badges are theirs to keep, but they will have to be tested each time for the virus.

They are all content with that and leave the base and head back south to the Hot Springs Village shelter. It isn't long and they are pulling in at the boys' house. They drop them off and head back to the country shelter.

Kelly gets out of the Op Track so they can pull through the large double doors. She hears Chopper barking off in the distance at the commotion and looking up toward the doors in the front yard. It is near six pm as they pull up to the front of their cabin and the rattle of the diesel engine in the Op Track rumbles to a stop. They both climb out, pretty tired from the trip, as the lights are beginning to dim, signaling the end of another day on the frozen world.

They go inside and Danny replicates a nice tall glass of Michelob Light and takes a pain pill. He heads into the living area and sits down on his large recliner. Chopper is headed his way and jumps in the middle of him as he turns on the television to find out what is going on out in the world.

"You big lap dog," he says to Chopper.

"You hungry?" Kelly asks.

"Yes, I would like some deer tenderloin if you wouldn't mind."

"Replicated?"

"No, if you don't feel up to cooking, you can replicate me a chili dog."

"If your heart is set on it, I will cook it for you, but I am pretty tired. All the deer meat we have is frozen up at the barn freezer and will take some time."

"Replicated dog will be just fine with me, babe."

They have their supper and find that the shelters in other areas are beginning to choose God or totally drop off the radar, operating within a literal evil underground or under snow network. Some have been rumored to have made deals with the devil. The news crew is describing the Tempe, Arizona, shelter, along with many others, as being an organized crime network. There are many who have turned to God and seem to be doing better, while others still have no hope. The world seems to be turning into an evil place in most places.

"You know, I hated watching the news because of all the bad things going on in the world. Now, it is near rock bottom except for those who have turned to God."

"What would you expect? We are living in biblical times, Danny."

"Deal with the devil? Hell, why would he make a deal with your dumbasses? He already has you?"

Danny finishes his chili dog and prepares for bed. He knows tomorrow will be a long day. He plans to pack up and go to the Hot Springs Village shelter and make several trips to LRAFB to load everyone's belongings in the spacecraft, and hopefully leave.

They go to bed and sleep well.

Morning comes very early for Danny and at four am he is climbing out of bed and headed for the coffeepot. He recalls on the way that his little Tilley is not there and he will have to make his own coffee this morning. A grimace forms on his face as he gets to the kitchen. There is only a light from a vent-a-hood above the cook stove and the lighting is just bright enough for him to see to navigate his way around.

He grabs the coffee grounds, pulls the cap open to find his scoop. He digs a nice big rounded scoop out and opens the lid of the coffeepot to find it full of fresh grounds and a filter. He lifts it and judging by its weight, it is also full of water.

"Well, that sweet Tilley must have known yesterday she wouldn't be here and made up my coffee. How sweet," he says.

He flips the switch as he has done so many mornings and walks out through the living area. He opens the door to the mudroom and steps out on the porch to feel the nice breeze. He takes a breath of fresh air and still smells the freshly plowed dirt out in the field. He has a seat in the chair and looks out at the yard. It is dimly lit with the security lights. It isn't long and Chopper smells or hears him and he hears the big dog bump the door to go outside.

"Okay, boy." He gets up and lets him out and leaves the front door cracked.

He hears the coffeepot gurgling and goes in to find his favorite cup. He places it under the replicator and says, "Baileys original cream. A double shot." The silver spigot dispenses a light brown liquid into his cup and fills it about a third of the way full. He grabs the coffeepot and fills the cup the rest of the way and takes a big swig saying, "Mmm, such good strong coffee." He realizes that Tilley did not make it. It was stronger than she makes and realizes that Kelly must have made it. He smiles as he has an appreciation for her doing that for him. He heads back out onto the front porch to enjoy some relaxation before the craziness starts.

Before long, he makes his way to Kelly's fire pit to the right of the front of the cabin and gathers some fallen limbs. He realizes if this isn't his last morning here that it is one of very few left. He lights up the fire and pulls up a folded chair from against the cabin. *What to do, what to do,* he thinks to himself.

He reflects on his time here at this shelter. How he thought that it would be home from now on. He considers the dangers of obtaining the spaceship. It would seem that it is secured. He wonders if First Sergeant Carter is aligned with his wishes and will support his group getting off the planet safely, or if he could, he would have already taken his spaceship.

He knows that worrying will solve nothing and the only way to get things going is to go and do, not sit and worry. He begins to think of all the awesome things he has experienced. The Op Track, Kelly saving his life when the tunnel buster about busted him up. The lessons the little model has given him. He sits petting his dog by the fire and begins to pray. "Lord, if it be your will, please support me to get through this evil shell of a world that has been left behind. In God's name, I pray, Amen."

He looks up and Kelly is standing there watching him pray. He smiles and says, "I love you."

She reaches down and kisses him and says, "I would enjoy relaxing here for a while before we must leave. Will we leave today?"

"I want to."

"Me, too. I am excited about the cruise ship and having a true maid again."

"Such a bitch to her."

"No, but she needs to remember her place. Her place is as a maid."

"She is more than just a maid, she is also a friend. Would it be so hard to look at her as such?"

Kelly shrugs and says, "I can see her as a friend, of sorts, but she is what she is….and that is a maid."

256

He picks up a fallen limb and stirs the fire. It flickers and lights up Kelly's beautiful scabbed and imperfect face. He heads back to the cabin to get a cup of coffee and Kelly stops him.

"More coffee?"

"Yeah."

"Let me get that for you." She smiles.

"A shot of Baileys please."

"Rum, too?"

"Nah, I should probably not get too carried away this morning."

She returns very shortly with coffee and a blanket. She lays the blanket on the ground. The next thing you know, they are lying side by side, nude, under the light of the security lights and the flicker of the fire lighting each other as they admire one another.

Danny says, "Chopper, you go into the house."

The big obedient pit bull begins to trot along and up to the porch. He climbs up in the love seat and lies down, looking out over the dirt garden, letting out a snort.

The two spend the morning's replicated sunrise making love one last time at the country shelter.

They later find themselves in the shower, then they replicate a quick breakfast; an omelet for Danny and pancakes for Kelly. They sit at the dining room table discussing what must be done. Kelly finishes a bite of pancakes and asks, "So, will we bust a tunnel and take the big truck so we can bring all of our stuff?"

"What in the world do you have to take? Do you have a truckload? The tunnel buster would take a month."

"That I would like to take or I need to have?"

"That you can't live without."

"I have clothes that I can't replace. I also have some trinkets. The spaceship will have everything that is needed to live, right? It's not like we are moving to another house and need televisions and things like that, do we?"

"It is exactly like a cruise ship. Don't forget we can replicate any pattern of clothes that you want on the ship. When we get there, we can purchase absolutely anything, as long as you don't make me make fifteen trips to Jacksonville."

"Well, let me pack. I want the bottom station on each side."

"Deal!"

The two make fairly short work of gathering their belongings. Danny drives the Op Track up to the barn and fuels it up. He pulls back down to the cabin and looks out at his classic Mustang that he has to leave behind. That will be the only thing he regrets not taking and is almost worth busting a tunnel to be able to bring it. In very short order, the two have the bottom two stations and the second tier station of the machine full of luggage.

Danny looks out at the dirt garden and at his beautiful lady. "I will always remember this time."

"Will Mr. Franklin pilot the spaceship for us?"

"I am sure he will. He just needs a little encouragement and some confidence. Anyone who piloted commercial airliners should be a shoe-in for piloting the spacecraft. To be honest, I have been reading in the evenings with your tablet before I go to sleep, about the controls. I believe that if push comes to shove, I could fly the damn thing. I have flown my own leer jet. I have about two hundred hours on it and the documentation for the spacecraft shows that it has an almost autonomous autopilot."

"I didn't know you had your license."

"I do, but it isn't something I'm really crazy about being common knowledge. Too much responsibility. I try to leave that to the experts, but if Franklin isn't on board, then I can and will be at the helm."

"That makes me feel better. I thought it odd that we weren't at his front door every day, trying to make sure he is on board. Will we return here?"

"Do you have everything you need?"

"I believe so."

"As long as Chopper will fit, then no, this will be the last time we leave the comfort of this shelter."

There is a pause as the two realize how much this place has shielded them from the world outside. They load up Chopper on top of the luggage beside Kelly, on the right side of the machine. The luggage extends from the front all the way to the very tail of the station and is about level with the second tier. The big dog steps around like he isn't sure where it is okay to sit down. Finally, he finds a spot on the luggage as Kelly comforts him. He looks a little apprehensive about riding in the machine again.

Soon the hatch is closed and they are en route. They travel past the Hot Springs Village shelter without even stopping. Danny has the Op Track running about forty mph as they plunge into the snow at the end of the tunnel, passing the road that leads into it.

"We aren't going to stop and get anyone to take along?"

"I don't really see the room, and the air base looked like it was pretty much secured."

Kelly reaches her hand over to Chopper and runs her hand down his back. He reacts to her stroke, as if to try to caress her back. It is a long slow trip as they pull into the large tunnel that has the divided road.

They pull up to the front gate with the large metal barrier stopping anyone from passing. An MP comes out to greet them. He is a tall fellow wearing fatigues that have a desert pattern.

Danny pops the hatch and shows him his pass as Kelly stands up on her knees while still at her station in the Op Track. He takes a look at Kelly's pass as well as Danny's and pulls out a pen that favors a sobriety pen. He places a miniature hollow rubber cover over the end of it and asks Danny to blow into it. The light illuminates green on the end as he begins to replace the protective cover, Kelly says, "No need to replace it. We won't

259

infect each other." The soldier then takes and hands it to her. She does the same and nets the same results.

"Welcome to our base, Mr. Nichols," he says as he turns and goes back into the guard shack. The metal barrier drops and they drive through. They navigate their way to the enormous hangar where the spaceship is stored. They exit the machine and Danny walks up to the beige building with a blue door with an Air Force insignia marked Hangar 10321. He places his finger on the touchpad to the right of it and the door clicks open. He disarms the alarm system and goes inside.

They look everything over to find that nothing seems to be out of place. They unload their items and go into the big ship and find a huge suite on the top deck. The deck has been finished with glass-front offices that are located along a corridor leading to a large hardwood door that has a golden plaque to the side marked Danny Nichols, CEO Chimera. The pair makes several trips back and forth and finishes with their business and lock up the spacecraft.

They exit and lock up the facility and head for Hot Springs Village to get another load. The empty Op Track seems to move a little faster. They have made this trek a few times and it is just a non-eventful drive on the snow. The sun is out, but the wind is heavy, as always. They pull up to the outside doors of Hot Springs Village and Kelly gets out to open the doors. Soon they are sitting at his mansion, with Tilley bringing her items to the front entrance.

"I am going to take the GT down one last time and tell Mr. Franklin and Tabatha to get ready if they are coming. We will make a trip with your stuff and perhaps one more with Mr. Franklin's and Tabatha's items, then us three, along with Mr. Franklin, Tabatha, and one of the boys will go back to the spacecraft. We will let the boys bring the Op Track back," Danny explains to Tilley and Kelly.

Kelly says, "With Chopper? We should plan to drop someone off and leave them and Chopper at the spacecraft," while looking at Tilley. "For the last trip. seven people and a dog will never fit."

"Oh, hell, Tilley and Tabatha are pretty small. I think they could take up one station, but you are right, it would probably be more comfortable if we can drop someone off to lighten the load for the last trek."

Kelly and Tilley begin to load up Tilley's bags. There aren't quite as many as Kelly had and fills about half of the lower station on the left side of the machine.

They hear the GT engine fire up and come whizzing by the side of the house on the cobblestone path, spinning tires. The taillights of the car disappear down the wooded driveway.

The two get the Op Track loaded fairly quickly. The girls know they need to let the boys know they need to be ready within a couple of hours so they can ride along and drive the Op Track back if they want to keep it.

Danny returns home to find the jeep is gone and doesn't find the girls. He goes in and replicates a tall glass of Michelob Light on his way and finds Chopper in the backyard. He is a little too excited to sit and relax much. He hears the jeep pull back in, with the two pretty ladies in it.

He walks out to the jeep and greets them, "Where did ya'll go?"

Kelly, stepping out of the driver's seat, says, "We went to tell the boys to start getting ready if they want to keep the Op Track. What did Mr. Franklin and Tabatha say?"

"Tabatha wasn't there and he said that she really was debating about staying here with the boys, but thought that when we got back, she would be ready. He has read all of the manuals on the ship and feels good about piloting it and has been waiting to see what we were going to do. He will be ready when we return."

"That sounds great. All of this sure seems like it is going awfully smooth."

"I know, it is kind of scary, huh?"

261

"I don't see why it has to go ape-shit crazy, we are just leaving on a spaceship. This has been done how many times now? Why does it have to be some major problem for us?"

"Because it is us. You remember the fire, the wasps, the idiots in Arizona trying to kill us? We don't have the skills and expertise of the WRC to do it all for us, but nothing ever just goes as planned."

"True. Well, so far so good."

Without much additional talk, they load up and take off for the base again. They arrive much like before and breathe into the illness meter and Tilley is issued a pass. They get to the hangar and unload Tilley's items. They find her a suite on the top level. It is next to Danny and Kelly's room, along the corridor to the right before they arrive at the glass-front offices.

Danny asks Tilley, "Would you care to stay here with Chopper or do you want to make another trip to the shelter?"

"You are going to have the boys with you for the final trip?"

"At least one of them."

"I will stay."

Soon, they are back at the Hot Springs Village shelter. They arrive to find that Tabatha is back at her dad's and they both have all of their belongings ready to go.

Once more they make the trek to the base. They drop them off and find them provisions on deck three. This is the deck where the cockpit is located and is the pilot's quarters.

The two arrive back at Hot Springs Village and go to the boys' house. They need more diesel so they pull behind the boys' place to find the diesel pump.

They both come out to see if they can both go or if there is only room for one.

Bryan walks up to Danny with the fuel pump in the top of the Op Track and says, "Yeah, just help yourself."

"Thanks, I will," Danny replies, and chuckles.

They both stand there watching him fill the tank and Adam asks, "Can both of us ride along?"

"Yeah, we dropped everyone else off already. When we get there, this time, you guys will be able to take the Op Track, have the keys to the country shelter, and can have all of my stuff here; basically, we will be gone."

Chapter 31
The Journey

They are now at the hangar and Danny begins to raise the outside doors. The boys have said their goodbyes and he watches the Op Track drive away. First Sergeant Carter arrives to assist with getting their craft out of the hangar. Four doors are opened that make up the front of the enormous hangar.

Sergeant Carter opens a second hangar that is about two hundred yards away and begins walking over to the craft, piloting a remote controlled Buckingham Dolly. He runs the four dual-wheeled unit under the front landing gear to connect to a pin on the front of the craft. A hydraulic ram whines as it seemingly strains to lift the front of the enormous vessel. Once up, with the front wheel off of the ground, it again begins a whine as it slowly pulls the large spaceship from its resting area. Soon, the enormous flat-black spacecraft is out on the runway, with the assistance of this remote controlled machine.

He drops the hydraulic ram and moves the whiny hydraulic unit back, headed toward the hangar where he retrieved it from.

Kelly, Danny, and David Franklin all stand there looking at the ship and Sgt. Charlie Carter stops the machine to shake their hands and wish them well.

Danny asks, "Do you have family here, Sgt. Carter?"

"No, it is just me. All of my family is on Goldilocks or with God now."

"Do you want to come along?"

"I thought you would never ask. You okay with me going?"

"Well, you don't really seem to be a mass murderer, and you didn't steal the spacecraft when you had full access to it. I don't really feel like you are a bad man."

"Yes, I would very much like to ride along. I am a pilot, you know."

264

"No, I had no idea. We really could use a good copilot."

"Let me go and get my things. I could be back in an hour."

"Hurry now," Danny replies.

They all go into the ship to fire up the engines and prepare for their voyage. The pilot, David Franklin, sits at the front of the cockpit, with the controls of a 767 aircraft in front of him, and begins to go through the checklist. He has gone through everything necessary to take flight, with the assistance of Danny and instructions sent from the WRC on Goldilocks.

Kelly, Tilley, Danny, and Tabatha all sit in the other seats around the cockpit that are meant for the copilot, commander, navigators, and engineer.

Soon they see the blue truck off in the distance, at the end of the runway, coming along at a pretty good rate on the front holograph. They open the side door on the left side of the craft. The truck gets closer and it appears that Sgt. Carter isn't alone.

The truck comes pulling up, stopping in a rush, and three men are in it. One looks like Ben Calhoun, with bumps all over his face. They have a black gun at the back of Sgt. Carter's head as they get out. The entrance of the spacecraft is somewhat dark inside due to the bright sunlight.

Suddenly, a crackle is heard as the pilot enables the outside shields. The group getting out of the truck has no knowledge of shielding and unknowingly walk up to this blue hue that makes up the shield barrier. A tall blond haired man, with winter gear and fresh sores on his face, walks into the shield first. His yellow hair instantly turns dark brown and becomes blackened in the front and his face is wiped away in black ash. He shakes in convulsions and falls back onto the ground. Sgt. Carter realizes the first man walked into the shields. This spooks Ben and Charlie reaches back and grabs the end of the barrel of the gun. He swings the man around, using the barrel for leverage, hoping it doesn't go off. When suddenly a blast

265

from the barrel is heard. The door of the spacecraft is still open and everyone is standing near the doorway, watching this unfold.

Suddenly, the man hits the shielded area with such force that he is forced all the way into it. On the ground, in front of the shield, all that remains of the man is a pile of ashes. The gun barrel makes contact with the high voltage barrier and Sgt. Carter is left with a metal rod essentially embedded into the shields.

"Turn off the shields!" Danny yells as he sees what has happened.

A slight buzzing noise is heard and Sgt. Carter falls to the ground, lifeless. Danny and Kelly run down the steps from the ship to check on him. Kelly kneels beside him and checks for a pulse. His hands are blistered and red. He is gone. He has no heartbeat and isn't breathing.

Danny drags his lifeless body across the path where they saw the blue hue and goes back into the cockpit.

"Energize the shields, David."

"Do you realize that this will probably vaporize his body," Mr. Franklin responds.

"I am sure they will. He has no family here, and he was ready to go to Goldilocks with us. The military may or may not give him a proper burial, but this way, I am sure that his corpse will be taken care of and won't be lying out here on the tarmac to rot and be eaten by animals, vultures."

"Very well."

He energizes the shields and in an instant nothing is left but a pile of ashes. Danny grabs a paper bag and a small wisp broom, that is in a cabinet to one side of the cockpit, and goes out and obtains all of the ashes that he can get. He returns to the cockpit and they all hope that this is it for opposition while they are trying to leave.

The large triangular propulsion engines begin glowing blue and the craft makes a vertical takeoff. They get about two thousand feet into the air and begin traveling. There is a hologram display at the front of the cockpit and it displays a huge canyon in the snow that contains the base. Past that, the terrain is nothing but a white blanket, with clusters of tall buildings peeking out as they pass casinos and towns in Mississippi and Alabama.

Danny asks, "Can you do this without a copilot?"

"I guess I will have to."

"I will help when you need me."

The terrain below is passing by at a very rapid pace. They are almost to the east coast, over North Carolina. The instructions dictate that the best path for travel to the ionosphere is to get to the North Atlantic and travel north near Nova Scotia, then begin a diagonal path south toward Africa, climbing altitude until the ionosphere is reached.

They pass the land mass and suddenly a crosswind, that this pilot has never before experienced, hits the side of the ship. It is so strong, it is traveling at a higher rate of speed than the ship. It blows the enormous vessel several miles off course, causing it to go into a roll at some point. It appears that the horizon has inverted. The gravity generator in the ship gives them a false feeling of being righted.

The pilot gains control of the ship once again as he descends to get away from these strong crosswinds. A bolt of lightning is heard and hits the bottom of the ship. They all sit, now strapped into their seats, as the holograph at the front of the room shows an image indicating they are upside down.

Danny asks, "Are we upside down?"

The experienced airline pilot is disoriented but insists, "We can't be, no one is hitting the ceiling, are they?"

"It has some kind of gravity generator, I thought. Why is the display upside down?"

"The camera image must have been damaged. I have the throttle set at eighty percent and the shields at maximum. I am ready to try that strong wind again." He begins to pull back on the yoke to begin a climb and take the craft toward space. He is, in fact, piloting the craft toward the icy ocean below.

Suddenly, the display shows nothing but white as they are disoriented and no one knows what is going on. The ship is flying upside down, but the gravity generator has the pilot confused. They reach the ocean surface upside down. They all feel that they are pretty much doomed as they see the ice coming up on the holograph. The pilot tries to abort the descent that he was fully convinced was a climb and had the ship committed to it.

Danny yells, "Abort, abort!"

Suddenly, they plunge into the water. The ice was a projected hologram from aliens that live within the ocean. These beings have been there for thousands of years and have gone undetected. The UFO sightings and abductions that had been reported for so many years were from these Grey beings.

No one can believe that their ship wasn't destroyed in this crash. They felt certain the ice would have demolished the spacecraft.

They find themselves in a pocket of air, thanks to the shields. The shields are protected against short circuiting if they have equal conductivity exposed over a large area. They are now sinking to the bottom of the ocean in an air pocket.

Mr. Franklin looks around, specifically at Tabatha. "Is everyone okay?"

They are all strapped in and looking scared.

He begins to try to figure out a way to make the air pocket more buoyant than the ship so they can return to the surface. The engines can't provide any thrust within the water due to the limited amount of air intake. He decides they should open the outer door and pressurize the cabin for space. He enables an override and begins to open the outside door.

Kelly says, "Are you out of your fucking mind? We will all drown."

"I am hoping that we can become buoyant by pressurizing the shield's air pocket."

"Brilliant idea," Danny replies.

They can see that the craft has stopped on the screen. The water is no longer passing by the shields and the altimeter is now showing a constant value, but they are not traveling back up. They are neutrally buoyant and stranded.

Danny exclaims, "Damn, I need a beer!"

Mr. Franklin says, "A copilot would be nice, too. Okay, let's all stop and take a breath. We are safe for the moment."

They all breathe a sigh of relief that they are still alive. Danny goes to the dining area near the cockpit and replicates a tall Michelob Light and a shot of Crown. He sucks down a few sips and heads back to the cockpit.

Mr. Franklin begins to move the cameras around and says, "Well, I guess we were upside down. We are right side up now."

"Ya think, dumbass?" Kelly responds.

The holograph switches to different images that show water all around the shields as they float around helplessly because the engines can't produce thrust in the enclosed cavity. A camera gets a glimpse of a large object that doesn't appear natural. Mr. Franklin takes control of the camera and focuses it on an enormous octagon made up of what everyone recognizes as a cluster of UFOs below them.

Danny is seated in the commander's chair and sees a communication request banner come across the control panel at his station. He places his finger on the video conference button and sees a bald, large black-eyed, small body, gray being on the display. *Oh shit*, he thinks to himself. He doesn't dare put it on the holograph, as he knows it will scare the hell out of everyone in the cockpit.

"We want you to surrender your ship," the being explains.

"We have shields and weapons," Danny replies.

"We are stranded here with limited ability for speed. We can only travel at light speed. The new planet your race is moving to is twenty years away for us. We can't sustain resources for that long. Please allow us to board and go with you, or share your technology."

"If there is some way you can help us out of here, we will send you our technology," Danny replies to them, as they are now on speaker.

Everyone is very alarmed and they all begin to get up to look at Danny's console to see who he is speaking with.

"We shall destroy your vessel if you do not send this information now."

"We will send it as soon as you aid us in getting out of the water. We also have weapons and we have our impenetrable shields energized. Your move," Danny replies.

The entire octagon made up of these ships begin to move beneath the transport. This Armada bumps shields with them, causing arcs within the water as they collide from below and begin pushing them to the surface.

The pilot tells everyone to be seated and buckle up because as soon as they can, they are taking flight.

As soon as the transport can propel in the air, the pilot turns on full power, shooting a two hundred foot blue flame from the back of the engines. The horizon on the display is right side up. They are climbing at full speed, away from the surface in an instant! He changes the holograph to a split display that shows the large UFO cluster behind them, splitting into smaller ships and leaving the water. It looks almost like salmon spawning as they exit the water and each begin firing upon them, realizing that Danny lied to them, but it is too late. The transport makes it to space and begins their long six-month journey to Goldilocks.

Kelly says, "Suckers!" Everyone kind of chuckles. This group has stayed hidden in the ocean, instilling fear in the human race, and has been responsible for abductions, as well as all of the unexplained mysteries of UFOs on Earth all of these years. And they had just been punk'd by them.

~~THE END~~

Imminent Domain

New World Order
Neal JB Verne

Contents

Chapter 1
Molding the Landscape

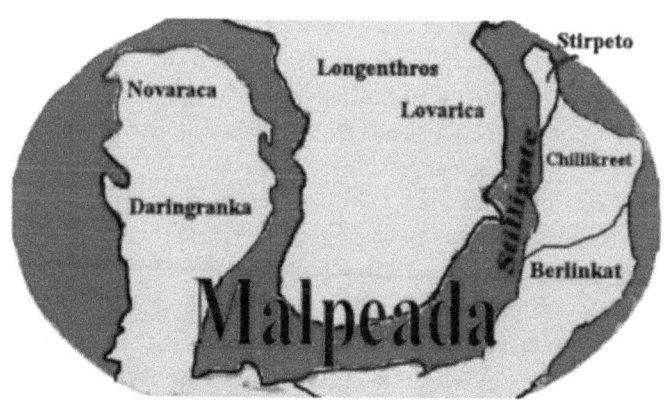

OLD WORLD

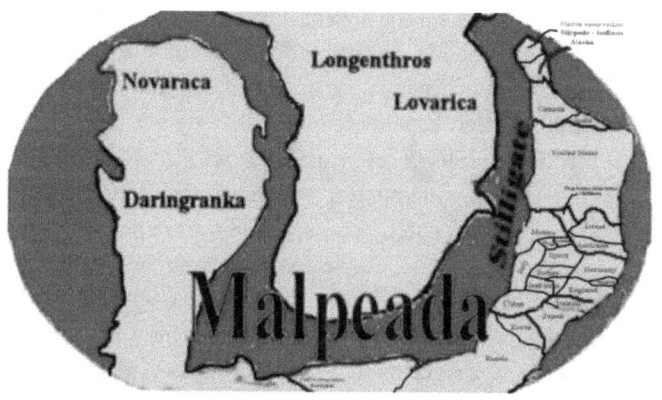

NEW WORLD

On Chillikreet, a fleet of bulldozers plow their way across virgin land. There are at least twenty-five of the D11

1

models that were transported by the WRC. The machines are US military camouflaged colors and each seems to have their own area to level. This particular land mass was claimed by the United States of America. President Lynch has given the order to begin preparing an area for a new White House and essentially a new Washington D.C.

The land being cleared is near a lake, has hills, and is densely covered with trees. Several roads are being constructed in conjunction with clearing the land. Tunnels are being dug for the infrastructure that is required and will hold electrical wire, sewer mains, and potable water supplies. There is a plethora of activity taking place in this area to construct the headquarters for one of the three new superpowers that are settling on this new land.

The superpowers of the new world are the original inhabitants: Malpeada, United States, Russia, and Japan. President Lynch sits alone at his makeshift Oval Office within the shields of the dignitary transport. The vessel is sitting on an enormous leveled, newly constructed, concrete lot near the new construction site. The area has a new lawn of Bermuda grass within the shields. The shield repeaters are placed all around the area. A sandy beach is just beyond the furthest repeater and it is blinking green, separated on each side by a double six-foot-privacy fence that encompasses the area.

He sits looking at a computer monitor. The monitor shows a large conference table. The camera he is viewing appears to be sitting on the corner of the table, near an unoccupied chair. The camera is complete with video. He hears President Gryntha Haulk speaking. He addresses the group concerning the technology their new guests possess. They speak of the people from Earth and the possibility of them turning their weapons against Malpeada. They are concerned about how they could defend themselves in such a crisis.

Suddenly, General Zelicwi walks to the camera, with a rolled up newspaper, and a loud *swat* and *pow* is heard. The general looks back to the group and says, "I got him." The president's monitor goes blank, with nothing but white noise on his screen. He still has audio for a few seconds and he hears Zelicwi saying, "We have ways of dealing with our guests if they become less than gracious." The sound coming from the device then goes silent.

The president's monitor has multiple drones that provide images from all across the world. The USA-AK-1 is the name of the new country on Alpha Kantabury I, and they have developed six prop drones that are nuclear powered and they are intercontinental. These drones carry a payload of smaller insect and reptile imitation drones that look like common houseflies, crickets, spiders, and frogs. These drones can travel anywhere on the planet. The camera that President Lynch had been viewing was a housefly drone. General Zelicwi swatted it and destroyed his live feed.

He calls out to his administrative assistant, Barbara Kennedy, on his speaker phone, "Please ask that General Brandon Evans contacts me for deployment of another insect drone immediately from our master drone in Daringranka's capital city, Novaraca."

Barbara calls General Evans. He says, "Let me guess. The president lost his feed to Malpeada."

"You guessed it."

"Why doesn't he let us do our job and give him the important stuff, rather than eavesdropping on our tap? We will get what he wants and won't have to endure, and hear him bitch about, these little mishaps that occur."

"I think he gets bored."

"Tell him the new housefly is back in the building."

A few moments pass as the president sits getting agitated as he gets a reply from his assistant. "Sir, you should have a link now."

The monitor becomes alive once more, with a blue square, then a pink square that fades into an image of the door outside the conference room in Novaraca. The camera hovers in front of the door for a few seconds, then suddenly the door

3

opens and all of the members of Malpeada's senior staff begin exiting the room. The camera then stops and the image turns sideways as the insect drone lands on a wall.

It then begins to follow President Haulk until he reaches an office. The door is slammed prior to the drone making its way into the room with him. Suddenly, the image lands on a ceramic floor and begins moving. The camera bobs up and down slightly as the drone walks under the door gap at the bottom. The camera reveals a large fine brown wooden desk and a white floor. This is about all that can be seen. He hears President Haulk on the telephone and much of the conversation was missed, but he hears, "I want this carried out now!" he yells, and slams the phone down.

Suddenly, the screen goes dark once again as his wife, Vice President Haulk, enters the room and steps on the drone.

While he waits, he switches the monitor to another identical insect drone located in Russia's dignitary vessel, well south of him. He sees the Russian President in a hot tub with three beautiful Russian ladies. All three are naked and President Lynch snaps a quick screen shot of it, then changes to another image outside the Capitol headquarters in Novaraca.

The image is floating in front of a large, white building. A limousine is sitting with the President Haulk and his wife, Vice President Haulk, climbing in. President Lynch is disappointed that he didn't get to hear more of what counterplans this country could launch, but decides it prudent to leave the espionage up to the professionals. He changes to an image of the construction that is taking place.

He watches one bulldozer in particular peel up soil that has never been touched. The green foliage is still attached to the black, fertile ground as the large dozer curls it up, as if it were peeling a banana. The dirt rolls up several feet in the air as the large machine clears a path. Suddenly, the ground gives way and the bulldozer falls into a pit beneath, and is completely gone without a trace. The only thing left is the wide tracks embedded into the dirt that was cleared, a hole where the machine fell through, and the enormous mound of dirt that it was pushing.

The drone moves the camera and zooms in above the hole to find molten lava at the bottom of a cavity that is at least one-hundred-feet deep. President Lynch says, "Heaven help us! Is this damn place hollow?"

COMING SOON IMMINENT DOMAIN: NEW WORLD ORDER
By Neal J.B. Verne